A MISSED MURDER

A MISSED MURDER

Michael Jecks

CRÈME de la CRIME

This first world edition published 2018
in Great Britain and the USA by
Crème de la Crime an imprint of
SEVERN HOUSE PUBLISHERS LTD of
Eardley House, 4 Uxbridge Street, London W8 7SY
Trade paperback edition first published
in Great Britain and the USA 2018 by
SEVERN HOUSE PUBLISHERS LTD

Copyright © 2018 by Michael Jecks.

British Library Cataloguing in Publication Data
A CIP catalogue record for this title is available from the British Library.

ISBN-13: 978-1-78029-108-6 (cased)
ISBN-13: 978-1-78029-589-3 (trade paper)
ISBN-13: 978-1-4483-0160-7 (e-book)

All Severn House titles are printed on acid-free paper.

Severn House Publishers support the Forest Stewardship Council™ [FSC™],
the leading international forest certification organisation.
All our titles that are printed on FSC certified paper carry the FSC logo.

Typeset by Palimpsest Book Production Ltd.,
Falkirk, Stirlingshire, Scotland.
Printed and bound in Great Britain by
TJ International, Padstow, Cornwall.

This book is dedicated to the memory of Dave Hatton

The man was plainly alarmed, as he should be. He was about to die.

He had a thin, weaselly face, his lips dry and pale, under a thin mop of grey hair. With features that were already pasty from lack of exercise and living indoors all year long, he looked little better than a corpse. But for all that, his clothing was not too shabby. His doublet looked of good quality, and he had a short cloak, more for decorative use than protection against the weather, which was trimmed with golden needlework.

'Who're you? What do you want?' he demanded.

I was in no mood for lengthy explanations. We were down at The Brokenwharf at that point, and for all I knew, Humfrie would soon be there too. I had to hurry, to get this fool away. Yes, it sounds daft, but having ordered this man's death, now I was desperate to save him.

'Just follow me,' I said.

A sour wind blew along the Thames, bringing with it the scent of rotted fish guts and ordure. At that time of the night, it was at least quiet. There was none of the constant calling and shrieking of the gulls trying to steal food from your hands, or the curses and bellows of the men emptying ships, the chandlers calling their wares and the thousand or more other peddlers of dangerous snacks. Instead, the air was thick with the smells of the great city.

It wasn't pleasant.

'Who are you?'

I drew myself up to my full height. 'I am the man who's trying to save your life!'

'Who'd want to hurt me?' he said. He had a wheedling, whining sort of voice that set my teeth on edge. I was sure that if I shook his hand, it would be as clammy and manly as a dead carp.

I gazed at him scornfully. 'Probably those who know you are overly keen on the Spanish controlling our country. Perhaps someone who knows what you have been getting up to with the Spanish ambassador? Master Renard is a devious fellow, so I have heard tell. But you are lucky, because I choose to save you.'

There was no need to mention that I only knew of him because I had been instructed to kill him.

I didn't think that would endear me to him.

He gaped and goggled a bit at that. It was obvious that I had shaken him with my confident assertion. For a few moments, I enjoyed the sight of his shock, but only for a few. Just now I had an urgent need to be away from this place. As did he.

The thing is, I had been ordered to come and do this. I didn't want to, God knows, but I could hardly tell my master, John Blount, that I was discontented with the thought of completing his instructions. There I had been, enjoying a number of ales with the Spaniard, sitting in plain view in a glorious little tavern, armed with the perfect alibi, and now – well, now it was all changed. Like God interrupting Abraham in his busy son-killing schedule, Master John had changed his mind. He countermanded his order to kill this rather sad-looking fellow. Which, for a man like me, who dislikes the sight of any blood, especially my own, should have been welcome news. But it wasn't. Not today.

'I don't understand? Why do you think anyone would want to hurt me?' His tone was that of an offended choirboy who has been told of an impending caning.

'Look, just follow me, will you? There's a man coming who wants to murder you,' I said, and turned. Over my shoulder, I added, 'That's why he got you to come here to this place, at this ungodly hour.'

The wharf's boards were cold with the early breeze from the east. Where the fish had been unloaded early that morning, they were wet and very slippery. Overhead, the sky was clear, and the moon's light shone silver, gleaming on the flecks of fish scales that lay all about. Ropes and nets lay where they had been dropped in an unholy mess of cordage. Once I had been told that shipmen were neat and tidy, else they might become entangled in their own ropes and injured. The same was plainly not true of dock workers. This place was a disgrace. Even a pirate would have been disgusted.

I made my way cautiously away from the river. Behind me came that querulous voice again. 'What makes you think I know Renard?'

'Because you are Jeffry of Shoreditch, and you are here. I sent you the message to come and meet him here today. You have already been paid two bags of gold to do the bidding of Renard. You sold your soul to that Spanish devil for the benefit of your purse, and now there is a reckoning.'

'Do I look like a man with money?'

'Your contract with Renard was overheard. My master heard it.'

'I wasn't going to do anything for it!'

Oh, the cry of the child through the ages: *It's not fair! It's not just!* I hadn't been expecting that quite so soon. Still, it got the conversation out of the way.

'You weren't going to do anything? Master Jeffry, no one pays two bags of gold for nothing to be done! If you didn't meet the terms of the contract, you would not have lived above two days! You think the Spaniards will be forgiving? No, I know all about you. I know that you have been paid to foment trouble for the good Lady Elizabeth. Renard wishes to see her dead, because he sees her as a threat, and you are commissioned to make his task all the easier, since you are a committed Catholic like the Spaniard.'

He blenched at that. 'This is nonsense! How should I know a man such as him?'

'Your wife was once a maid for Queen Mary's mother, wasn't she? She served Catherine of Aragon long before you married her, and she has reinforced your popish opinions.'

He winced and withdrew a little. 'My wife died a long time ago. You are here to kill me?'

'No!' I said, perhaps a little more emphatically than I needed. 'I am here to *save* you.'

'You're going to kill me! I have a little girl, master, and

two boys! My wife is dead already! Don't make them all orphans!'

Ignoring his whining, I made my way to the entrance of the alleyway. The usual path down here to the wharf was Denebury Lane, but that was watched by too many houses. This little alley was a narrow walkway, barely three men wide, with a small kennel in the middle, a gutter, down which the rain could flow, washing the detritus of the street before it. The alley gaped like the maw of hell, black and foul. Anyone could be in there, I thought to myself. Humfrie, Blount, or any number of footpads. It was tempting to call this old fool and have him march before me, but I truly did not like the thought of being the hindmost. My craven back crawled with the thought, as if a shovelful of worms had been deposited there and were wriggling their way down towards my arse.

'Oh, ballocks to this!' I muttered, and plunged into the alley.

It was dark. I stumbled over trash and garbage, mostly moderately quietly, until I pitched into something on my left. It was a pillar or section of wall, and my shoulder caught a nasty blow. I turned to face it, rubbing my injury and cursing builders who stick bits of building into darkened alleyways, and when I turned to continue on my way, I struck my knee against a barrel sitting beside the wall. Swearing again, I kicked it and pressed past. It was then that my ambition of maintaining silence was thumped hard on the nose. On top of the barrel there rested a circular tray of some sort; I saw the barrel, but not the thing on top, nor the collection of odds and ends of metal that were placed on it. They sounded like a lot of metal hinges, with a few horseshoes, and perhaps a light chain thrown on top for good measure. The pan itself decided to land on an edge and proceeded to spin about its rim, making a whirring row that must have woken Satan and all his demons, until it finally gave a tinny little rattle and was silent at last.

I stood stock-still, listening with every fibre of my being. There were mumbles and sleepy grunts from one of the nearer buildings, with someone muttering about 'Clumsy, godforsaken, drunken bitch sons' from a window not far away. Here at the wharves, the men had to be at work before dawn to begin their labours, so most would be abed before dark to rest before beginning the new day.

Relieved not to be accosted, I turned.

In the place of the walking corpse, there was a trim fellow. He wore dark clothing, a cap with a feather, and a cape that swirled as he marched to me. His square shoulders and barrel chest told me all I needed to know. If I had needed another clue, the thin-bladed dagger in his hand would have told me enough.

'Oh, ballocks,' I said.

This was the man sent to murder the man whom I had been saving.

He had succeeded.

'Master, what are you doing here?' he asked, not unreasonably. After all, the whole point of his being here was that I would be at the other side of the city engaged in loud play with Willyam, Leadenhall Bob and the Lawyer, as well as other members of my drinking club.

'Never mind that for now. Where is he?' I hissed.

This was Humfrie, and he was, I suppose, sort of my father-in-common-law. Not that it was through any choice of mine. I distrusted the old rogue. He was one of the few men I have met who seemed to be able to read me, and I don't feel comfortable around such people. Others made assumptions about me, but Humfrie appeared to be able to *read* me.

He stood an inch or two taller than me and had the frame of a man who has worked all his life, slightly bent, with a head that hung low between his shoulders.

'Where is he?' I demanded again. 'What have you done to him?'

'Over here. I knocked him on the pate and he went down like a ninepin.'

I saw a huddled shape at the edge of the wharf. It was Jeffry. Hurrying to him, I grabbed at his shoulder and pulled him on to his back.

I stared down into Jeffry's face. The old man looked still paler in the moonlight. In the silvery light, he appeared waxen, with a blueish tinge to his features. He could have been dead, but when I set my ear to his breast, there was a slow thudding heartbeat. A sudden loud snore reassured me, and I sat back on my haunches with relief.

'What now?' Humfrie said.

I shrugged and gave the cool cheek before me a slap. It sounded no louder than the waters of the Thames slapping and swirling about the piles supporting the wharves. A rat jumping into the water would make more noise. I slapped him again.

Bleary eyes opened and tried to focus on me. 'What? Did you knock me down? Why did you knock me down?' he demanded petulantly. 'I thought you were . . .' His eyes took in the sight of Humfrie over my shoulder. 'It was him, wasn't it? Who is he?'

He scrabbled at the ground to put some distance between himself and Humfrie, like a crab on ice, clambering to his feet. I rose and held up a hand placatingly. 'There is no need to—' I began, but then my foot found more trash left behind by the wharf's godforsaken stevedores. I had stepped on a rope's end, and it rolled. It felt just like a large rat, and I squealed like a rabbit bitten by a fox, springing forwards.

Jeffry was startled. I suppose he saw my hand reaching for him, and what with my shouting, he thought I was going to harm him. He gave a squeak himself, and the fool sprang backwards, away from me. I was too late.

The problem, as he was about to learn, was that the wharf ended where he had been. His feet landed on empty space.

Jeffry opened his mouth to speak, as though he thought he was about to land on firm boards, and then his eyes widened, and suddenly he wasn't there any more. There was only a disappearing wail.

In my defence, I did try to grip his shirt as he fell away from me, but he was gone before my hand could reach him. There was a quiet plop as he tumbled into the waters and disappeared from view.

I stood at the wharf's edge and stared down, filled with a sort of disbelieving horror; the river had swallowed him up as effectively as a frog gulping down a fly. If you haven't seen it, it's an impressive display of *now you see it, now it's gone*, and the frog looks smug after he's swallowed his morsel. The river didn't look smug. It just looked filthy and grey, the same as usual. A turd floated past.

'Oh . . .' I said. Then I added, 'Oh, *ballocks*!'

'Cor! He went down quick, didn't he?' Humfrie said with a kind of wonder. He had joined me and was staring into the depths with keen interest.

'I tried to . . .'

'Yeah. Nice,' Humfrie said, adding with a display of professional pride, 'No injury when the body's found, if they do find him. How'd you know he couldn't swim?'

'I didn't.'

'So just a lucky guess, then, eh? Good move. Mind you, I would have stabbed him, just to make sure. I suppose I should have thought of that before I left him to speak to you.'

He looked mournful at having missed his opportunity.

I left him there, still peering over the edge of the wharf into the turbid waters only a couple of yards below.

There was a man I used to know who swore – well, a lot really, but mostly about the health-giving virtues of a morning's dip in the Thames. I was always rather wary of him. He was one of those fit, healthy types, who would only ever eat and drink what he thought was best. Rationally, he stuck to good, healthy English foods, like plenty of beef, dripping, suet and bacon, washed down with a half-gallon of ale. His arms were impressively corded with muscles. He would clamber into the water every morning and emerge later further downstream, puffing and blowing like a wrestler after a bout. Of course, I would have thought that swimming in amongst the detritus of the city would be less than appealing to any man who didn't want to leave the water smelling of old shit, but be that as it may. One day, he went for his swim and came out of the water white as a ghost.

'There was a body in there,' he said. To hear him, you would have thought that there was something unusual in this. Then he explained that the body was caught by one of the piles of the wharf, and as he passed by it, the corpse waved to him, in a mildly friendly manner, as though wishing him Godspeed,

or welcoming an old friend whose acquaintance he hoped to
renew soon.

My fellow caught a chill, and within the week he was dead.
I always wondered whether it was the turd-water he had drunk
while swimming in the cesspool that was the river, or whether
his erstwhile companion of the deep had in fact beckoned him
to join him.

Whichever was responsible, I was firmly determined never
to go paddling in the river after that. Even using a wherry
made me anxious. Not that I had ever enjoyed crossing water
in boats; I could get seasick crossing a puddle.

This was a ridiculous situation. My brain was wandering
with the shock, and I made my way back to the alley, mind
churning the whole way. All I had to do was stay at the alehouse
where I'd been, and my alibi would be complete. Now, instead,
I had actually been there when the man had died. If anyone saw
me near this area, it could go badly for me if his body was ever
found. I hurried on my way, back into the narrow passageway.

I reached the place where I had struck the pillar, a dim
shadow in the deep blackness of the alley. A doorway this
side of it made another black sweep in the gloom, but I was
keeping away from both. My shoulder still ached from where
I had hit the pillar earlier. I gave it a wide berth and went to
hurry back to where I had left the Spaniard snoring. I'll explain
about him later.

Anyway, I was dashing along the lane when my boot hit
something. Instantly, there was a swirling clamour of metal.
In my attempt to avoid the damned pillar, I had forgotten the
blasted things I had knocked from the barrel. It was a clattering timpani, a rising chorus of metallic pandemonium.
Startled, I almost stained my hosen. I sprang back, and only
after a moment did I take a breath and continue on my way.
But then something struck my brow. It was sharp, I thought,
and massive. And that was about all I thought, because as I
fell on my arse I could feel my consciousness slipping away.

Sometimes, when I have been injured, I have been able to
recall the moments leading up to it. Other times, like this,
there are only sparks of memory that flash and fade.

I know I collapsed, I know I landed on my back, and I

know my head hurt because I had struck it. But apart from that, all I know is, as I lay there, I began to slide into what felt like a pool of warm, thick, black oil that had opened up beneath me, and now swallowed me whole.

The evening had started so well, too.

I was out with a club of friends, drinking, when the message was given to me. And what a messenger!

When I first saw her, the main thing that impressed me was the low cut of her bodice and how insufficient it appeared for the restraint of her natural attractions. Why, I thought, a swift slice with my little knife at one of the laces would bring down the entire edifice. It was a rather ignoble thought, perhaps, but it was enough to bring a smile to my face. Any man would have thought the same.

She was a woman in her middle twenties, I would guess, and slightly shorter than the average, with fine features and a slightly – not to be ungallant, but you know what I mean – a slightly vacant air about her. Those large, luminous blue eyes were slanted downwards away from her delicate nose, and she had full lips, as soft and as pink as rose petals. Her face itself was a pleasing oval, with a high brow and delicately arched eyebrows of a pale colour. The hair that I could see was a delicate golden with strawberry tinges, and I was convinced that there were freckles all over the bridge of her nose and over both cheeks. She was absolutely adorable, and although I was rather occupied at that moment, she was definitely a diversion I would have sought out with enthusiasm, given the chance. I watched her idly as she stood near the doorway, peering about the room with a perplexed expression on her features. She reminded me of a puppy I had once seen at a neighbour's house when I was a boy. It always looked like this: desperate to please, but unsure how to do so.

Others did not have the same feelings about her, if they noticed her at all. Beside me was a scruffy churl who called himself Leadenhall Bob. He cast a short glance at her and sniggered. It was probably her obvious lack of funds. Bob was a mean, thieving devil at the best of times, and he saw only her obvious shortcomings as a potential victim of his charms:

her skirts were threadbare, her feet clad in cheap shoes that were more scuffed than an apprentice's after playing football in the streets, and the coif laced under her chin was deserving of a lengthy wash; it was almost entirely grey. There was no point investigating the contents of her purse, plainly. The rest of our party didn't so much as glance in her direction. My own charge, the Spaniard called Luys, seemed to find it impossible to focus on her. He allowed his head to slump back to the table and began a mild, melodic snore.

We were sitting in the White Bear at the time, at the later end of the evening. I was there with a company of friends – Leadenhall Bob, Lawyer Abraham, Willyam of Whitechapel among others – and with us were a few young women of variable virtue whom we had found in the street and who were keen to entertain us while we had the funds. I was in the fortunate position of having money just now, because I had my new job, but these fellows were men I had met in the days before my recent good fortune, when I was a cut-purse never more than a few steps from the gallows tree. Willyam and I had heavy leather tankards of rich, dark ale, and Bob, too, but the Lawyer stuck to wine.

Willyam had a little packet of golden rocks. 'What are they?' I asked.

He uncovered the packet. It was a square of soft pigskin, and inside were yellow stones, all strangely smooth-sided. 'These? They are called Persian pyrites.' He held one up. 'It looks like gold, doesn't it? I thought it was when I first saw it.'

I took a piece. It did look like gold, certainly, but was considerably lighter. 'Where did you find this?'

'Oh, you know.' He grimaced. 'Just some dark fellow with a hood over his face, but his purse on his hip. He never saw me, but I was hopeful the purse had more than this in it!'

'I see.' A man who dipped his hand into someone else's purse would occasionally find something unexpected. 'What is it worth?'

Willyam shook his head with resignation. 'Nothing. It's just a stone. Soft, too. Although I've heard that you should be careful holding it in your hand. It can burn. If you hit it with metal, it will make sparks like steel and flint.'

'Exciting,' I said. Ale was of more use; that was my own thought. A stone that sparked was good when lighting tinder, but little help for anything else. Besides, I was more interested in the woman who had entered.

I didn't know then just how much trouble she would cause me.

'I say that those who said Spain would make a good bedfellow are all liars,' Bob said, casting a disdainful look at the snoring Spaniard.

Lawyer Abraham tipped his head and peered at Bob from hooded eyes. He was not trained in the law, but with his rangy frame and balding head, he had something of the look of a lawyer, and the manner, too.

It was Willyam who answered Bob's question. 'Why?'

'They come over here, taking our houses, fondling our whores, and don't let any Englishmen into the King's household,' he said, eyeing Luys without favour. 'I say we'd be better if the Queen was still unmarried.'

I didn't want to get involved in a long debate. Bob was the sort of man who would decide he didn't like something in politics, and would chew at it like a dog with a bone until all about him were well-nigh ready to slaughter the fool. He had once been employed in a bishop's household and thought that allowed him to pontificate about the doings of the great and mighty.

Willyam shook his head. 'What of it? You've lost that boat: it's sailed already. Queen Mary, God bless her, is married to her Philip of Spain, and that's that.' I'd known Willyam for a half year, and most of the time he was amusing company. He was thin-faced, with a chin you could use as an awl. His eyes were too close together, but he couldn't help his looks. He had a good brain and, better, light fingers. Willyam had once been a servant in a great house, I had heard, before his interest in other people's money had led to his losing his post and almost being taken to answer probing questions in court.

'There could be another rebellion,' Bob muttered darkly. He was a shortish man, with curly brown hair and a thin mouth, who, in all the time I had known him, managed to look disgruntled about one thing or another.

'There could. Or there could be a visit by serious-minded men with weapons, to take loose-jawed fools who talk too loudly to the Tower to explain why they had something against the Queen's husband,' Abraham drawled.

Willyam glanced at me. 'Very true. We can't afford to have disputes about the Spaniard's rights to be with the Queen, now that she has chosen him, can we? Besides, who would you have her take in Philip's place? The French Prince? Spain is surely a better ally.'

'Ally? They'll be bringing us into their wars, you mark my words. They aren't satisfied with coming over and forcing us to drink their wine; they'll want to have our army join them, and then they'll bring their popish priests over, and . . .'

Willyam shook his head and glanced at me, giving a roll of his eyes. It was the same every time Bob had too much to drink. He was determined to complain to all and sundry about the shocking marriage of the Queen to her Prince. But that was months ago. Their baby was expected at any moment. I said, 'They are married, Bob. Your complaints can achieve nothing! What, do you expect her to copy her father and try to divorce Philip? She is happy, from all the reports.'

'How can she be happy with him?' Bob muttered, submitting to the wine by slumping back.

'Easy,' Willyam said. He held his hands out like an angler describing a monster fish. 'The Spaniard is hung like a donkey!'

The woman at the doorway was a great deal more interesting than such conversation.

Although at that moment I was engaged with a curvaceous young whore called Lizzie, who had sprawled herself over my lap in an act designed to give me a good view of her cleavage while she muzzled lewdly at my earlobe, which was guaranteed to send me into a frantic fever of lust, this new face was distracting.

'Who is that?' I said.

Lizzie chuckled in my ear, and her hand explored beneath my codpiece. 'Why, don't you have enough to deal with already?' she said breathily.

It was more temptation than I could bear. I bent to her, but even as I did so, there was a call from the barman. 'Anyone here called Jack Blackjack?'

Looking up, I saw the woman at his side. She gazed about her at the room with every indication of concern.

'You been planting saplings in that lady's garden?' Willyam asked with a sneer.

Lizzie sniggered, then pouted up at me. 'Aren't I good enough?'

Lawyer Abraham turned and subjected the woman to a close inspection. 'Well, I always knew Jack preferred blondes,' he drawled.

Bob lifted his head with apparent difficulty. He was like a puppy which begins to doze while sitting up, and his head was now unconscionably weighty as he peered at her. 'I wouldn't mind her warming my bed.'

Willyam winked at me. 'But what if she was a Spaniard, eh? You'd want her to make a move homewards quickly enough, I'll wager.'

'I could make an exception for her . . . for at least ten minutes,' Bob sniggered, but then his head began to droop again.

'After the wine you have had,' Lawyer Abraham said thoughtfully, 'I think your exception need only last a moment or two.'

'And you would have to hope she would want a curly-haired simkin like you!' Willyam said. He took a longer pull at his ale.

I looked at the woman again. She was looking around the room, and then I saw her give a fleeting frown as she gazed in the direction of our little table, momentarily meeting my glance.

Willyam turned to look at her, and I saw him give a fleeting smile, a confidential, sly little easing of his lips as he caught her eye. I knew what Willyam was like, pretty much. I hadn't known him that long, but he was always the one who would try to push his way ahead of any man who took the fancy of an attractive little tart. A forceful fellow, with the morals of a true dipper, which is to say that he was a thoroughgoing thief with the morals of an alleycat. What he cared about more than anything was whatever was good for him. Still, he bought his own round when it was his turn, and in the last months I had not had that many friends.

However, Willyam looked as he truly was – a scruffy near-vagrant – whereas I was clad in a new dark-blue doublet, with tight-fitting hosen, a short cloak of dark blue lined with blue silk, and a cap of scarlet, with an extravagant feather springing from the side. I was, in short, the picture of a wealthy young nobleman. Willyam stood no chance.

I extricated myself from the sultry Lizzie, stood, straightened my codpiece, tugged my doublet and made my way to the woman. As I approached, I pulled my cloak slightly, to show off the lining to better effect, and smiled.

She looked me over, and I could see that she was already springing from the idea of a brief conversation to pummelling some sheets with me. I am lucky with my face. Where men like Willyam suffer from narrow-set eyes or skin pocked by youthful spots or other complaints, I have a good head of hair and a face that inspires trust. I have dark-brown eyes, and I make an effort to use them well, lowering my head as if in deep sincerity when I speak. My straight nose and regular features never fail to win over women of all qualities, and usually their husbands too.

'Mistress,' I said, and bowed elaborately. 'I am your most devoted servant. I saw you enter, and . . .'

'I must speak with Jack Blackjack, Master. Do you know where I might find him?'

The man from the bar sniggered and walked away as I smiled lecherously. 'I am he. You were looking for me? What is your name, pretty maiden?'

She looked doubtful. 'I was told to look for a man who had a square face, brown eyes and a little scar on his left cheek.'

I smiled at her. My face has always been my fortune. Women look at me and see a bold yeoman they want to coddle. God would never have given such looks to a black-hearted devil, they think.

Turning my head, I indicated my scar. I always think it gives me a devil-may-care appearance, a proof that I am a bold, adventurous type – although I won it from falling while fleeing a furious miller who wanted to exact vengeance for my deflowering of his daughter. Deflowering, indeed! That little hussy had been more practised than half the women in Piers's brothel.

'Who told you to seek me?' I asked.

'Master Blount.'

The name was enough to make my cods shrivel.

John Blount is, I suppose, my master. He is a loyal servant to Sir Thomas Parry, the comptroller to Lady Elizabeth. Blount last year found me and deemed me to be ideal for his purposes. He had come to believe that there was a need for a man who was determined, bold and ruthless: an assassin.

You see, the nation was embroiled in ructions again at that time, about a year ago. The fool Wyatt was raising Cain in Kent, and leading an armed mob against London to push Queen Mary from her throne and replace her with Lady Elizabeth or Lady Jane Grey. Behind the scenes the men aiding each woman vied for control, and men vying for power can grow dangerous. Blount sought an assassin to use as a final resort in certain cases. In me he thought he had discovered his perfect killer. He little knew that the sight of blood always leaves me weak and enfeebled.

However, his scheming meant I would be better served by accepting his offer of a position than refusing it. To refuse would place me in a delicate situation. I would be in the uncomfortable position of knowing his plans. That, I was sure, would not be a secure berth for me: a man seeking to hire an assassin would not balk at removing an irritating witness to his plans. Then again, there was the other weight in the balance: I was poor, with no home, no friends and no prospects. Blount was holding out the offer of a house, new clothes and food, as well as a goodly salary.

If the worst came to the worst, I could always take his money for the present and then flee, I thought. It seemed to me to be the best of all worlds. Money, women, a warm home . . . who could refuse it?

However, Blount was a hard man to escape from, and it was not easy to disappear. If I fled London, I might survive, if I wanted to. The kingdom outside London always struck me as wet, miserable and filled with fools who could barely speak English, or not in a comprehensible manner. London was my home. Yet if I were to escape his clutches and remain in the city, I had an uncomfortable conviction that he would find me.

It was not a pleasant reflection.

All this, and more, passed through my head as I gazed at her.

'Who are you?'

'A friend. Do you want the message or not? I've spent half the day trying to track you down. Your servant was little help. I've been traipsing all around the city since noon.'

'Noon?' It was about an hour before midnight now, I reckoned. My day had been extraordinarily busy. I had not seen this woman before. She looked still more fretful as I stared at her. 'Why did he send you to find me?'

'How should I know? Look, I have a message for you: he wants you to ignore the Spaniard's man and instead deal with . . .' She reached down into her cleavage. I tried to keep my eyes from her bosom, but not very hard. 'This man.'

I took the slip of parchment with a sense of utter hopelessness. There was a name on the strip of parchment, but I could not read it. Not because the name was written in code, an especial code that a friend of Blount's had devised, but more because my eyes were rheumy and incapable of focusing accurately after so much ale, especially in the dark. 'What does this say?'

'It says Michol, who hails from near St Olave-towards-the-Tower. Can't you read?' she asked, somewhat sharply, and snatched it back. 'Give it to me! It says, "He has a square face, dark hair, is in his early thirties."' She went on to describe a genial-looking man, his clothing, his hat, his manner. He sounded a contented soul.

'You are sure of this?' I demanded.

She peered at me with a faint air of bewilderment. 'Of course.'

'He didn't say something like "When you have completed your task with the Spaniard's fellow, then see to this Frenchman?"'

'No, of course not! Why should he? No, he said to ignore the Spaniard or he would be angry.'

I had no answer to that, of course. Because the simple fact was that I had plans in train already. The Spanish spy, our friend Jeffry, was to die that very day, in almost exactly an hour.

It was that which made me suddenly sober up. There was a cold sweat breaking out on my brow. The careful preparations I had in place already to ensure that this specific man would die were foolproof, and yet now I was being ordered to cancel them and make for a new target.

That was all very well, but if the wrong man were to die, there would undoubtedly be consequences. It would no doubt be my fault, or the blame would be laid at my door, and that would have to mean that I would lose my house, clothes, and perhaps more.

It would be painful, I was sure.

'Where is he?' I asked, a little hoarsely. 'Where is Blount?'

'He was going to meet with someone. He said he would return in a few days,' the woman said. She was clearly nervous, her eyes flitting around the room, resting briefly on the men at the table.

A few days! He was doing exactly the same as me: trying to creating a strong alibi. He would be keeping his own head down and out of any possible nooses, while leaving me standing on the scaffold!

The woman's lip curled. I glanced over at the table. The Spaniard was still sprawling, with his cheek resting comfortably in a puddle of spilled ale. He wore a smile. At his side, Willyam had taken advantage of my flight to accommodate Lizzie with a new lap, and he had his hand inside her bodice while she squeaked and laughed, and Bob and the Lawyer were engaged in an argument, no doubt once more about the Spanish or the French.

Perhaps it was just that this woman was unused to such low dives. A group of men over at the far wall were cheering on a couple who were enthusiastically coupling, while bawds and drunks egged them on with crude shouts and curses. There was a gaming table where men were gambling with money they could ill-afford to lose. It never ceases to astonish me that men who can barely claim the coins to put food in their bellies will still keenly throw the few pennies they possess to enrich a man who owns a pair of skimmed dice.

I stood there for what seemed like an age. Suddenly, a hand landed on my shoulder. I gave a startled convulsion, like a deer who hears a hound baying in the distance. It was Lawyer Abraham, saying Bob was growing tedious, and asking did I want more ale? I shook my head somewhat dumbly and stared about me again. This was terrible news. I found my eyes returning to the woman. She had a steady, confident gaze and held my eye while I considered.

There was only one thing to do.

I fetched my snoring Spaniard and left.

I am supposed to be an assassin, but don't hold that against me. I have never killed anyone on purpose, except during the Wyatt rebellion the previous year, and that was because I couldn't escape the city beforehand. Believe me, I didn't want to be involved.

It was never my intention to become an assassin. But when Blount offered me cash, a house, new clothes and the chance of a lifestyle I could never have imagined, I would have been a complete fool not to accept it. I don't know anyone who would have paused to consider before snapping up the offer. And I could always run away, I thought.

But that little detail of actually being expected to kill people – that was always going to be a problem. Yet the new house, the clothes, the money . . . they were a strong compensation.

It so happened that I was on friendly terms with a young woman called Jen. It was an entirely pleasant relationship up until the moment her husband found out.

He was a fellow called Thomas Falkes, truly a villain of the foulest water. In terms of twisted crookedness, he could outdo the screw on a cider press. He could compete happily with the worst men in London, which means the worst in the whole of England. Worse even than the politicians and lawyers of the city, most of whom were in his purse, for his purse was deep. He was a swindler, blackmailer, procurer of whores and fence of stolen goods. There was no crime so small that he wouldn't conceive a means of profiting by it. But for all that, he was very keen to protect his own woman, and when he heard that I was regularly taking her mattress-galloping, he took umbrage and attempted to investigate my interior organs after skinning me alive. I escaped that and hurriedly left the city. When I returned, he was no longer in business – I think John Blount had devised a means of keeping Falkes occupied for the nonce – and I returned to squiring young Jen.

She was worth the effort. Jen was a slim thing, pale as a pewterer, with red-gold hair so abundant that its weight seemed to keep her chin tilted upwards. She had vacant blue eyes, and lips that were always on the verge of smiling, as well as a pair of bosoms that could suffocate a fellow if she rolled on to him. Still, he would die happy.

Aye, Jen was a lovely little thing, sweet as a piece of sugar-candy, and of course she was deeply in love with me. She loved my intellect, my easy-going nature and, no doubt, my good looks – for Thomas was an ugly brute with the manners of a night-soil collector. Compared with him, I, with my smart clothing and good manners, must have been a source of great joy to her. Yet still, although she was plainly devoted, there were occasions when she could lose her temper, and when she did, it was a sight to behold. In the last few months her rages had grown more regular, and only yesterday, after her latest eruption, I had decided to set her aside. Life was troublesome enough.

The first time it happened was some seven months ago. We were in a tavern, and I happened to cast a glance at a young doxy in the corner. It was little more than that – scarcely more than the time it takes to blink – but Jen began to screech at me, declaring that I must be the savagest man in all London to take a woman like her and then eye every whore in town. It was entirely unreasonable, and I was swift to make my feelings known, you can be sure, but later we made up and all was satisfactory once more. Still, it told me that this was a wench to be wary of. And I was right.

The day before, I happened to meet another woman. We repaired to a tavern, where one thing led to another, and I was about to lead her to an upper chamber for a little horizontal wrestling when I heard a piercing shriek. It was Jen. I suspect she had followed me. Perhaps she had followed me every time I was out and about.

Fortunately, there was not too much at hand, for Jen had a propensity for flinging objects in a manner that made them as devastating as a king's cannon. If she could be harnessed, she could destroy whole towns, I swear. On this occasion, I was able to dart out of the path of the majority of her missiles, and others at the tavern took hold of her and forced her to withdraw, to general merriment. She was tugged from the chamber, her bodice moving thrillingly, and I took my own leave, with the doxy on my arm. The last thing I heard was Jen's threat that she would set her father on to me.

Well, really, I thought with a light chuckle. How fearsome.

And so that morning Humfrie came to visit me.

To be honest, my problems with Jen had slipped into the background at the time. You see, before Humfrie arrived, I was called to visit my master, John Blount, and his news was enough to drive thoughts of Jen, Jen's father, and the wench in the tavern, into the middle distance.

'I have a man I need you to remove,' Blount said as I entered his chamber.

Not the best welcome I have ever received. It sent a shiver down my spine to hear it, as you can imagine.

Blount's house was on St Martin's Lane, nearer St Martin's Le Grand than Aldersgate, only a short distance from St Paul's. A fairly modern house, it was narrow, three-storeyed, with beams and wattle liberally spattered with limewash. Blount lived in a studied, bleak manner like any puritan. His servant, the man I had come to think of as the Bear, from his huge size, let me in and directed me to the rear parlour where Blount was wont to meet his agents.

It was a smallish chamber, bare apart from a table, chair, stool and a number of candles. A simple wooden cross hung from a nail in the wall. There was only one window, and that gave a clear view over a small garden and orchard to the church of St Nicholas.

'Who?' I asked, after clearing my throat several times to bring my voice down to below the mouse-like squeak that threatened. All the while my breakfast attempted to reappear. I have never got used to the idea of removing people. It sounds clinical and straightforward, to borrow the terminology that Blount and others would use, but for me it only meant men, blood and bodies. I had no liking for blood, as I have said, and the idea of attacking men was also unappealing. I have always found that men, when they discover themselves the unwitting victim of an unprovoked assault, will often grow determined to defend themselves, and that usually means that they will launch their own offensive against me.

'You must have heard of the Queen's favourite adviser? Renard? He is from the Spanish imperial court and waits on Queen Mary at every opportunity, even more so now that she has married Philip, the son of the devil!'

He could still make himself angry like that on occasion. Whenever I heard him speak of the Spaniards, he grew warm. I could almost believe that he had some bad experience with a Spaniard when he was young, for he could barely speak of them without spitting.

'What of him?'

Blount sat at his table. His dark eyes were flaming coals deep in their sockets as he glared at me. A heavy brass candle-holder held a single stick that dribbled and sputtered, making his high cheekbones seem even more pronounced with shadows that moved. 'He is the enemy of your Lady and mine. Sir Thomas Parry has learned that he still agitates against Lady Elizabeth and has instructed a man to see her destroyed.'

'Who is this fellow?'

'A low-born son of a churl, called Jeffry of Shoreditch. He has been paid to foment trouble for her.'

'What of the Queen? Or Philip of Spain? Do they have a hand in this?'

Blount sneered at me. 'You think even Mary could think of such a foul deed?'

'She saw to Lady Jane swiftly enough.'

'Lady Jane Grey was foolish enough to marry a man who had the brains of an ape, without the subtlety. She tried to take the throne when Edward died, and then allowed Wyatt to stir rebellion in her favour.'

'In *her* favour?'

'Whether it was the truth or not, only God can know,' Blount said. 'Be that as it may, Wyatt fomented rebellion and the Queen believed it was in order to install Lady Jane on the throne. She has spent the last year attempting to prove that Lady Elizabeth also had a hand in the uprising, but there is nothing to associate her with Wyatt, which is why her head still rests on her shoulders. But if this man should succeed, it may go evilly with her. As for her husband, he would scarcely dare to attack Lady Elizabeth. No, this comes from another quarter – from the ambassador himself, I'll wager.'

I would have questioned him further, but he gave me no time and ran on immediately. 'Now, I must see him dead quickly. I will not permit any danger to the Lady Elizabeth. Ideally, remove him before this day is ended.'

'Oh.'

He looked at me severely. 'Your task is to find this man, pursue him by any means necessary and execute him before he can proceed with his foul plot. There is to be a bonus for you in the matter, too,' he added, disapprovingly.

It was a strange aspect of this grim-featured man that he could happily chat about murdering others, but the subject of money was distasteful to him. I was being rewarded, it was true, but I never saw the harm in a little extra incentive. 'Yes?'

'He has been paid two purses of gold to pursue his foul stratagem. Sir Thomas has agreed that you may keep them. But you must complete this assignment urgently. Is that clear?'

'As clear as a millpond,' I said. My interview was evidently at an end, for Master John had already dismissed me from his mind and was studying a sheet of paper with a frown.

I left.

My first act was to hurry back to my own house, where I began to select a collection of valuables that would serve me well once I had fled the place.

Fled? Of course, fled. I cannot kill men willy-nilly. I have seen men expire, and it's not pleasant even when you aren't responsible. The idea of hunting a man down and killing him in cold blood was appalling. I could no more do that than fly to the top of the tower of St Paul's! No, I had promised myself ever since the horrors of Woodstock last year that as soon as I was instructed to commit another murder, I would be off, and my meeting with Blount was enough to convince me that my time had come.

It was a shame if this man Jeffry was truly determined to harm poor Lady Elizabeth, but that was not my fault. No one could say that *I* was responsible for his actions. And Lady Elizabeth had many resourceful, clever and bold men at her command even now. Her pale complexion and youthful charm had won over many who were determined to be her enemies, from all I had heard. There were plenty who would seek to protect her, no doubt.

Politics is a mess, of course. While thinking of Lady Elizabeth, I could not help but remember a rather more dumpy maid I had seen last year, sitting alone in a chamber, looking rather lost. She was the Queen herself: Mary. And now Queen Mary was a married lady, wedded to the heir to the Spanish empire, King Philip of Naples, no less, and ready, so it was said, to produce her first pup. Some said it was a disgrace that the English throne should be allied to the Spanish, but it all made little difference to me. Whoever ran the kingdom, my life would continue as before, I hoped. And now this Jeffry of Shoreditch wanted to hurt one young woman to enhance the position of the other. All because the Spanish ambassador thought it was in the interests of his master, the King of Spain, I supposed. Philip would not want his English crown to be threatened by the machinations of Lady Elizabeth.

Her face came back to me. I had met her at Woodstock last year, when she was still incarcerated there, and she had made quite an impression on me. Slim, pale, with extraordinary eyes set in that fine face, she was entrancing. And ruthless as an adder. She was more scary than Mary, in my opinion. But there was also something in her that I could see would attract a certain type of man. An adventurous type would consider her a challenge. *I* wouldn't! Once you get to playing hide the sausage with royalty, you know your life expectancy will reduce daily. Lady Elizabeth may be worth a tumble, but I

had the distinct impression that she would exact her pound of
flesh from a man who attempted such familiarity.

I had my things packed away and threw them into a satchel.
My purse holding all my worldly wealth was at my belt. The
strap went over my shoulder, and I was about to leave when
I recalled my secret stash. There was a loose brick in the
chimney, and behind it was a small collection of pennies. I
was about to reach inside the chimney, when my servant,
Raphe, appeared.

'You going out, Master?' he said.

Raphe was a tow-headed lad of some seventeen years. He
was no bottler of skill and ability, nor was he competent as a
steward. When I first took this house, I had a steward called
Atwood, but he made me nervous. Soon Master Blount
appeared and suggested this fellow instead. Atwood left
shortly afterwards, and Raphe arrived.

It was tacitly agreed between me and John Blount that he
would remain. Personally, I wondered whether the lad was
Blount's bastard son and he was keen to keep the fellow
occupied. It struck me early on that his function was less likely
to be that of servant, more that of spy: watching me. Standing
before my door, he eyed my satchel with undisguised interest.

'Yes. I have a task to perform for Sir Thomas,' I said loftily.
The house was, after all, owned by Blount's lord, Sir Thomas
Parry, the confidential servant and comptroller of Lady Elizabeth.
Any plots that John Blount was involved in must be known to
his master, and if they weren't, they should be. I wasn't going
to be the secret agent of Blount against his master!

I left the last pennies behind. Raphe was rubbing his jaw
thoughtfully, his weaselly eyes fixed on me, but I didn't care
as I marched to the door. I was going.

It was not yet the hour for a midday meal, so I thought to buy
a meat pie for later. I could eat it while walking, and put many
miles behind me. But where could I go? I couldn't remain in
London; that was sure. Blount had men everywhere, and there
was nowhere I could hide, except six feet under, which is
where I might well end up, once he exacted retribution. In
preference, I thought I should make my way south of the

Thames, perhaps get advice from Piers at the brothel known as the Cardinal's Hat. He would be able to help.

I bent my way towards London Bridge along Fenchurch Street, mind fizzing all the way. There was the thought of the two bags of gold which Blount had said I could take, which did make my feet slow whenever I thought of them. Two bags of gold, after all, was a treasure to any man. I hoped Piers would be able to help me think my way out of this mess. I reckoned I would need all the help I could get. Yet the thought of being paid two bags of gold . . . it was a hard decision to leave the city when there was an incentive like that. In my mind's eye, I could see the purses. They had a glorious heft to them. I could all but feel them – the wonderful mass of both, one in either hand.

As though in a dream, I strolled down St Margaret's Lane, and it was only when the missile narrowly missed my shoulder that I realized there was a disturbance.

There are some people who come to London and are welcomed with open arms. Usually, it is the type of character who turns up with full purses, like the ones I had been imagining, just begging to be emptied. Some foreigners are gratified to be greeted by the smart set. They are glad to be entertained by new friends, visiting taverns where games are played on which guests can play chance and hazard the devil to take their money. He usually won't, but his minions – the thieving scum of a dozen English towns – will happily do so for him. Dice that have been shaved or fitted with weights, cards with markings, or a bystander who keeps a careful watch on the visitor's game and alerts his companion with unnoticeable signs – all are used in the shady streets of London. The visitors are welcomed and leave poorer, but a great deal wiser.

Men who visit London from abroad are the best of all. From early on being pleasantly surprised by the welcoming kisses of the womenfolk, to discovering the delights of the stews and brothels, they find the city attractive. It is bustling, loud, noisome, dangerous, but fun, exciting and thrilling, all at the same time.

However, the visitors who come arrogantly declaiming the

people of the city, who declare the place a foul pit of deceit and crime, are never welcome.

I was aware of the noise shortly after the second missile. Others might stand and gawp, but I knew my London mob, and when something flies past my ear, I don't wait to see what it was; I duck and find shelter. There was a 'car' beside me, one of the long, thin vehicles designed for London's narrow streets. This, twelve feet in length and three wide, offered some protection. Swiftly, I shot around to the side of it, and then became aware that the missiles were nothing more than small bread rolls.

Now that I could concentrate, I was aware of a series of cries and roars. Looking ahead – in my dreaming I had not noticed this before – there was a wall of men and women blocking my path and the road. A pair of ungodly little heathens of some nine or ten years were egging the adults on.

On the car above me, the carter was grumpily staring over the heads of the crowd, muttering to himself. While he watched, his pony lifted his tail and added his own pungent comment to the delay.

'What's happening?' I called to the carter.

'More of Philip's men. God's pains, why these Roman Spaniards have to come here – fondling our women, taking English positions at court, renting the houses we need! We should send 'em all back where they came from,' the man complained. There was a shout, and suddenly something came flying through the air. This was different. Perhaps the stores of bread rolls were diminished now, but whatever the reason, this time it was a cabbage that came flying. It struck the side of the car near the driver himself. He knelt upright and bellowed, 'You kiss my arse, you peasant, bleeding rufflers!'

I could see nothing of swaggering Spaniards, but I was prepared to watch while the London mob took advantage of a small group of them. It never hurts to watch a foreigner coming up against Londoners in full cry. I once saw a Frenchman take umbrage at a comment from a costermonger and seek to punish the fellow. The costermonger, who had made only a mild comment on the Frenchman's ancestry, called for assistance, and the Frenchman found himself confronted by some dozen before he fled. However, today I was in a hurry. I had to get a move on, else I could be stuck in London for a long while. I pushed and shoved, and generally made a nuisance of myself, but made no headway until there was a sudden shriek, and the crush seemed to melt away like snowflakes on a fire. In no time, I was alone with a body lying in the road and three Spaniards who stood gaping all about them with alarm.

There was a muttered oath – I assume, for it was not in English – and a long rapier flashed towards my throat.

Those who have followed my previous adventures will know that I am never keen to find myself in the presence of the injured, all the more so because often it is assumed that I myself may have some form of responsibility for the body lying before me. Looking down at the point of the blade coming closer, and hearing rapid, heavy boots approaching, I sought to step away and make myself scarce, but even as I turned to flee, I saw two things that made me reconsider: the fallen man's purse and the little movement of his hand.

I am not foolish enough to forgo a possible reward. This was a wealthy young Spaniard, from the look of him. He had a dark complexion, with a narrow, well-formed face and fine little beard that followed the edge of his jaw, and which had been neatly trimmed. His hat was richly coloured and decorated with tiny pearls, while his jack was bright scarlet, with sleeves slashed to show a bright yellow silk interior.

But it was his purse that had caught my attention. This was one of those fellows who trusted no one. He kept his worldly wealth on him, or so it looked. The purse was made of beautiful leather, I thought, with a red hue, but patterned with the impression of some kind of repeated symbol, like a coat of arms. The leather looked soft, but very strong. Of particular interest to me was the way it bulged in such an enticing manner. My occupation until last year had been that of professional cut-purse, and I was very successful in my calling. I knew my targets: those who were younger, who were as green as fresh-stripped bark, who had little experience, and, ideally, those who were so new to the big city that they hadn't had time to rinse the mud from their shoes. Those who stood gawping at the tall buildings, who gazed on the spire of St Paul's cathedral as if expecting it to topple at any moment, who didn't notice the shit in the alleys even when they stood in it; these were my targets. And who could be easier to fleece? Why, a Spaniard, newly arrived with a purse full of gold.

His hand clenched, then spread, and he gave a groan, rolling on to his breast, placing his hands on the dirt of the road and pushing himself upright. Reluctantly (for he had fallen into piles of ordure from dogs, pigs and horses), I squatted at his side and murmured soothingly into his ear. I ignored the blade that was pointed at my throat. It was the action of a nervous man who had just been the centre of unwelcome attention and was wary of any newcomer, rather than a serious threat.

Mind you, this new fashion for carrying lighter swords is a growing problem. In the past, a foister like me, who was practised at picking pockets, only had to worry about the poor gull carrying something like a riding sword or heavy-bladed broadsword. Those things took time to pull from a scabbard and couldn't be used just anywhere – they were too cumber-some – but these Spanish toys were light, swift and lethal. A man could be stabbed twice before he realized he was in danger from a Toledo steel. I didn't like them.

'It's good enough, fellow,' I said to the man on the ground, patting his back. God's wounds, but that purse looked heavy! 'They all fled when they heard me arrive. You poor man! What sort of a welcome is this for a foreign guest, eh? It was your head, was it?' It was easy to see that he had been struck. The blood was gathering in his hair. His hat must have protected him a little, but he had been clobbered well. No doubt the brute who had done this was already enjoying a quart of ale at the expense of his comrades, celebrating this victory over the hated foreigner. He would have had more companions with him if he had but grabbed the purse as well, I thought. This is the difference between a fool who enters fights for no reason and a man like me, who attempts to avoid the use of violence.

'What's all this?' a harsh voice demanded. It was the catch-pole. He stood with two companions, all grasping staffs viciously shod at either end with iron designed to break a man's head. 'Who are you?'

'I am Peter the Passer,' I said. It was a name I have used often enough before, but it was never dishonoured, so far as I knew. I pointed back along the street. 'I live just off Alegatestrete. I saw a mob here and hurried up to help. Some fools attacked this poor fellow. Look, they tried to smash his skull.'

The constable nodded suspiciously. His face looked as though someone had tried to batter Ludgate open with it. His nose was flattened, his brow heavy, his jaw massive. I had the impression that, were I to punch him, he would be unlikely to feel it, and my hand would be broken permanently. 'Who did this?'

'I didn't see. I was at the back. When this fellow fell, and they all saw you coming, they scattered.' I saw the carter, who was still standing and watching with apparent interest. 'Ask him. I was with him when the crowd began to grow agitated. Better, ask these fellows. They will confirm my words.'

'If they speak any bleeding English, which I doubt,' the constable said.

He went to the carter and asked, while I remained, helping the fellow on the ground to sit up. He had a permanent wince on his face, and he laid his hand on his head as if to contain his brains before they spilled loose. 'Did you see who hit your friend?' I said to the others.

The sword had gradually dropped, and now the man who held it shamefacedly thrust it into the scabbard. He stared at me, then at his companions, and shook his head. I got the strong suspicion that the constable was right: these men spoke nothing of our language.

Looking down at my charge, I saw that his eyes were narrowed with pain. 'I do not know,' he said, in passable English. 'They were just idlers and vagabonds.' He felt quickly at his hip, before the tenseness suddenly left him. 'But at least they did not try to rob me.'

'No,' I smiled.

The catchpole was glad enough when I offered to take the Spaniard off his hands.

Why did I want to do it? The weight of his purse was a
great incentive, but just then I needed to get away from London
and hide somewhere so that John Blount couldn't find me. I
wasn't going to put myself through the strain of trying to kill
some fellow in cold blood. That wasn't the sort of man I was.
But, as they say, a pickpocket can take a purse from a man,
but no man can take a pickpocket from his haunts. Well, it's
what I say, anyway. I was made to be a thief, and I am an
uncommonly good one. It was a hard trade to learn, and now
I have grown to manhood, I find it difficult to resist the temptation of a good weighty purse like this Spaniard's. I felt
confident that I could have his purse swiftly enough, if I was
given the opportunity.

Yes, it was a foolish idea. He had men with him, and finding
them alert enough, and distrusting, should have warned me,
but I was not thinking straight. In my mind was the command
to kill this Jeffry, the horror of complying with Master Blount's
instruction, and the thought that I must get away from London
permanently. Yes, if I stole this purse in my own home, the
Spaniard would know who had taken it, but the beauty of my
plan was that even if he knew, it wouldn't matter, because by
the time he appeared knocking at my door, I would be far
away in Kent or Surrey.

So it seemed a good idea to bring the man to my home. It
would have been better, were it only me and my gull, but I
could not help the fact that the other three tagged along with
me. They seemed still to hold some sort of grudge against me,
as though I was as much of a threat as those who had assaulted
them in the street. I would never do such a thing, of course,
but they clearly did not trust me.

'Who are you?' I asked my companion as we walked.

His face was pale under his brown complexion, but he
walked with his head held as high as a knight. If only he had
used the odd vile oath or two, I would have thought him a
nobleman. 'My name is Luys de Aguilera.'

'And you're over here with the Queen's husband?'

'Yes. We came with King Philip, and we are here still to
support him and his wife.'

He shot a look over his shoulder as he spoke and I gained

the clear impression that, whatever else, these four were not here just to fetch and carry for the Queen's man. He muttered something in his rattling language, and the men nodded grimly. I got the impression, I don't know why, that this man, with his showy style and apparent riches, was no less a scoundrel than me. In particular, I was convinced that his name was not Luys any more than mine was Peter the Passer.

'Here we are,' I said.

Luys stared up at my house. 'This is a big house,' he commented in his strange accent. It almost sounded as if he was surprised to learn that I had such a large property. I could have been insulted, had I given myself time to think. But maybe that was only his accent, and I was doing him a disservice.

Instead, I threw open the door and helped my charge inside. Bellowing for my servant, I asked Raphe to bring me a footstool, and soon had Luys installed in front of my fire with blankets all about him to keep him as warm as possible.

While I was seeing to his comfort, his companions stood in a huddle, eyeing my belongings, my pewter and other items on display. My suspicious friend, who had been so keen to draw his sword and point it at me, stood with an expression of grim uncertainty on his face, as if expecting at any moment to be set upon once more. Plainly, he thought I kept a small brigade of ferocious ruffians in my home in order to do away with chance visitors, the fool.

I called to my servant for ale, and then glanced at the three and changed my mind. Foreigners from the Continent, so I had heard, preferred to drink wine. With that in mind, I gave Raphe instructions to go to the vintner's on the corner and buy a small barrel of good Guyennois wine. Thinking, I pulled out my purse and fiddled, hoping that the three would take the hint and offer to pay, but they were clearly well born, and therefore as tight-fisted as a Scotsman. Reluctantly I put my purse away and told him to promise to pay for the wine later. I hoped to be long gone before the vintner appeared to demand his bill be settled.

'You would offer hospitality to us?' Luys said.

'Of course,' I said. Although I had given the wounded

gentleman my chair, I yet had a stool, and I plonked my arse on it. No sooner had I done so than there was a slither of steel and that damned rapier returned to my throat.

Now, generally I dislike being threatened. It grieves me to risk my good looks and limbs, let alone my life, but this man's routine resort to cold steel was seriously annoying me. I looked along its blade, to the man's eyes. He was older than my battered companion, with a face that had surely seen a certain amount of excitement. He had a ragged scar on the right of his face, and his mouth held a sardonic grin as a result. His brow swept back, and he had a significant widow's peak that gave him a strangely feline look. But it was the appearance of a wild cat, not some casual mog from the street; he looked more like a feral brute that would scratch my eyes out in an instant.

However, I had shown him kindness, I was investing in wine to entertain him and his injured friend, I was delaying my departure (yes, only so I could steal some of their wealth, but they didn't know that), and, all in all, his habit of threatening me was growing worse than tedious – it was also rude.

'Master Luys, would you tell your dog here to remove his blade, or I will shove it so far up his arse that he'll have to sharpen it by opening his mouth,' I said coldly.

Luys chuckled at that, wincing as he did so. He rattled off some words like a fusillade of artillery, and the man relented. The rapier withdrew an inch or two, and he stared at me resentfully before thrusting it back into his scabbard. Turning to Luys, he snapped something that sounded appallingly rude, but, for all I knew, he could have been commenting on the weather. Luys returned with something that sounded conciliatory, and Rapier Man gave a gesture of disgust. Strange how some gestures are easily comprehended. He threw his hands up, rolled his eyes and gave a little gasp, and I could see at once that he was telling Luys, 'This Englishman cannot be trusted, but you ignore my good advice and prefer to pander to him? You should have your brain examined. It's scrambled by that blow.'

Raphe entered with a flagon of wine and goblets. He filled them, passing them to our guests, and one to me, and I had to tell him to refill the flagon and bring it back. If I could, I would have had the vintner's barrel in here too, because if I understood men at all, the thieving scrote, Raphe, would drink half the barrel in the parlour while we were in here.

Luys drew me back to the present, glancing at me. 'My companion is determined to think that you are a dangerous fellow. He said that we should beware of you, that your kindness and . . . your good looks could be a clever ruse to disguise evil intent.'

'He does, does he?' I said coolly enough, looking up at the man.

'Ramon is not very trusting. It is not surprising after what happened in the street.'

'It is odd that he should seek to distrust the one man in London who came to help you.'

Luys gave a quick grin. 'It is that which makes him mistrust you!'

I grimaced. This Ramon was a fair bit brighter than Luys, then. I was sure that he was a servant here to protect his young master. 'I think him a very cynical fellow.'

'Cynical?'

'It means he seeks to find the worst of any man he meets, rather than treating them as another Christian soul,' I said, allowing a degree of hurt to enter my voice.

'Do not mind him,' Luys said.

He was the son of a Spaniard who was in the King's court, he told me, and keen to learn all he could about this land. The customs, the habits of all the people – these were his study. 'You see, I must learn about the foods, about the drinks, about the . . .' He blushed slightly.

'The women?' I said.

'Indeed, these too,' he said, and I instantly saw what form of fellow he was. Here he was, a young fellow set loose in the greatest city in all Christendom, and he was desperate to get to fencing with a bawdy basket. He would be desolate if he didn't find a wench.

'Are you free this evening?' I said. If I had to, I could put off my disappearance for one more day, I thought, staring at him to prevent my eyes from sliding down towards his purse.

'I could be,' the lad said, glancing up at Ramon. He didn't have to say what was going through his mind. Ramon had to be left behind.

'Meet me here this afternoon, and I shall take you to a safe place,' I promised. And I smiled.

It was approaching the time when sensible men would be seated at their grand tables ready to fill their bellies, and I had plenty of miles to cover if I was to escape the city, yet I was now in two minds about fleeing or making the most of the opportunity represented by that purse, as I saw the Spaniards to the door. They gazed up and down the street before setting off purposefully southwards.

That purse. It filled my mind with dreams of gold and jewels, and I could barely contain myself.

Raphe entered the chamber, glowering about him with the look of a terrier who had heard a rat. I ignored him, as a well-bred man would. I did not even comment about the reek of wine on his breath.

'I suppose Master Blount will be happy to hear you're looking out for Spaniards,' he said as he picked up a goblet with a grimace. Anyone would have thought he considered the vessel polluted with poison, the way he took it up.

'What has he to do with anything?'

'Nothing. What would I know?' he said with that strange, wheedling whine that is the proud manner of speech of the lowest orders of servant.

I was about to kick him from the chamber when a moment's reflection caused me to hesitate. 'What makes you say that about Blount? What do you know about him?'

'I know little enough. I know what you are paid for,' he added.

I jerked the dagger from my belt and held it high, as though to plunge it into his breast. 'You know my profession?'

He looked up at the blade with a wavering uncertainty in his eyes. 'I had heard something.'

'What?'

His gaze flashed from the blade to me and back. 'Nothing, I'm sure. It's nothing.'

'Are you well enough paid for being here?'

'I . . . yes!'

'Then if you want to keep your . . . your *position* here, and not lose things you would prefer to keep, you will watch your tongue.'

He nodded. Clearly my little pause had given him time to reflect. If he had once been told that I was an assassin, he would think twice before irritating me again.

'Now,' I said, 'why did you say that about me looking after Spaniards? What do you know?'

'Master, I meant no harm!' he declared suddenly, and I thought he would piss himself. His face was anguished when he stared at me. 'Don't hurt me! I know about Master Blount, because he told me to keep a close look on you, in case you should come into danger. But he also told me you had a new task, and I was to watch in case a Spanish intelligencer might set men to keep an eye on you. That's all!'

'So you made a comment about me serving Spaniards because he thought someone could be watching me?'

'I only meant to say that you were watching those who were trying to watch you, Master!'

Although it took a little time for me to work my way through the logic of that, I kept a firm grip of him and maintained my glare. 'And what of these Spaniards watching me?'

'There is a man, sir – not short, but not over-tall either. He is a strong-looking fellow, with the build of a miller, but the look of a bull. He holds his head low and looks ready to charge.'

'What of his clothes?'

'He wears a cowl, a dark hood over a fustian robe of some sort. Makes him look like a miller clad as a cleric.'

'Where have you seen him?'

'Out in the street, sir.'

I let him go. 'You have been drinking too much of my claret and it's addled your brains, such as they are! Stop worrying about men in the street and start thinking more about your job, if you don't want to be thrown from my door!'

For good measure, I kicked his arse as he fled the room, then I sat in the chair so recently vacated by Luys, and chuckled to myself. A little while ago I had watched a man demonstrating his skills as a juggler. One trick had impressed me, and now I copied him, balancing my dagger on my finger and keeping it there a while, thinking that if Raphe knew I was supposed to be a lethal assassin, I might as well pander to his impression. Then the blade slipped, and as it ran down the side of my finger, it cut deep, before clattering on the floor. I picked it up, stowed it in my sheath and sucked my finger.

The man in the road was no Spaniard. He was surely a London cove, one of those involved in the underworld. I knew that Blount had a couple of men who were often with him. Perhaps this was the one I always thought of as the Bear on account of his size. Raphe was no judge of character or man, and he would look on anyone as tall compared with himself.

It was plain enough that Master Blount was keeping an eye on me, but less, perhaps, because he thought me a careless wastrel with no competence in the task he had set before me, and more because he thought me a serious agent who was dangerous, but also in danger. So he had set Raphe to guard me, had he? That was good to know. And from the sound of things, another bully London fellow in case Raphe was too dim to do it properly. At least Blount was protecting his investment in me.

Not that it helped me with my immediate problem: whether I should take my package now and flee, or wait for the Spaniard to return so I could relieve him of his purse. One thing I was certain of was that I was not going to see to the execution of Jeffry of Shoreditch. I could not do that, not even for two bags of gold.

These were the issues that tormented me. Fly now, or fly later with a rich man's purse.

I should have been better occupied in finding a low tavern and drinking myself to a dribbling stupor. It would have been more productive, as my next guest was to prove to me.

I confess that I was not alarmed when Humfrie turned up at my door.

The knock, when it came, was a fairly quiet affair. I mean to say, I was expecting the knock of Luys's companion, which would surely have been a loud rapping with the pommel of a dagger, or the slightly dulled thudding of a gloved fist. Instead, this was a tentative little tap, as of a single knuckle. I was a man of some status now, a man of substance, so I left Raphe to answer it.

'Yes?' I enquired loftily when he was brought into my parlour.

The visitor wore a felt cap with a large feather in it. His hats always had feathers, I was to discover. His jack was old and rather threadbare, and he had a cloak of some dull, brownish material that reached to his shins. It looked very coarse. He walked into my room and stood there, gazing about the place as if he was completing his own inventory. Apparently, it came up to expectation, for at last he deigned to notice me and approached me, removing his cap as he came.

At first sight, he struck me as the sort of man who would work in a smithy. He was not big, exactly, but not small; he had strong shoulders, but they weren't too wide; his hands were powerful, but hardly fearsome. All in all, I would have said that he was a competent-looking fellow, but not the kind to set the world afire. A man accustomed to using his hands, but not a fighter. He was more a labourer, I would have guessed.

'Yes?' I repeated.

He continued to walk towards me without speaking. His cap was in his left hand now, and as I looked up into his eyes, I saw a cold glitter in them. It was like looking at moonshine gleaming on black ice in the middle of the night: it was as cold and unfeeling. Suddenly, I regretted Raphe's departure. He had walked away as soon as he had ushered my guest into the chamber. Learning who this was, I would have hoped the black-hearted fool would have realized that I might have needed his help, but I could hardly wave at him or frown while Humfrie stood there before me.

'Yes? Hello?' I said.

He had come within a pace of me and now he stared into my eyes.

His was a face that had been lived in. There, in the gloom of the early evening in my house, his face seemed to be made up of wrinkles and creases, with the dirt deeply ingrained in all, as though someone had set off black powder near his face and the soot had burned deep. His eyes were a deep blue, almost black. His skin was like well-tanned leather that has been soaked and dried a dark colour, like aged oak, and I got the impression that if I were to hit him, it would hurt me much more than him. He did indeed look a hard man.

'You are Jack Blackjack.'

It was tempting to deny it. There was something about his eyes that was alarming. 'You have the advantage of me.'

'Yes,' he said.

This was unsettling, I confess. I essayed a light laugh, but even to me it sounded a bit too much like a lamb's bleat. 'So who are you?'

He smiled. The slow parting of his lips reminded me of a snake. 'I am the man sent to kill you.'

You will understand that this was not news I wished to hear. Suddenly, I had a vision of Thomas Falkes. He had his fingers in so many pies all about the city that it would not be a surprise to learn that some of his companions were murderers. Perhaps one of them had decided to take revenge on me for the insult and any injury done to Falkes. Was this the man whom Raphe had seen, the man who had been watching me?

I began speaking hurriedly, backing away, thinking that I might dissuade this assassin, but he cut off my babbling by pulling his cap away from his midriff where it had remained since he took it off. Behind it, I saw now that he was gripping a dagger. It was not long, but it appeared thoroughly service-able, and, more to the point, it was very close to my belly. The candlelight lit the edge, and it shone yellow and malevolent like poison. 'Be silent,' he said.

'I . . . You . . .'

'Shut up,' he said.

'You are an assassin? Have some . . .'

'Shut up. I was sent here to teach you a lesson, for my little Jen takes offence so easily and she wished me to punish you.'

'Jen? My darling Jen?'

'I am Jen's father,' he said quietly. 'I am called Humfrie.'

What, this fellow was going to try to fleece me for the enjoyment of those womanly parts that should have been kept back for her husband? Well, if he tried to take any sort of high-handed line of that nature, I was prepared to be blunt. After all, it takes two to play hide the sausage. And then I reflected that he held a sharp dagger and looked thoroughly competent to use it. I doubted he would cut himself playing balance the blade. And he might think that I had unfairly forced his daughter into my bed. Many a man could be persuaded to feel a degree of righteous indignation at the thought that the little girl who was his pride and joy had been rudely deflowered of her virtue, without considering that the little strumpet had been wagging her backside at every young man who had a purse or a codpiece larger than an acorn.

He gave me a look that told me perfectly clearly that just now she was definitely *his* 'little Jen', and not mine.

I took the hint and was silent.

'She tells me that you were out whoring. It made her cross.'

I gulped a little at that. 'Oh, it was just a—'

'You know who she lives with?'

'Yes,' I said. There was no point trying to hide it. Everyone knew of Falkes.

'Aye, well, he has disappeared this last year, almost. He may be dead, for all I know. But until his corpse appears, the fact remains that she's married.'

'She's married? Why, if—'

'I'm not thinking about you. You should want me to keep it that way,' he said.

Raphe poked his head around the door and asked whether we wanted anything. I tried to indicate, without speaking or gesture, that I wished him to slug this man on the head, but he didn't seem to comprehend and walked out again.

Humfrie continued, 'Yes, she is married. Why she's so desperate for me to punish you, when she's the one who's been playing marbles with another man's ballocks, I don't know. Still, she was ever a wilful child. Just you be careful of her. I don't want to have to keep coming here. In future, if you can't keep your tarse in your cods, at least go somewhere quiet if you want to swive a wench, and don't let Jen see you in plain view.'

I think it's fair to say that I goggled at him. 'You aren't going to hurt me?'

'Do you want me to?' He lifted the corner of his mouth at that. It looked entirely sardonic, although I wasn't sure that I liked it. After all, he was implying that he didn't feel it would take much effort to execute me. 'No one's going to pay me to come here and injure you. I only hurt people for money, not for pleasure.'

I suppose he saw my look of surprise. His grin grew, but although his eyes creased, I didn't see any humour in them. 'Did you not know? I had thought Jen would have told you before sending me here. You say you know her husband, Thomas Falkes?'

'Yes.'

'So you know what sort of a man he is. He employs me. Or did, before he disappeared.'

'That . . . um. I know what he did.'

'Falkes is a special man. He is an extorter of money, a fence, a man who will rob a cart of its wheels, who would steal the food from a beggar, but he does more serious business too.'

'I know. Jen has told me.'

There was a faint surprise in his face on hearing that. 'Really? So you know sometimes he will use harsh methods.'

'He had a man's legs broken for fiddling him of a little profit, I heard.' The man had tried to keep back a small amount of money from a whore he was pimping for. When Falkes heard, he had the man's legs broken, his shin bones and thighs, before he ordered his men to cut off both index fingers, so he would never again 'put a finger into another man's pie', as he said. I swallowed at the thought.

'I see you do know, then,' Humfrie said. He set his head to one side, surveying me. 'I kill men for him – for money. Falkes retains me to remove his business competitors.'

The smile that broke out on my face made him scowl, and I quickly disposed of it. 'I see.'

'What's so funny?'

I quickly fitted a serious expression to my face. 'Nothing.'

He looked about him again. 'Jen tells me you are respected. You have a pleasant home here.'

'I like it.'

'It would be a shame if it got damaged.'

I shrugged. Today, with all my thoughts of running from London, damage done to my house was the least of my concerns. What was it, after all? Only another man's invest-ment. It could burn to the ground for all I cared. I wanted money, specifically Jeffry's money, but I could do nothing about it. I would have to kill Jeffry first.

And that was when I had a brilliant, shining idea. It was one of those that occasionally strike me, one which has such brilliance that it quite took my breath away. This time, when I laughed, he did not ask why, but his eyes narrowed, and he was suddenly very still and tense.

I waved a hand at my chair and stool. 'Master Humfrie, would you mind sharing a little wine with me? I have a proposition for you.'

I left my house later with a feeling that all was well with my world. Humfrie showed himself to be a thoroughly accommo-dating man, and when I explained that I had a certain task for him, and that there could be more similar jobs in the future, he looked suspicious for a moment, but when I went on to say that all those he pursued and removed were sworn enemies of the realm, he was far less concerned. He seemed to think that if he made enemies of these people, it would likely be less dangerous than being involved in some of the business disputes that his involvement with Falkes had led to. Remembering Falkes, I could easily see that he might be correct.

The Spaniard calling himself Luys arrived just as a fine rain began falling, and I promised him an evening to remember. Which, all things considered, was literally true – for me, if not for him.

We went first to the White Bear down near St Botolph's, where I bought him a quart of the best strong ale I could find. I had some of the weaker. I wanted him drunk as a duke, so that the next stage of my plan would be executed efficiently. It was a mere chance that we stumbled into the three drinkers at the same time. I had known the three while working the streets as pickpocket. Willyam was agog at the sight of my companion, while Lawyer Abraham looked at him with amusement and Bob seemed barely to notice him. They all noticed Luys's purse, though. Men of our quality don't miss things like that.

On hearing that we were going to the Cardinal's Hat, Lawyer Abraham and Leadenhall Bob expressed an urgent need to see the ladies too. Willyam was soon persuaded by the other two, and we set off for the river. There were several wherries plying their trade. Later, many of the wherries would cease their activities as the light faded and the curfew was called, but there were always some who would continue on into the night. They swore and rowed incessantly, but they were easier than fighting your way over the bridge, with its narrow thoroughfare and houses at either side. As long as they were offered the price of a pint or two of ale, they were more than content.

Soon we were at the other side, and I was happy. I made plenty of noise, and when we passed by the bear pits, I made myself unpleasantly memorable to one of the masters of the mastiffs. I sneered at his monsters on their chains and, egged on by my companions, I laughed at the thought that they would manage anything in the ring. The master saw me and offered to introduce me to the nearest slavering brute, and if I didn't fetch myself away, he would release the thing and see what I thought of him then.

I took the quickest route from the pits, you can be sure. Besides, my aim had been achieved. I wanted to ensure that there was a strong alibi. Since Raphe knew that I was commissioned to have something to do with Spaniards, I wanted to make sure that everybody knew exactly where I was, because Humfrie had sworn to achieve his aims this very evening, and had told me that he would do away with Jeffry at nearly midnight at The Brokenwharf. Which was perfect, I thought. It was at the other side of the river and some distance away from the Cardinal's Hat.

I had left Raphe with a message for John Blount, informing him that the nuisance would this very evening be removed, and now I needed as many people as possible to remember where I was. Then, when the body was discovered, as it must be, no one would be able to blame me. I would be safe. And it also occurred to me that John Blount would wonder how on earth I had managed to be in two places at the same time.

It didn't matter that he would be confused. In fact, that was one of the attractions of the situation. The more that even he could not reason how I had achieved the murder, the more valuable I must appear to him.

It was all to the good, I thought. But I wasn't aware how the Fates were about to punish me for my confidence and arrogance.

We strolled from the bear pits down the road to the Cardinal's Hat. All the way, Luys appeared to be casting glances about him, as if he constantly expected to have a gang of wastrels leap upon him and carry him off, or perhaps merely murder him.

'You're safe here with us,' I reassured him, but my words did not seem to ease his mind. The raucous singing and lewd jokes of Bob and Lawyer Abraham were hardly designed to calm the nerves of a Spaniard. They are known to be ever timid, not hardy like Englishmen, so I patted his back in a brotherly sort of way, and led him to the door of the Hat.

It was one of those afternoons when the place had a number of visitors. The usual roughs at the door had been allowed to go and sink some ales, and in their place was a man built like St Paul's cathedral, along with Piers.

'Ho! Piers!' I cried. I was glad to see him.

He gazed back with a frowning expression while he swayed slightly.

Piers was one of those men whose age was impossible to guess. I certainly couldn't. He had greying curls over a drawn, rather haggard face. His blue eyes were still clear, but the mass of veins about his cheeks and nose spoke of the brandy and wine that had been his downfall. Once he had been a moderately successful barber in London, but his wife and children left him as his drinking became ever more problematic and the money did not support them. I think they went back to her father's house, and Piers could devote himself to drinking himself into a stupor every evening.

It was the lady who owned the Cardinal who brought him back from the brink. She wanted a reliable man who was not interested in the bevvy of beauties she controlled, who could protect them when customers grew too demanding, and who could cut their hair. Piers had all the requisite skills, when sober, so he was given the job and permitted to cut their hair after his first wet of the morning, but not after the second. One was adequate to stop the shaking of his hands, but by the time he had the second, he was dangerous with a pair of scissors.

Today he looked worse than usual. His grey features were waxen, as though he had a constant sheen of sweat over his face. Still, he allowed us all inside, and soon I was sitting with Bob and Lawyer Abraham while our Spanish friend and Willyam went inside to enjoy themselves.

Later, when Willyam had returned, smiling like a hound who's eaten a cat, I was tempted to enter a chamber with one of the less expensive wenches.

If only I had. I might have missed a lot of pain and trouble.

By the time Luys was ready to plead exhaustion and beg to be released, we were all growing fidgety. There was one fubsy wench there who could see my eye on her, and who had lips that pouted delightfully, and whose breasts were like plump melons, and although I was tempted to go and investigate the depths of her cleavage, I had not yet managed to separate my charge from his purse. I was keen to keep a clear head.

We took our leave of the brothel, not without a regretful glance at the pouting beauty on my part, and began to make our way back to the river. The wherrymen were mostly gone for the evening, but I saw one man asleep in his boat, curled up with a blanket over him against the evening's chill, and he grumpily agreed to cross the waters one last time. We all scrambled in – Luys almost falling into the water, he was so wearied after his exertions – and we were sworn at foully by the master of the craft.

Soon we were crossing the river, the wherryman aiming at a point far upstream, while the current pulled us downriver. As if by a miracle, he deposited us at almost the same place where we had taken a boat earlier that evening. Before long we were happily ensconced in the White Bear once more.

The evening's drinking continued well. I had thought to get Luys wicked drunk in a hurry, and then to relieve him of his purse in a game of cards or dice, and make my cheerful way home, and all appeared to be succeeding surprisingly well. I had pushed food and strong ale into him, convinced that the two together would induce a sense of well-being and comfort, such that when a game was proposed, he would be agreeable. It usually works. Soon I was happily groping the lovely Lizzie, while my Spaniard was outside spewing.

I should have gone with him, obviously. I knew that even as he rose from the table, his face blotched and pink, and hurried from the room. But the fact was that Lizzie was an entrancing distraction, especially since I had remained celibate while my friend made free with the assets of the mistress of the game at the Cardinal's Hat, and all I could think of at that moment was the delicious young strumpet wriggling on my lap.

Luys came back, wiping his mouth with the back of his hand, and I winced to think how he must reek. English ale is strong food for those with English hearts and stomachs, but this foreigner clearly had weakly blood from too many years drinking wine. Still, I had to appear concerned. 'Are you well, Luys?'

'Yes, I think some of the ale was off,' he said, but there was a frown on his face.

'Is something troubling you?'

'There was a man out there, just now. He did not know that I could see him, and he was only a shape in a doorway, but he kept watching this place.'

'What sort of a man?' I asked.

'Heavy, ugly,' Luys belched. He grinned at me and took another draught. 'He was like a man I saw before, watching outside here before we crossed the river.'

He gave me another grin and then slowly subsided until his cheek was companionably resting on the table.

I did not like the sound of this. Raphe had mentioned a large, ugly man outside my house, too. Was it Blount's man, Bear? If not, who was this fellow, and was he following me? I tried to elicit further descriptions from Luys, but at the moment he was smiling happily and seemed incapable of waking.

It was a little after this that the buxom angel appeared, just as I was thinking of slipping Lizzie from my lap and removing the purse from his waist, but with the messenger's appearance all thoughts of my Spaniard's purse – and Lizzie – fled. There was no point thinking of such matters when John Blount was likely to want to see me racked and disembowelled for killing the wrong man. Especially since after disembowelling me he would really go to town on my remains. Of that I was certain. I didn't feel well.

I had intended to remain here with Luys, but now I had other matters to occupy me. I left my little gathering to go and find Humfrie before he could kill Jeffry. That was the thought uppermost in my mind as I drained my tankard and gave my farewells.

'We'll look after your Spanish friend.'

Willyam's words struck me hard. I couldn't leave the poor fool with Willyam and the others. They'd empty his purse in the blink of an eye. It was only professional politeness that had kept them from doing so already. No, I would have to protect him, clearly. But how to do so, when my house was in the opposite direction to the quay where Humfrie was going to kill Jeffry? I resolved that I would take Luys with me and hope that his presence would not harm my effort to save Jeffry.

I roused him with difficulty and got him to stand, just, with one hand outstretched on the wall, the other at his belly. When I pulled at his arm, trying to persuade him to come with me, he was as reluctant as a hound on a leash for the first time. He kept on muttering gibberish, or so it sounded to me. Perhaps he was just speaking in his own language. In any case, after some oaths and mentions of his suspect parentage under my breath, I did succeed in getting through to him.

'Tired. Need bed.'

'Aye, well, let's go then,' I said, and steered him into the road and towards the river where Humfrie was.

'You are a best friend to me,' Luys slurred.

'Yes.'

'Men say these English are only sons of pigs, but you are kind. I like you.'

The insufferable fool threw an arm over my shoulders. He reeked of vomit.

'Good,' I said.

'You not son of a pig. You nice man.'

'Thank you so much.'

He continued in this vein for most of the journey, beery, vomity, garlicky breath wafting all over me. By the time we reached the little alley leading to the quay, I was myself about ready to throw up. With relief, I heard him say that he was rather sleepy, and I let him sink to a sitting position at the entrance to the alley. While I watched, he stretched out his legs, finding a pool of what I hoped was water – although, this being London, I wouldn't vouch for it – closed his eyes with a sort of beatific relief, and began to issue a whistling alternating with a low rumble, rather like light rocks rolling down a hill.

I left him there. The rest you know.

I came to with that almost-glad-to-be-alive feeling that I have been growing to know so well. It was *almost* because at the back of my mind there was a sort of feeling that, now I was awake, what or whoever it was who knocked me out would feel entitled to continue with his Battering Jack project. It was not something I wished to carry on.

There was a brief period of pain. My head was a mass of bruises and pain, and I did not attempt to sit up yet. That shows how much I have been learning. There are correct ways of recovering from head injuries, and there are painful ways. I have had more experience of them in the last year than most hardened boxers would win in a lifetime.

This time there was a loud hissing in my ears. It was irritating, but sticking fingers in both meant I could hear nothing – nothing but the hissing. It was apparently there to stay for the nonce. When I opened my eyes, there was an interesting display of stars in the darkness. At first I thought it was the sky I was looking at, and I enjoyed the display for its own sake, before realizing that as I blinked the display was beginning to fade. By the time I felt composed enough to sit up, the stars were almost gone.

My hat had been struck from my head and was lying upside down in the kennel. I leaned over, picked it up and eyed it distastefully. There was a distinct odour about it that did not bode well. That was when I realized that my hosen were damp, but fortunately I think it was only a little water from the river that had lain in the cobbles of the alley. Finally, I moved my shoulders. Although there was a little wetness on my back, my new doublet felt undamaged, and I could not discern the smells I feared.

It was then that I remembered what I had been doing in the alley. I stood and had to pause, toppling and grabbing at the pillar that stood some two yards from me. I was like a seaman sailing on a wild ocean, clutching at a mast for support. As my head span and bile rose up my throat, stinging as it came, I grew aware of a stiffness at my face, and when I touched it, I realized I had been bleeding profusely. Blood had coagulated all down my left cheek, and had run into my ear and hair while I was unconscious. My head hurt.

I was, then, still in the alley where I had fallen. The dish full of metalwork that I had earlier knocked flying was the cause of my stumble, I realized. I had stepped on assorted tubes, chains and other things, and, being unexpected, the sensation had caused me to try to leap away, only to fall clumsily and hurt my head. So much was clear. Now it came to me that my Spaniard was probably still snoring at the other end of the alley, and I set off to find him. It would be just my luck if the fool had woken and made his own way home. Bearing in mind how drunk he was, I should not be surprised if he were to walk straight into the river and drown. Well, if he had, I was not going to worry about him. I had more important things to consider.

Before Humfrie left, we had arranged to meet the following afternoon at a small tavern not far from St Paul's churchyard. I had an urgent need to discuss with him what we should do about the absence of Jeffry, and to discuss the new target, and he suggested lunching together. Now I was considering possible options again as I made my way carefully along the dark alley.

If there had been a watchman there, he would have been able to follow my progress, as a series of clatters and curses tracked my wake. My shins were barked on low barrels and a table, my hand was scraped badly on a section of exposed stone on one building, and my head pounded painfully all the while. I truly detested that dark alley. The darkness was fearful. In it

I could easily imagine all kinds of horrible wraith or monster. Perhaps that was why no watchman went to investigate. Most watchmen were older men who had a lifetime of excitement behind them, and who did not get old by seeking out danger intentionally. Walking into a drear little alleyway that led to the Thames was no way to ensure a long and fruitful life.

Nor, apparently, was resting at the top of an alley. Because, when I reached Luys, the first thing I saw was that his lovely, weighty, intriguing purse was no longer with him. The second thing I saw was that Luys's purse was not the only thing missing.

So was Luys's life.

He was lying in the same place as when I had left him. His face had the same dropped-jaw daftness that I had seen before I went to talk to Humfrie, and if it were not for the fact that his chest was not rising and falling, I would have thought him still sleeping, nothing worse than that. But even in the dark I could see the bloody stain that blackened the front of his jack. It spread from his breast, almost in the middle, but not quite.

I had to turn away. This was appalling. I hate blood, I really dislike bodies – and some bastard had taken the purse as well. On top of the accident that had all but broken my head, and the sudden death of that damned fool Jeffry, this was enough to make me want to heave my guts up.

My belly complied.

Even as I hurled up all the ale and food of the day into the kennel, I was thinking despondently about the chances of escaping this series of catastrophes. Without the purse of gold, escaping far away was more troublesome, and escape I must, if I were to evade the righteous anger of Master Blount for killing the wrong man. I knew Blount, and the excuse that '*You* told me to kill him originally; it's not my fault you changed your mind' would not cut his pat of butter. He would want to know why . . . and that brought up another difficulty, which was that he must hear from his messenger that she had got her message to me on time. So that meant Blount must assume I had killed Jeffry *after* I had been told not to. That would look like intolerable disobedience to him. I knew him quite well by then: he looked on me as a mere automaton and nothing more. I was a servant, and was I to become trouble-some, he would remove me. I had no illusions about concepts of honour or loyalty. Blount was a hard, violent man. I was his murderer because, by using me, his own plots and evil plans failed to be spotted. After all, if he was always in plain sight, he must be considered innocent. It was the same as the arrangement I had fixed with Humfrie.

'Oh, God's ballocks,' I muttered. This was not good. I looked at Luys again. 'And now you, too.'

With a shock, I recalled the Spanish servant. He was a bodyguard, if I had ever known one. The memory of his flashing rapier blade intruded into my thoughts. I had a sharp picture in my mind, absolutely precise and clear, of his cold eyes gazing at me along the length of the steel. They were colder than the blade itself, and the idea that he could hear of the death and robbery of his charge might lead to his making enquiries about me. A Spaniard, one of the horde of foreign gentlemen in the household of the new King, would be sure to seek vengeance.

Have you ever swallowed water from a stream in winter? It goes down easily enough, but you feel every inch as the chill freezes your insides, and when it hits your belly, it's like having a lump of lead there. Well, that was how I felt now. My guts were chilled, and I could almost believe that my internals were turned to ice. Those eyes. So cold, so threatening. They seemed to be telling me that he would remove all my limbs for fun before starting to make me regret this death.

Too late. I already did.

This was the moment when Luys talking about the man who had been following him, or us, came back to my mind. Raphe had spoken of some cove outside my house, too. Who was he? Blount's Bear, a Spaniard seeking to protect Luys, or a London rogue who wanted to see me implicated in the murder of one of the Queen's husband's servants? There was a rattle along the road, and I shot a glance in that direction, but it was just an old Tom cat, from what I could see, rootling about in some trash. For a moment I imagined a large, bluff fellow standing beyond, watching me, but when I blinked he disap-peared. Perhaps he had never been there.

What could I do? I was racking my brains when I had a sudden inspiration. Until I met Luys, I had been determined to leave London. My bag was still packed. Luys's purse was a loss, but it was only ever an attractive addition to my funds. This, now, was proof that I must get out of London. Permanently. Perhaps I could escape the fate that seemed to be beckoning.

Of course, there was the other money: Jeffry's. I had not seen it on him. What if it had been found by Humfrie and moved to his own belt? I doubted it. It is one thing for a foreigner like Luys to walk the streets in a new land with a purse containing half a treasure-ship of gold, thinking he could not trust the servants to keep their thieving hands from it, were he to leave it at home; it was quite another for a Londoner born and bred to think that it would be anything better than instant suicide to walk the streets with that kind of sum in plain view. More likely, Jeffry would not have carried such wealth on him. He would have concealed his money somewhere safe.

Now I was torn. Should I run, with the little I had saved, or should I hunt for Jeffry's money and take it? It would help me with my retirement, were I to find it. It could support me for many years.

I thought I heard a noise again. What, would I spend all the rest of my life wandering, worrying about a man over my shoulder with a knife? Far better to have wealth behind me before fleeing London. I must find those purses.

With that resolution, I set my face to home.

But as I went, I was aware of a sound, a pattering, as of light shoes running in the dark behind me. I glanced around and saw a large shadow – like a man in a robe with a cowl, I thought.

It was enough. With a hand clapped to my bloodied brow, I ran, and barely stopped until I reached my house.

There was a thin mist the next morning when I arrived at Shoreditch. There was no breeze to stir the air, and I found my nostrils were immediately assailed by the smell.

It is a miracle to me that more people don't die there. The Shoreditch is a mean little rivulet, which runs down a shallow depression in the foul, marshy ground. Over the years it has become home to a poor, weakly population; they are not healthful or virile. All have the complexion of people who have lived amidst the fumes of contagion and malady. For although the place was, I am sure, once full of fit and exuberant people, the fact is that the sewers of a large part of East London run straight into the brook. If it were as sizeable as the River Fleet, the effluent would be dissipated somewhat, but here, on the eastern fringes of the city, the stream was too low for much of the year. All the effluent from a hundred channels ran straight into this stagnant, overwhelmed water course.

The result was that the poor denizens of the area fought against the evil odours through the whole year. Turds floated down the Shoreditch, moving sluggishly towards the Thames, but often through the year there was too little water, and you could see them forming dams wherever a twig or branch had fallen in and caused an obstruction. There were two that I could see from where I was standing.

There was a wooden bridge that was just wide enough for a London car to pass – a wagon or cart would be too wide. I took this, warily stepping on the creaking timbers. At the farther side was a growing community, with small houses and scruffy hovels clustered around a church with four gables and a low tower. There was an old abbey there, too, but that was in the process of being demolished. It made a sad sight in the thin mist.

Why was I here, wearing a light cap to replace my hat that was in desperate need of cleaning, a linen pad over my broken forehead, and a headache that was constantly rumbling at the front of my skull? Because Jeffry had a home out here. Perhaps he had a place in London, too, and I intended learning where he lived, so that I could search for the two purses which I was coming to think of as my own.

My head hurt. All the way, I felt every step through the lump at my skull, which seemed almost to ring with the swelling, as if with every step the clapper of a great bell was slamming into it. I felt quite nauseous when I awoke. Walking here, near to the open sewer that was the Shoreditch, several times I had to clap a hand over my mouth and pause, for the threat of vomiting was always close.

As I approached the church, I met a priest and engaged him in conversation after the usual greetings.

'Jeffry? I can think of several. What does he look like? Oh! *Him!*' His expression did not seem to express approval. 'Yes, I can tell you where he lives. He is up there, to the left of the old priory. See that house – two storeys tall, with limewashed wood? Next to that is his place.'

I thanked him and made my way to the houses he had indicated. The limewashed house was all a modern house should be: clean, well maintained, and with a roof of chestnut shingles bleached by the sun to a silvery grey. It was a lovely-looking house. If it wasn't for the smell of the open sewer, I would have considered it an appealing accommodation. But that wasn't Jeffry's.

Jeffry's house was next door, and if I say it was tatty, I would be doing a disservice to the word. Many years had passed since it had last seen a brush and limewash. The daubed walls were cracked, and many of the internal wattles were exposed. Anyone living in there would have to become used to every breeze blowing through and learn to wear many more clothes than others. The whole place had a look of general dilapidation, and there was an air of sadness about it, like an old whore who's reached her middle years and cannot support herself, but won't admit to herself that she has decayed.

This was the house that the priest had indicated. I strode to the door and rapped loudly. There was a scuffle inside, a shout and some screaming. Gradually, the door opened, and a small, tousle-headed figure peered up at me without speaking.

'Is your father at home?' I asked. I smiled.

The little figure remained staring at me without speaking.

'Hello?' I said, wondering whether the little brute was deaf.

'Who are you?'

A woman had tugged the door wide and stood staring at me from the doorway.

She was a woman in her late twenties, perhaps early thirties. She had long brown hair that peeped from beneath a simple coif, and she was wiping her hands on an apron which was a sheet of linen tied about her waist with a piece of twine. She

set her head to one side like an inquisitive robin. She had very
dark eyes and a thin mouth that was pursed into a straight line.
From the look of her, this was a woman who was desperate. I
could see that she was gaunt from lack of food, and the lines
about her face spoke of her hunger and overwork.

'Why do you want him?' she snapped. 'He owe you money,
too?'

I admit, I had not expected this. For some reason it never
occurred to me that the man could have been married. I have
no idea why, except that the fellow did not look to me like
the sort of man who could capture even a tired drab like this.

'I am sorry, mistress, I was hoping to find your husband
here.'

'Husband?' She gave me a cynical stare. 'Why? How much
does he owe this time?' She looked me up and down. 'What
was it – betting on a horse race? A cockfight? Baiting? Dog
fighting? You don't look like one of his ordinary men.'

I was unsure how to proceed. I have never been confused
with a gambler's money-collector before.

'You dress different to the other ones. Does that mean he's
found a new gambling den?' she said. She curled her lip,
tugging the little child to her. 'Come here, Sue. Don't let this
one touch you.'

'I'm not from a gambler,' I protested.

'No. You don't dress like one. They usually clothe themselves more flamboyantly.'

I bridled at that. My hosen were the best quality, my
dark-blue doublet was rather splendid, if I say so myself, and
my cloak was a fine example. True, my hat had suffered last
night, but that was why I wore the little cap instead. 'I do not
represent a gambling den.'

'Good. I don't like to disappoint people, and the number
who come here threatening me with being thrown from the
house unless I pay 'em is getting a pain in the buttocks.
We have no money. *Nothing.* If we did, would I be here
slaving away all hours? Eh? No, we'd have a maid in to
do some of the work so I could look after Sue and the
others. A girl to help cook and do washing and the like.
But I don't have anyone, and all the while the little brats

are squabbling and bickering . . . So who are you, and what do you want?'

'Well, I had heard that . . .' My inventiveness dried up. I had been thinking to explain that her husband had found some purses. I was the man who had lost them, perhaps, and I would pay a reward for their return – something of that sort – but even as I tried to frame the words, it was clear that it would not do. This woman was no fool, and she would know that a fellow like me, with my good clothing and elegance, would not come to such a mean place with a view to enquiring personally. I would have sent a henchman to ask. Besides, there would be little point in asking. If the man had found a purse, he would not spread news of his discovery; he would conceal the money and seek a means of hiding it from all the people who would come demanding their share.

'I'm sorry,' I said, backing away. If I mentioned purses to this woman, at best she would be bound to think I was accusing her man of stealing them. At worst, she would be as silent as a dormouse to my face and then turn the place upside down to find them. And she would have a better chance of finding them than me. She knew her own house.

She was frowning at me now. 'What, that's it? What did you want with him?'

'I was wondering where your husband was. I have a friend who wishes to speak with him.'

'He's not my husband. He's my father,' she said. 'And he's not here. If you really know someone who wants to speak with him, which I doubt,' she added, glancing at my doublet and cloak, 'you'd best look at all the gambling dens in the city. Where you find two men betting on how long it will take a fly to crawl over a loaf of bread, or which of two snails will win a race up a wall, you'll find him when you look to the man who loses every bet.' She sighed and glanced at the doorframe, then to the door, and there were tears brimming. 'He's already lost the house. He sold it in return for paying rent to the new owner, but now he has lost his job, and the money that was to pay for us to stay here has been pissed away, too. But he swears he will make good with one last deal. Except he has no stake money now. So, I'm sorry, Master, but I have no idea where my father is, and, to be frank, I don't rightly care. If you're looking to have him pay you, you'd best save your effort.'

'You say he reckoned to make good? When did he tell you this?'

'He said he was going to get money tomorrow. But if he did, it'll have been spent enriching some devious thief who will gamble with him and take the shirt off his back.'

'Did he say who was going to pay him this money?'

'Why? What is it to do with you?' she demanded, eyes flashing.

In an instant, I felt a curious sympathy for the man Jeffry. This woman would be terrifying when truly angry.

'It is nothing. I was just interested. If he were to be so lucky, I could try my own luck.'

'*Luck!*' she said bitterly. 'When will men like you and him learn that there's no such thing as *luck*? There's being careful and slaving and saving so that you can put food on the table. *Luck* is a toy of the devil. It curses men whenever they try to gamble. It persuades you to try your chance at one more wager; it means men will risk everything for one more throw of the dice; it means their families hunger and they lose their houses. And so, Master, if you are keen to find him, perhaps you should go and look into hell yourself? Mayhap you will find him at the gates playing hazard with the demon acting as porter!'

She slammed the door shut.

You may be assured that it was a quiet and introspective Jack who made my way homewards, holding my nose at the open sewer and hurrying away from it before the foul miasma could affect me and give me a dose of malaria or worse.

I walked up to Moorfields and watched archers practising at the butts. Some were highly competent and sent their darts to their targets with an ease that made their achievements look ludicrously straightforward until others attempted to emulate them.

No doubt if Jeffry was here, he would be trying to bet on how many times this man or that would strike the bull, or miss the target completely. I had seen such men often enough. Usually, I had laughed at men who despairingly demanded to 'double or quit' as their losses mounted. Jeffry was clearly like them: he would make a wager and struggle then to control his frustration and self-pity when time after time he lost. Perhaps every so often he would make a small victory, and his joy would be unbounded – but then he would convince himself that his luck was changed, and he would dive in with ever more extravagant gambles. I had seen it so often before. Once a man was ensnared by the gambling fever, it would not let him rest until he was utterly in thrall to it and then, like any parasite, it would drain him. Only when everything was lost would he stop, and that was only because by then he had no means to continue.

Which left me feeling miserable. The man may well have acquired a large sum of money and then thrown it all away. Which meant that I was no nearer finding a source of funds.

Except it wasn't only him. I had seen a woman today who should have been a happy, laughing maid. Instead, she was old before her time, her youth and vitality eaten up by the effort of keeping a household going with no money, when her brothers and sisters were all hungry. It was a depressing memory. I had not liked her – and the feeling was mutual, obviously, from the way she looked at me – but that didn't stop me thinking that it would be pleasant to find a coin or two just to give them to her and see her eyes light up. Her face could almost be pleasant if she tried wearing a smile, I thought.

But I had no money. Not to spare, anyway. It was infuriating. In a day I had almost got my hands on three well-filled purses, and all had disappeared without trace, so it seemed. Now I had the difficulty of deciding whether to run or to stay and brave Master Blount's ire. And my head was hurting where I had struck it last night.

Thus it was a morose Jack who returned to his street and aimlessly walked homewards. And then I stopped and stared ahead of me with a sudden feeling of excitement. Of course, Jeffry had disappeared, but I had the perfect alibi. All who knew me knew that I was at the brothel or the White Bear. No one had seen me at the wharf with Jeffry excepting Humfrie, and he wouldn't put any suspicion on me, surely.

So there was one way I might be able to recover my

position. I had the new instruction, to kill this fellow Michol. If I achieved that for Master Blount, then surely he would soon forget the missing Jeffry?

I walked on more swiftly now, determined to find Humfrie and ask him to help with this new commission. As I passed the door to my house, I happened to glance to my left, and I saw, only fleetingly, a face that was so like that of the woman who had brought the message from Blount that I almost stopped to speak with her. But no. I had more urgent work, and, besides, it was probably only the way that the light was reflecting off the roadway, or a complete figment of my imagination. After all, in times of stress, my mind will often turn to women. And this one was definitely appealing.

No! I didn't have time.

I continued on my way down the road to St Paul's.

This was an area I knew well. All we foists and dippers knew this place. There was a constant changing of faces as visitors to London came to view the great church. I looked at it now. A long building with a towering steeple. It was impressive inside and out, which was why people came from far and wide to enter the nave and pray. Pilgrims in their sackcloth, the occasional fanatic crawling, almost all barefooted, and others better dressed – such as two merchants I saw, rich and gaudy in all their finery, riding fine horses and casting their eyes to left and right with that careful view that could see a profit at twenty yards, but not the outstretched hands of the beggar two paces away. They were the sort who would sniff at the sight of a young tatterdemalion and claim that the wretch brought his hardship on himself with whoring and profligate spending, and then go to a tavern or brothel and spend as much in one evening of gluttony as the beggar would in a twelve-month for all his food.

Yes, this was a popular place for cut-purses and others. It was a constant changing scene here, with newcomers who were unused to life in a big city. Gawping at the high buildings, staring at the fine work in the goldsmiths' shops, practically drooling over the spices on sale, the jewellery, the clothes, and everything else. After all, what would a fellow from the wilds of Essex or Kent know of the wonderful products in a city like London?

The tavern was up near the St Paul's Cross where the preachers often came to harangue the populace. It was always fairly full of people from out of town. Men like me enjoyed it for the quality of the purses to be taken, but as I came to know Humfrie, I found that he had no such interests. He liked busier places where he could sit back and watch people milling. It made him feel good to see so many people walking about and enjoying themselves.

He was inside the tavern as I entered. The tavern held a trio of small chambers, and I walked from one to another. Humfrie sat at a long bench in the rearmost room. On a low table before him sat a wooden trencher containing a hunk of bread and the remains of a thick stew of meat and sausage. A blackjack of ale supplied his needs for drink.

'Humfrie,' I said. 'I am glad to see you.'

'Master Jack. I am glad to see you too. I hope you slept well, eh? Let me buy you a quart of ale. You look as though you have been busy today; you could do with a drink.'

His polite prattle was incongruous, but I let him continue. He beckoned a maid who whirled away and soon returned with a large jug for me. She set it on the table, taking Humfrie's money and disappearing again.

'Last night was a problem.'

'Really?' His eyes opened with amusement. 'We were commissioned to perform a removal. I think it went rather well.'

'That's because you haven't heard what happened!' I said, and took a long pull of my ale.

'I am listening.'

I began, speaking about the sudden appearance of the woman at the White Bear, her shocking message, my urgent rush to get to Humfrie before he could slay the man, and then the sudden death of my Spaniard.

'That is unfortunate,' he said at last when I was finished.

'Last night,' I whispered, eyeing the crowds on all sides. 'Did you find his purses?'

'Purses? I didn't know he had any,' he said.

I didn't comment on that. To be honest, I hadn't told Humfrie to look out for purses, because I wasn't sure that he wouldn't take them for himself. He would have expected nothing else.

'If he still carried them on him, that would explain why he sank so swiftly,' I said. 'When you found him, where was he?'

'Do you know the bowling alley Falkes owns just off Candlewrightstreet? It is his gambling den. I found Jeffry in there. I spoke to him, told him I had a message from Renard, the Spanish adviser, and he soon came with me, once he stopped his chat with Mal the Loaf.'

'Who?'

'Don't you know him? He's known as Mad Mal, or Mal the Loaf. He works at Falkes's bowling alley near to St Andrew's at Baynard's Castle, but in truth he is one of Falkes's enforcers. Mal has a speciality: his weapon of choice is a breadknife. That's why he's called Mal the Loaf. He can do terrible things with his knife. Fingers, toes, even cut off a head.' Humfrie allowed a frown to pass fleetingly over his face. 'He likes to see people suffer.'

'Isn't that what he is supposed to do?'

Humfrie held his hands out, palms up in a sign of openness. 'Well, of course, Master Falkes sometimes wanted to see men punished for one reason or another. I always avoided the instructions where he wanted a man injured.'

'But you don't mind killing them?'

'Well, you see, Jack, there are some men who take pleasure in inflicting pain. That's not for me. If Master Falkes wants someone removed, I go and do it, because I can do it quickly and without fuss. But I don't like to see someone in tears and squirming. No, I will remove a head, garrotte, break a head with a bar or mallet, and throw a body into the river, but I don't like pulling fingernails or teeth.' He shivered. 'Ugh. I hate the thought of pulling teeth. You ever had it done? This one here – it was horrible, it was,' he said, lifting a lip and displaying a black gap where his canine had been. 'I had a week's agony with it till I went to the tooth butcher and he yanked it out.' He stared contemplatively at his ale, remembering, before taking a long pull. 'I'll never forget that. And I won't do it to someone else. No. Besides,' he added thoughtfully, 'if you hurt someone and leave them alive, you always have someone who might seek revenge. The dead don't bother.'

So that was it. I had allied myself to a soft-hearted fellow who was convinced that death was kinder than, say, breaking a limb. Which was fair, since a broken leg would all too often lead to a slow and painful death.

I have met other men like him. Although butchers, for example, often seem to take delight in slaughtering pigs or cows, tormenting the poor, terrified creatures before killing them, not all are like that. In the countryside once, I saw a warrener who had netted a rabbit. While I watched, he took up the trembling creature, resting it in the crook of his arm, stroking and petting it as if he intended taking it home for a prized daughter to have as a companion. And then, as the rabbit relaxed and stopped shivering, he suddenly whipped its head back and it was dead.

That was much like Humfrie: he would have been proud of a commission quickly and efficiently achieved. He did not kill for pleasure. It was a job, and he preferred to perform his tasks with efficiency and the minimum of fuss.

'He went with you all the way from Candlewrightstreet to the river?'

Humfrie shrugged. 'I told him to come at midnight, said it would be worth his while, and he was eager enough.'

Something else was bothering me. 'Why would Jeffry be talking to this Mal?'

'He was planning something that involved a breadknife, I expect.'

'Why, when Thomas Falkes has disappeared?'

'Perhaps Mal has his own commissions. I don't know.'

There was one other thing that bothered me. 'Was Jeffry worried by Mal? Did he look as though he was anxious? Like a man who is about to be introduced to Mal's knife?'

'No, he looked like a man who's just been given the keys to the Queen's strongroom.'

Humfrie was watching me with a slight frown. He looked like a benevolent patriarch eyeing a wayward youth. 'What is it?'

'I was hoping to find the money.' I didn't say that I wanted

those two bags of coin to assist my own escape from the city.
I could have cursed to think of the three purses I had lost in
the last day. It was ridiculously frustrating.

That brought to mind the other matter. 'Oh, I all but forgot.
There is another man to be dealt with.'

Humfrie smiled and nodded to urge me on. 'Who is this?'

'A Frenchman. His name is Michol, and he is an intelligencer
and messenger from the French court.'

'First a Spaniard's man, now a French? Your master has a
problem with foreign visitors?'

'If *he* has a problem, so do you and I,' I snapped. 'If he
once grows to believe that we have outlived our usefulness,
he will destroy us as swiftly as that!' and I snapped my fingers.

He raised an eyebrow and shook his head slowly. 'I hope
you have not told him about me, Master. I would be most
displeased if you have.'

I wasted no time to reassure him. 'I can't tell him about
you. If I do, he will remove me for certain. But if I am gone,
so is your source of income. Don't forget, your money comes
through me.'

'Yes. So you have the money for this second problem Master
Blount wishes me to remove?'

'Eh? Oh, the Frenchie? Yes, I have money,' I said, and fixed
a smile of such transparent insincerity to my face that I'm
surprised he did not recognize its falseness.

Perhaps he would have done, but at that moment there was
a loud peal of bells from the church. I was confused. This
was not the time for any church service. We surely had not
been sitting here talking until Nones, and Sext was some time
ago.

It was not only me. Humfrie frowned, and others in the
tavern were suddenly quiet. I felt it like a clutching at my
heart. Church bells ringing could mean either good news or
very bad indeed. Only last year rebellion had swept the land,
and now that England's Queen had married the Spanish heir,
both were considered the enemies of France, who might have
sent a fleet to invade, I thought. All of a sudden there was a
ragged rumble and graunching as stools, benches and tables
slid across the floor as men lurched to their feet and ran to

the roadway, staring up at the church towers as though an answer could be read emblazoned on them.

Up and down the street, people were appearing in doorways, windows, erupting from alleys, all staring about and asking what was happening. The din was deafening, and no one could hear a word anybody else was speaking. It suddenly stopped when the bells fell silent, and a boy – an apprentice, I think – sprang on to a cart and blew three blasts on a horn. 'The Queen! Our blessed Queen has given birth to a healthy son!' he cried.

I turned to Humfrie, and the two of us stared at each other. True, if there had been another man to clasp with joy, I would have grabbed him instead, but for now Humfrie would do, and we threw our arms about each other in a hug and danced about the road, even as others followed suit. No one would forget that day. At last the succession was assured. All the confusion and arguments and fighting over the kingdom were done, for a child had been born.

'A son! A son! We will have a king!' I heard a man shouting with glee.

Humfrie raised his eyebrow. We had relinquished our grip on each other and now we somewhat shamefacedly made our way back into the tavern and our ales. 'That man is a fool,' he said.

'Who?'

'The one declaring his joy for a royal son,' Humfrie said. We sat again, and he took a sip of his ale. 'It matters not whether it is a son or daughter. Either way, the child is welcome. It means we can have some certainty over who will inherit the government of our land.'

'But a son is better,' I grinned. I was feeling happy.

'Perhaps, for some,' Humfrie said. 'But boy or girl, it means we need not fear for a Scottish invasion or Lady Elizabeth wresting the throne from Mary.'

I hadn't thought of that. 'Why a Scottish invasion?'

He gave me a long, quizzical look. 'We have a Queen married to a Spanish gentleman. If Queen Mary were to die without a child, we should have a battle between those supporting Lady Elizabeth and Mary, the Queen of the Scots.

Mary of Scotland has the better claim, since Lady Elizabeth
has been declared illegitimate.'

It was ironic, I always thought, that Queen Mary should
have been dispossessed by her father. When he chose to divorce
Catherine of Aragon, he used a law that meant his marriage
was not legitimate, so Mary was born out of wedlock. Then,
when he married Anne Boleyn and had Elizabeth, he named
her his princess and dispossessed Mary. When Edward VI,
Henry's son, died, his will maintained that Lady Jane Grey
was his heir. But the Catholics were strong, and with their
support Mary was able to take the throne, overturning Henry's
divorce of her mother, and thereby declaring Elizabeth illegitimate, no longer a princess, and shunned. A pretty foul act by
someone who knew how harsh life could be, I always thought.

'Mary of Scotland is Catholic, I suppose?' I said.

'Aye. But she was raised in France,' Humfrie said. 'The
Spanish will not be pleased to think that England could be
allied to France. That would cut their empire in two, with
France and England slicing through their shipping trade. They
will do all they can to prevent Mary of Scotland from winning
the English crown.'

'What else would they do?'

'Put Elizabeth on in her place, I suppose,' Humfrie said.

'But she is not Catholic.'

'You think religion will matter when it comes to hard-headed
politics? The Spaniards are realists. They are practical. They
won't give a tuppenny knee-trembler for religion if it means
they can maintain their empire, keep the sea lanes open, and
retain a firm grip on their money.'

I was not convinced. Still, for now, it was good to know
that the kingdom was secure. With one boy-child born, the
happy royal couple could make another babe, and then another,
guaranteeing the kingdom for their line. Then there would be
no need to worry about civil war, rebellion or invasion. It was
a profoundly satisfying situation.

There was a crackling and great shout from outside. Some
fools had already collected a pile of wood and old trash from
the alleys and streets; now a man had struck flint and steel
and set the lot ablaze. When I glanced through the doorway,

I saw thick yellow and blue smoke rising. There was singing, and men entered the tavern demanding ales or wine.

'Last time I saw a bonfire like that in the road,' Humfrie said sourly, 'it set light to three houses.'

Back at our table at the inn, I repeated that Master Blount required the man Michol to be . . . removed. Humfrie required the same payment as before, which I was happy to agree, and then we parted, I to head east towards my home, him west to watch the festivities attendant on the birth of a royal son.

My thoughts turned to the fiasco of the previous day. If that fool Jeffry had been given two purses of money, as Master Blount had told me, surely the man would have taken it straight back to his daughter and other children to pay off his debts, rather than continuing to Falkes's gambling den to sink himself further into debt? But I knew enough gamblers to know he wouldn't. He would have taken any money straight to the nearest chamber where he knew he could bet. His daughter had said as much when she told me that he would be the one betting on which of two snails would win a race. He was an inveterate gambler. Luckily, that is an affliction I have myself managed to avoid.

My feet led me along the road aimlessly. The idea of going to speak with Mal the Loaf was unappealing. I wanted to know what had happened to those bags of money, but that didn't mean I fancied chatting to a mad felon with a bread knife while he investigated my internal construction. No, in preference to chatting to Falkes's favourite torturer, I would jump into the river after Jeffry himself.

It was a hideous situation. All that money had been within my reach, but it had slipped between my fingers. And the last of the three purses hurt the most. That Spaniard, Luys, had been *my* target. It was outrageous that someone else should amble along, knock him down and swipe what should by rights have been mine. All because I had suffered the misfortune of a fall and cracked my head. I touched the lump gingerly. It was painful.

I stopped in the roadway, my hand still on my pate.

A sudden thought had broken into my mind, and it was so shocking that I was quite floored by it.

The coincidence that I had suddenly fallen and been struck on the head as I fell, just as a man decided to kill and rob Luys, was too startling to be a matter of chance. What, if I were a gambling man, would be the odds of a man like me suddenly falling over a number of items on the ground, and falling in such a manner as to break my head? Yes, it had been dark, but now I came to think of it, did I slip and then strike my head, or was I struck on the head and so fell? And on what did I fall? Was there a box there whose corner I had hit? I didn't recall a barrel or chest when I came to. But it was dark in that alleyway. Someone could have been standing only inches from me, and I would not have known it. Not until his blow fell.

This was all speculation. It was wild and foolish to consider that such things might have happened. There was no reason to suspect that someone had been there, had deliberately knocked me down, and then gone on to murder the Spaniard. No reason whatsoever. It was probably just a sad, unfortunate sequence of events.

I had just come to this conclusion when I looked up and saw, some yards away, three men who looked oddly familiar. I could not place them for a moment. They were all involved in a close discussion, heads bent together. And then I saw a man behind them, a heavy-set fellow. There was something about him that looked familiar, so that even as he turned on his heel and strode away, I stood craning my neck. Which was unfortunate, because as I did so, one of the three looked up and caught my eye, and I recognized Luys's bodyguard, Ramon. I quickly placed a smile on my lips as I saw recognition flare in his angry eyes. His expression reminded me of the look he had given me the day before: so distrustful and suspicious.

Situations of this sort are never easy. It is best to talk quietly, calmly and reasonably, I have learned over time.

Either that or run.

I ran.

*   *   *

People, people everywhere, and each one of them seemed to be in the way. I barged into bakers, butchers, merchants, priests and the odd child, while behind me I could hear from the growing angry voices that the Spaniards were themselves slamming into similar numbers. An elbow caught me in the ribs, and I felt a blow on my shoulder, but I wasn't going to stop just then. All I could see in my mind's eye was a pair of dark eyes staring at me along the long, straight perfection of a Toledo blade. I didn't want to see that in reality again.

There was an alley, and I darted into it, hoping that I might find the escape I needed. With luck, they wouldn't see me, I thought, but it was the wish of a hunted fool. Of course, one of them saw me, and I heard a shout as they entered the alleyway.

Now, I have experience of running. It is one of the most basic skills of a true dipper like me. Every so often, the hand in the stranger's purse will jar as the owner moves, and that hand can be discerned, grabbing all it can. At times like that, it's best not to wait and discuss the matter, but pull your hand away and leave by the shortest route. That was what I was doing now. The key thing was to be away. Not to run *to* somewhere, but just to be somewhere else, somewhere that was not *here*.

The alley was narrow, and the buildings overhead jutted out over and above me like massive cliffs reaching up to the sky itself. The sun tried to penetrate, but failed. Garbage and trash lay all about, and I tried to keep from the gutter and the human faeces that lay there, waiting for the next fall of rain. A girl was about to step into my path, but I waved my arms, already too breathless to cry out, and she stopped, gawping at the tall man who ran past ahead of three more who were chasing after him. Four more steps and I was past her; another ten at most and I'd be out into the next road.

I didn't look behind me. You don't look behind, ever. Don't think about the pursuers, but think of where you are going. You aren't going to be here for long. Whoever is behind will remain behind, and when you have reached your destination, they will be nowhere in sight.

A hand, flailing, trying to grab my shoulder. One finger caught my cloak, ripping the fabric, but could not maintain the grip as I hurtled onwards. A moment later, a hand caught my doublet. Even as I felt my onward rush slow, I thrust both arms behind me, letting the doublet slide from me, cloak as well. There was a swift cry and tumble of limbs as the sudden release made my pursuer fall. My relief gave me an added burst of energy, and I suddenly broke into the clear light of a broad thoroughfare, panting and mostly blown as a horse after a race. I cried out for help, saying murdering Spaniards were trying to rob me, that they had raped my wife, killed my son, and now wanted me, too . . .

I heard a low growling, a demand of 'What're you chasing him for?' and several garbled comments from the Spaniards. I don't know if they managed to explain themselves in English sufficiently to satisfy the Englishmen in the road, because having hurled my accusations, I wasn't hanging around to see what the result would be. I kept on running, now eastwards, now north, now west, pummelling the roads like a madman, desperate to be away from that area.

In the end, I pelted along until I reached St Paul's again, and I stood on Ludgate Hill, staring about me and wondering whether I had lost them. A glance behind me was enough to give me a sense of relief I haven't felt in many a month. There was no sign of them, only the constantly moving crowds, women hawking the wares they held in their baskets, men bellowing, dogs barking or snarling, children running about the place, a horse neighing in complaint at the throng, and bonfires, two of them here, both with blue-white smoke, and all about them men singing or drinking, women linking arms with a few of them, grabbing their costrels or jugs and drinking along with them, others trying to pass by, glaring at the men trying to grapple with them with eyes flaming and angry, slapping at the hands reaching for bodices and bums, while the owners of the wayward hands laughed and jeered.

I bent, hands on thighs, desperate to breathe, sucking in the air and panting shallowly as I tried to slow my thundering heart. My head was a ringing tumult, my bruised and battered body pounding as if all the smiths in the realm were hammering it. The sweat, which I hadn't noticed while I was running, was soaking my shirt at the small of my back, under my armpits, and down my breast from the neck to my hosen, and now the slight breeze was making it chill. The doublet and cloak were gone for ever, I was sure. It was enough to make a man weep. The dark-blue material had been beautiful, and now it would go to the benefit of a Spaniard!

I shivered, and would have gone to stand nearer the bonfire, but if I did, the crowds singing and dancing would have enclosed me and trapped me, were the Spaniards to have reappeared.

Instead, I made my way to the church. I wasn't going to enter it, because in the hottest of summer's days St Paul's is cold, but I went around by the churchyard and down towards the river.

It occurred to me that I wanted to see where I had hit my head. I was growing more and more convinced that someone had been there and had tried to break my pate for me. The same man who had gone back to kill poor Luys – the man who had robbed Luys of his money.

I shivered again.

The wharf looked different in the daylight. Overhead, grey clouds made the river look miserable and thick, like a roiling pottage that's been left for too long. The smell wasn't so bad yet. I thought the fishermen must still be out in their boats, or the wind blew from the wrong direction. Or maybe they had joined all the other Londoners that day in celebration on hearing that an heir had been born to the Queen. Half the city would be nursing hangovers in the morning, I thought, but the grim, relentless pain of a drinker's head was better than the dreich life of daily fear of war or rebellion.

Standing at the edge, I looked down, my arms wrapped around me. Ridiculous that at this time of year I should feel so cold, but without my doublet I was shivering. The wind seemed to blow straight through me, as if taking the time to go round was too much effort. It was not something for me to worry about just now, though.

I stepped closer to the edge of the wharf and peered down into the waters tentatively, as though Jeffry could be there waving at me. He wasn't, of course, but the thought of him suddenly springing up at me, grabbing me and pulling me in after him, was so convincing that for a moment . . . well,

I nearly thought it was going to happen. But no, all I could see was water slowly making its way to the sea, great ripples where it met the piles of the wharf itself, occasionally yellowish scum or bubbles soggily moving past. It did look disgusting, even without the pale, pasty face of Jeffry looking back at me.

The rope's end that had been left was still there. It looked such a silly thing to have caused a man's death. That reminded me of the alleyway and the things in there.

Where I fell, I recalled, there had been a barrel and a load of metal items on top. The items had all been thrown to the ground. As I walked along the alleyway, I could see lots of things lying all about: broken spars, a stool with a snapped leg, a chain, two large metal hooks, a besom with a handle that was splintered only a foot from the twiggy brush, coopers' bands and assorted seamanlike things that I did not recognize, and then I saw the barrel. It stood out because it was the only one of a size that matched my memory. I walked to it, remembering how dark and gloomy this place had been the previous night, and stood over the thing, looking all about me. I had fallen about *here*, I thought. It was near the barrel, and I vaguely recalled the position from when I sat up. My head was throbbing again as if in sympathy with the location of its injury, and I looked at the ground all about with a resentful glower. The metal plate was a sort of round tray, on which discs, chains and horseshoes were collected. Someone had obviously come here and picked them all up again, and now they were sitting on top of the barrel once more. Good.

But the main item that I was searching for – some sort of box, lump of rock or timber, that I could have knocked my head against to make me fall – of things of that kind, there was nothing.

I spent some while scrabbling about the ground where I fell. The pillar I had walked into was perfectly obvious now, in broad daylight. Indeed, I wondered how on earth I could have missed the thing. It was taller than a man and almost a foot in diameter. I had not banged my head on it, though; that was immediately apparent. The pillar was rounded, and I could not imagine that it would have cut into my brow to produce my injury. Also, it stood a clear two yards from where I had fallen. There was nothing else I could have hit, apart from the ground, and that was too damp and soft to have sent me unconscious, surely, with such speed.

The conclusion was inescapable: someone had been here, and the fellow had knocked me down.

Just for a moment, I thought perhaps it had been Humfrie. He had seen an opportunity to remove me. True, I was his paymaster, but he might have considered that an extra assassin in the city was one too many. Or he could have thought that his daughter would benefit from hearing that he had complied with her request to see me destroyed. It would please her, I was sure, hurt though I was at the thought. But somehow I felt it was unlikely. Surely he would have looked surprised to see me today, if he'd tried to kill me. And he would have made sure of me, not just left me unconscious. Besides, Humfrie had been behind me when Jeffry stepped into the river. If Humfrie wanted to kill me, he would have done it then. Without fuss, without my even knowing: I would have been dead in an instant, like the rabbit in the warrener's hands. There was no reason for him to wait until I was in the alley again. The man in the alley must have been someone concealing himself from me. He was hiding from me, because he knew that else I might recognize him, perhaps. And he was in front of me. It couldn't have been Humfrie.

Perhaps it was a felon from the waterside, who hid when a stranger came and then knocked me down to rob me.

Except . . . it had not occurred to me before, but the man who gave me my broken head did not rob me. My purse was still on my belt; all the money I held was inside it. So it was not a robbery. Perhaps it was a bungled attempt, from a fool who was scared when I tumbled to the ground, and who . . . but he would not have gone on to kill Luys. No, the man who did this to me and killed Luys (the two were inextricably linked in my mind) meant to kill us both and rob Luys of his money. What need had he of my purse, when Luys's held more than enough money to sink a ship?

So he knocked me down here, in the dark.

There have been times in my life when I have been

threatened, and although I do not like to appear arrogant, I have to confess to a certain courage. I think it is this that makes me so appealing to the other sex. They can see in me a confident bravery that they miss in other men of their acquaintance. However, just now, standing in that alleyway, with my head thumping as if in time to a drum beat I could not hear, I have to confess that even my courage began to fade.

Someone must have been there in the alley and struck me. Perhaps it was as I kicked the rubbish on the path; perhaps it was afterwards, when I sprang back in alarm at the noise – it didn't matter to me. The fact is that someone must have known I would pass by, and had struck me. They could have *killed* me! Perhaps they *meant* to kill me!

That was a horrible thought, too. The idea that someone would have waited there in the alley just to knock me down . . . well, it was enough to send me walking moderately swiftly out of the alley. It would perhaps not be unfair to say that I hurried.

Who could have wanted to hurt me? I was only an ordinary fellow, not a violent felon like some. Not that it would help me. Here in London, the streets were paved with less gold than those who aspired to come to the city and make their fortunes imagined. Rather, they were drenched in the ruined hopes and dreams of the thousands who arrived every year. London was a city that fed on people. It sucked them in from all over the country, and it set its fangs into them and took the life juices from them like a vampire, until nothing remained but empty husks. Like Jeffry's daughter, old long before her time, grey and dismal as a plague victim. She was just one example of the sort of effect that London could have on people.

Not that it affected me in that manner, of course. I was one of the fortunate fellows who had come here with nothing, and now, only a little later, I was one of the wealthier men in the city. I had a new house, servant, clothes, doublet . . . my doublet! That was gone for ever, I thought mournfully. The idea that I had lost that splendid garment was painful to accept.

I reached the entrance to the alleyway where I had found Luys. Glancing down at the place where his body had lain, I could not help but shudder to think that here he had breathed his last.

So: had my assailant come here, found Luys, killed him, and then taken the alleyway in hopes of killing me too; or had he hurried down the alleyway, met me and knocked me down, before returning up here to kill Luys and rob him?

Whichever was true, the simple fact was that the assailant had been determined to execute me. Of that I was certain.

And I did not like the thought at all.

My way home was beset by delays.

There is no holding back the London mob. If they are displeased, no man can mistake the fact. It is easy to discern the difference between a smiling yokel in his field, waving at passers-by, and an apprentice who has drunk his fill of ale to give him courage, and who now waves a boning knife or cleaver about his head in angry display. The trouble, of course, is recognizing the signs and knowing when to duck and run, because the average student lawyer or apprentice butcher is rarely more than a quart of ale from causing an altercation that could grow into a full-scale battle between the city's White Coats and the mob.

The opposite, fortunately, is also true: the London mob is rarely more than a quart or two from unbridled joy. They can suddenly turn from sullen anger to puppy-like happiness for little reason, so to see them in such ecstasies of delight was a relief. As I walked homewards, I had several drinks pressed upon me, and I was forced to dance with a lively little strumpet who told me that her name was Sarra, and who wriggled most deliciously as she danced. I was fain to remain with that group for longer than I should, just for the pleasure of occasionally gripping her wiry little figure.

But the bonfires were a warning. As they began to die down, I was aware that I had been out too long already and the people all about me were growing maudlin or aggressively drunk. There was one man who wore a dark cowl that hid his face, and I grew more and more aware of him every time I grabbed the appealing little maid, but then he disappeared, rather to my relief. He looked too much like the man described by Luys

and Raphe, I thought, but there was something else. At first I
thought I recognized him, and that itself was unsettling. Then,
a little while after he departed, I noticed another man: slim,
young, wiry, with a dangerous look in his eyes. He was glaring
at me fixedly.

'Who is he?' I said, nodding towards him. 'He looks like
he just bit into a sloe.'

'God's faith! It's my husband!' she gasped.

When I saw him rise to his feet, clearly intending to remon-
strate with me, I quickly took my leave, the wench grappling
with me quickly and pressing her lips to mine before she
allowed me to continue on my way homewards.

There were people everywhere. On all sides I could hear
the Queen's health being toasted, and that of her husband and
her child. It was the first time I had realized that people were
fond of the Spanish Prince. Philip had been derided when he
first appeared in the country: first because he was a Spaniard,
and second because he was a Catholic. After Henry VIII and
Edward VI, the people were mostly content with the new order
and the new Church. The idea of going through all that arguing
to return to the Catholic Church appealed to very few, although
the zealots were starting to demand that all should accept the
Pope as head of the Church once more. Mary would push for
that, I was sure. Everyone knew she was a committed Catholic,
whereas Elizabeth had always appeared to be equally as determined to remain with her father's new Church.

Be that as it may, Philip had been hugely unpopular when
he first arrived. He brought his own household with him – his
own cooks, his own servants, his own guards – and it caused
natural annoyance. He seemed to imply that there was something wrong with English stewards and English bottlers,
English cooks and English . . . well, everything English. It
was not to be borne.

But now, now he had sired a future king. That was a glorious
result. We could all accept him, or so that appeared to be the
general consensus. And the people of London had taken him
to their hearts.

I hurried past the louder, more inebriated groups; it was with
them that I thought I must be in most danger. At last – and it

seemed an age later – I found myself at the entrance to my own road. I began to head up it, when I heard a hiss from my left.

'Eh?' I began, but then my powers of speech were cut off.

I have mentioned that my good, manly looks are instantly appealing to women of all sorts. Don't get me wrong, it is hardly a burden, but just occasionally it can surprise. Take this as an example: there I was, walking on my way home, somewhat weary, considerably battered, and still wondering how on earth to win some more money, when a woman launched herself at me. I had a single moment to notice her well-filled bodice, her appealing face, lips that could suck a football down a reed, but the surprise, as her lips met mine, did make me try to recoil. Her hand went behind my head, holding me there, and while I felt I was trapped, I confess that I didn't struggle terribly hard to break away. In truth, I succumbed to the moment.

'It's pleasant to meet you again, too,' I managed, when she finally came up for air.

It was the lady who had brought the message from Blount at the White Bear that evening.

Her eyes were flashing and glorious, her bosoms heaving, and her lips looked like strawberries just ripe for plucking, juicy and delicious. I grinned broadly as she withdrew into a doorway, and followed her with enthusiasm, although my lust had been somewhat abated when she grabbed hold of my head to press her mouth to mine. She had grabbed it sharply, and it was throbbing unpleasantly again. Still, I knew the perfect cure.

'So, Maid, you couldn't keep away from me, eh?' I said, gingerly touching the lump on my brow. 'No need for an alley, woman; my house is close by, and we can be comfortable there.'

She paid little heed. 'Master Blackjack, have you completed the task that Master Blount gave you?'

'Ah, well, there was a slight delay on that, but come to my house, Maid, and we can discuss—'

'No! You do not understand! There was an urgency behind the message. Master Blount did say it was important that you hurry. Did I not mention that?'

'Yes, but—'

'So I told you, but you chose to ignore his order?'

'Let's go to my house – we can have some wine, and perhaps . . .' I added, reaching for her left tit. She slapped my hand away. There was a gleam in her eye now, right enough, but it had nothing to do with thoughts of playing at mattress jousting. Rather, this was genuine anger. It left me confused, I have to admit. Probably because of the head wound. Usually, I can be as quick as any.

'He will be furious when he hears this,' she hissed.

'Let me explain to him,' I said.

'What then? He will think me a useless drab, no good for anything – not even supplying a message accurately or giving an indication of its importance!'

'No man would think you useless,' I said, my eyes falling to her undoubted charms.

'You only ever think of one thing! You see? Even you think I'm only good for lying on my back!'

'Oh, I can think of many other . . .' I hesitated. The look was in her eye once more. It had the appearance of danger that, say, a glint from a sword's blade would have in a dark alley. 'I only meant that I would defend you before him. He would listen to me, Maid. What is your name?'

She looked at me, and I instantly saw the fear in her eyes. Perhaps I had mistaken the menace. I have known hounds which, when particularly terrified, will growl and snarl and lunge, and I was beginning to see that this woman was the same. She was all fire and fury when she was alarmed, but all she needed was, like a hound, reassurance and comforting, and she would soon come around.

'Maid,' I said soothingly. 'It's not something for you to worry about. I can look after you. Let me speak to Blount for you, and I swear I will help. Your head is too pretty for—'

Well, a hound, while you calm her, can still bite.

She rounded on me, and this time my eyes had not time for her breasts, because I was trying to keep track of her fists. 'You *dare* to speak to me like that again, and I will have your ballocks on a platter! You think you can talk to me like an infant, you great lummox? Get out of my sight!'

I recoiled at her anger and was tempted to try again, putting my arms about her, perhaps – but discretion prevented me. Not from fear, of course, but I didn't want to provoke the poor little thing. 'Your name?'

'I am known as Agnis. You can call me Mistress Fletcher.'

'Oh, you are married?'

'I was. He died.'

She was being very short now. I was confused. Her moods appeared to swing from one extreme to the other without hesitating in between. 'Mistress, I . . . why did you welcome me with such enthusiasm, if you don't want to bed me?'

'Is that all you can think of? I was kissing you to stop you being seen by the men watching your door, and the thought in my mind was to prevent you being seen without calling you, which would have attracted their attention as well as yours!'

I gaped. Delicately, she took a forefinger and pressed it to my chin, shutting my mouth. 'You look almost endearingly foolish when you do that,' she said.

There was no need for such rudeness. I was merely considering her words. 'Who were they?'

'I have never seen such men before.' She glanced at my linen chemise. 'Are you not cold? Where's your doublet? Surely you wore it when you left your home.' She looked up at me. 'No one would leave home without his doublet, would they?'

'I was being chased by an unpleasant fellow with a rapier,' I said. It was the most important aspect of his dress that I could think of.

'Was he tall, very dark like a Spaniard, with a scar on the side of his face just here?' she asked, pointing to the right side of her own delicate features.

'Yes, a ragged one,' I said.

'And his friends were similarly gaudily dressed?'

'Yes.'

'They are the men waiting outside your house.'

I peered up the street, and I could feel my ballocks shrivel as I recognized the flash of scarlet. It was the Spaniard's colour. They all seemed to like the colour of bright red blood, I thought.

Whatever else might happen, I was not going to saunter up there and try to get to my house before he could use me as practice for a game of 'Let's spit the pig', using his rapier as the spit. No, there were many places I would prefer to visit than my house.

My first thought was the White Bear. Willyam, Lawyer Abraham and Bob would be likely to help me. The men at my door seemed to have little idea about concealment. They stood loitering like a gang of dock workers waiting to learn whether they were hired or not, and only rarely cast a glance along the roadway. When one looked towards me, I ducked away again.

'Come along,' I said, and took her hand.

'Where? What are you doing?' she protested as I pulled her with me.

'Hush! We're going back to the White Bear, where you saw me yesterday. I'll buy you a drink and you can tell me more about the man Michol whom Blount wants killed, and in the meantime, the Spaniards can cool their heels outside my door for as long as they like.'

'I don't want to go to the tavern.'

'Please? If they see me alone, they'll realize it's me; walking with you, they will see only a couple, and I will be safe.'

'Oh, very well!' she said with a bad grace, and we set off.

The tavern was full to bursting, with many a new face reddened with wine and ale. I have no doubt that somewhere in London there was a sober man bemoaning the outbreak of indecent insobriety, but all I can say is, I didn't meet that man today. When I entered, I saw that Willyam and Lawyer Abraham were at the same table we had occupied the previous evening. Willyam looked up and smiled at Agnis as I walked to them, dragging her with me. 'Where's Bob?'

'He hasn't turned up. Have you heard the news?' Lawyer Abraham said.

'That the Queen is safely delivered of a boy, yes.'

'Oh. It's good, isn't it?' Willyam said. He was as flushed as any number of the people I had seen earlier in the street. 'I mean, just look at all the folks outside.' He rattled his purse, grinning at Agnis. 'I can afford to buy you a good meal. Are you hungry?'

I knew what the purse meant, of course. While the people had been outside with their joy at the news of the Queen's son, Willyam and the others, like any gathering of foists, had gone to where the crowds were at their thickest, and deprived as many people as possible of their money. It was always at events of this nature that people discovered they had lost much of their money, and it was all because of the professional pickpockets. That was why I tended to wear my jack well buttoned and my money tightly bound in my purse.

Except now, as I put my hand to my money, I realized it wasn't there.

Have you ever seen a fellow undergo a severe shock? I was once in a tavern when a fight broke out. The winner of the little battle was flushed with booze and victory as his enemy collapsed, when someone told him the other was the son of a duke. The fighter's face went absolutely white in an instant, as did mine now.

'Oh, Christ's pains!'

That was all my money! Everything I possessed to enjoy a swift flight had been inside it. Without it . . . well, I preferred not to think what would happen without it.

'What?' she demanded.

'Some thieving scrote has cut the laces of my purse! Look! The prick cut the laces with a razor! All my damned money has gone!'

'Nice try!' Willyam laughed. 'So you want us to buy you an ale? Go home and fetch your money, fool!'

Lawyer Abraham was hardly more sympathetic. He roared, slapping his thigh with delight. 'You mean you got dipped? Someone cut your purse and took all your money? Hahaha!'

'I'll buy you an ale,' Agnis said. I turned to her with relief. She had a small purse and pulled out some coins. 'These will be enough. Buy me wine, if they have any in this place. It'll taste of piss, I expect.'

I saw a serving maid and hailed her. Soon Agnis and I were sitting at a certain distance from the other two. I was unimpressed by their lack of sympathy and understanding about the loss of my purse, and more keen to maintain the friendly relations I was building with the fair Agnis. She had, at least, shown sympathy in the way that she had offered to buy me a drink.

Where had I lost my purse? The only place I could think of was at the bonfire, when I was dancing with the little wretch Sarra. She had hands that wandered well, and I could easily imagine that at some point she had pressed her hand to my money and danced away with it. The accomplice, who kept glaring at me, seemed to be about to come to defend his woman's virtue – that was the impression he had intended to give me, to drive me away. She must have slipped him a nod when she had my purse, and he immediately started to scowl to stop me thinking about whether my belt was lighter than before, and to send me over the horizon before her 'jealous husband' could tear my head from my shoulders. Yes. It all made perfect sense. She had distracted me perfectly, and then he had completed the move by driving me away in fear of a lover's jealousy.

'What will you do now?' Agnis demanded. 'You can't go home with those men at your door, and you have no money. Will you get some from these fine friends of yours?'

'What do you think?' I said, casting a dour glance at the pair of them.

Lawyer Abraham and Willyam were discussing the absence of Bob. 'Where is he? He should be done by now,' Lawyer Abraham said.

'Bob knows what he is about. Perhaps he has just found a good spot and doesn't want to leave it until he has milked all the pretty cattle in the market!' Willyam said.

Personally, I found their conversation rather immature. To hear them laugh, and their gleeful bantering comments about fools who could dip and dive but not notice when their own pelf was being cut away, was irritating.

I finished my drink and stood. Agnis rose too, and joined me as I took my leave and walked from the tavern.

'What will you do?' she said again.

It was a good question. I fixed a serious expression to my face. It was one that lent me a certain contemplative look, I know, and always tended to secure sympathy from women. It showed my more soulful side.

She sighed. 'If you're going to look as mournful as a lost hound, I suppose I'll have to take you in for a while,' she said.

The house to which she took me was one of those older dumps out near the river, a short way along Tymberhuth Street, a narrow lane that runs parallel to the river just up from Tymberhuth's wharf. I said nothing, but it was a scant double stone-throw from where Jeffry died, and as I entered the building, I could not help but think that his corpse could even now be settling underneath the piles just out in the river. It made me shiver.

Her chamber was a small, foul room in the upper storey of the building. Below were storage houses for bales of material, ropes and metalwork of all sorts. There were four flights of stairs – or, rather, two staircases and then two rickety ladders – to scale before reaching her room, which was the topmost garret in the eaves. At least, I thought, she could pull up the ladders if she needed protection from attacking hordes. As an attempt at humour, it failed to lift my spirits. I didn't mention it to her.

However, when I gained my first sight of the room, I was glad first to see that it contained a large bed. It looked the sort of substantial, rope-sprung bed that would take a fair bit of punishment. There was one aspect of it that did surprise me. I mentioned this to her.

'Yes, it was my husband. He built it himself. All the work was done below, in the street, and then he brought it up, piece by piece, and put it all together here,' she said.

'It must have taken him an age,' I said, marvelling at it. It was a good six feet long and almost four wide, built of good, strong planks, with legs to keep it free of the floor. The ropes that supported the mattress were woven from one side to the other and then from top to bottom, and the mattress itself must have been fairly recently filled with fresh hay and some sweet-smelling herbs, for the chamber had the smell of summer, and reminded me of lying in a pasture in the sunshine. I could remember several times lying on my back in the fields up above Whitstable, before I escaped my father and made my way to the city to find my fortune. Once, there was a girl called Susan, who had smelled rather like this, too. But then her father got to hear that she had been idling her time away with me, and I caught a blow that blackened my eye for a week. I believe she married the smith. She probably has a miniature tribe of squalling brats by now.

More fool her, I thought.

Agnis had taken off her shoes. She had dainty little feet, and she sat herself on her bed and let them dangle. 'So, what now?' she said.

I gave her my best grin and moved towards the bed.

'Oh, no. You're not here for fun and frolics, Master Jack. You are here because, from the goodness of my heart, I have agreed to allow you to stay here one evening. You will sleep down there.'

'What, on the floor?'

'If you don't like it, there's always the pavement outside. Or you can make your way homewards and see if you can get into your house before the men outside cut your throat.'

I didn't like that thought, or the cool, convincing manner in which she shared it. I looked at the boards of the floor. They were warped and splintered, and there were gaps between each of them. She saw the direction of my look and must have relented somewhat. 'I can let you have two blankets and a coat to lie on, if you need.'

'Thank you.'

'Who were those men?'

I grunted as I took the blankets from her. They were thick, and I hoped they would protect me from the cold. 'Spaniards. I met them in the road when one of their number was attacked by some members of the mob, and helped them. But their friend – well, he died last night. I think they blame me.'

'Why would they blame you?' she asked, eyes narrowed suspiciously.

'He was out drinking with me, and he died while, well, while I was doing something for Master Blount.'

'What?'

'You don't want to know,' I said with mournful conviction. Jeffry's pale face sprang into my mind again and I shuddered. Agnis had passed me an old, heavy coat, and I pulled this on now. It served to keep the worst of the cold from me.

'Was it to do with the message I gave you?'

'Yes. It was the first command. I was trying to prevent its execution.'

'I don't understand.'

'It is best that you don't. And now Blount has given me this second instruction. And I have to fulfil that too, or he will be most displeased.'

She looked at me long and hard. There was one last blanket and a cloak. She tugged the cloak about her, lay back on her bed and threw the blanket over her as best she could, then turned her head to me, eyeing me seriously. 'You are in a mess, really, aren't you? I'll come and help you with your task, if you like.'

'You don't realize what I must do,' I said miserably.

'And you don't know what I am capable of,' she replied. 'It is agreed. You will perform this task for Master Blount, and then he will hear direct from you how helpful I was. You must swear: swear that you will tell him how much I helped, and that you could not have achieved the task without me. You must tell John Blount that.'

'Yes, yes, I'll tell him,' I said. I shivered again, lying down on top of one blanket and pulling the other over me. It smelled of mustiness and rat's piss, but at least it was likely to be warm, I thought. I crooked an arm and rested my head on it.

'How did you get to know Master Blount?' she asked.

'Me? I was just unlucky!' I said shortly. 'I used to be happy, but the rebellion came along, and we met, and he thought I . . . well, he saw something in me which he thought he could use, and so he hired me.'

'What did he think he could use?'

I felt the bitterness rise. 'Just because you think me contemptible, doesn't mean others don't see my skills,' I said with some heat. 'I am known for certain abilities, which are of great use and value to those who are in need.'

'Naturally. I am convinced of it.'

I accepted her words at face value, although I could not help but think that there was a certain lightness in her tone, as if she was keen to suppress amusement.

She might be a pretty little thing, with a pair of bubbies a man could pillow on for many a long year, but I got the distinct impression that this wench would be hard to live with. She was too self-confident, too certain, and treated men with too much contempt.

I closed my eyes and tried to sleep.

I have always been a good sleeper. At home at Whitstable, I would close my eyes and instantly fall into a dreamless slumber. If I were to sit down after eating my meal at noon, I could close my eyes and instantly be gone. It only required that I should rest my arse somewhere and close my eyes. Others, when we were harvesting or gleaning, would watch me jealously, because they were incapable.

Be that as it may, that night I could not sleep at all. I rolled over and over, I lay on my back, on my front, on either side, and still sleep evaded me. My face was cold, so I covered it with the blanket, but then my feet grew chill. I brought my knees to my chest, but then the floor boards dug into my hip. I turned to the other side, and that hip found a protruding nail or splinter, and sleep was despatched permanently.

As the sun began to throw its light over the river, I sat up and pulled both blankets over my shoulders. Crossing the floor, I sat near the window on an old chest. The room had little in the way of decoration. There was this chest, a stool, and a section of an old bench, which she used as a table. It was a mean little chamber, and it led to me wondering how she had survived since her husband's death. He must have died some little while ago, I assumed, for the lines of hardship were well engraved into her face. She had not enjoyed an easy time of it since his passing.

But she was very pretty when asleep. As the sun rose, it coated her face with a golden hue that made her features stand out with a kind of rosy tint. Her luscious lips became more moistly plump, her great eyes, now closed, seemed even larger and slightly slanted, and as she breathed, that splendid breast of hers rose and fell like . . . well, like a truly magnificent breast. I could only stare with longing, thinking how much better I would have slept, cuddled up with that warm, sweet-smelling body.

'Enjoying the look?'

She had not opened her eyes, and I could not discern any change in her breathing. How she knew I was watching her, I do not know, unless she assumed I was some sort of lecherous boor. Which would be a little harsh.

'The view of the river is fine from here. You can see over most of the buildings.'

'Yes. It was one reason I liked this room.' She opened her eyes and gazed at me. 'You are early to rise. I had assumed you would be lazier than this.'

'I like to be up early,' I lied.

'So you didn't sleep,' she said, as if I hadn't spoken.

'I always sleep well.'

'You make as much noise as an elephant, tossing and turning, grumbling under your breath, and then snoring. I thought you'd never go off.'

I forbore to respond to that. My disdain must have been apparent, though, because she gave a little giggle. I've known others who use a similar distraction to conceal their embarrassment. I would forgive her.

'What will you do today?' she asked.

That was an interesting question. I could go and see whether my house still lay under siege, I considered. I really wanted more money.

'Will you go and find out what you need to about the man Blount wanted you to deal with?' she asked.

'Well, no. I don't think that would be a good idea.'

'He did say it was urgent!'

'Yes, but I have other things to do. I need to get some money, for example.'

'You must see Blount, then. He can help and provide some coin for you.'

'Yes,' I said reluctantly. 'But I think maybe I should wait until I have achieved another objective for him, first.' In my mind was Blount's face when he heard that I had killed Jeffry, but not done anything about this man Michol. He would be most displeased. 'In any case, I need to find out more about this Michol.'

'Shall I go to ask Blount for money, then?' she asked. She had thrown the blankets aside now, and swung herself from her bed. She went to the farther side of the room, where I saw now that there stood a bowl and jug of water in a second dormer window. She poured a little water into the bowl and splashed it liberally over her face, rubbing at the back of her neck, wiping beneath her chin, and then pulling up her chemise and reaching beneath to rub at her armpits.

I watched as she performed her ablutions. She did so with complete confidence and no shame. It was a delight to watch her, and only when she took up a strip of cloth and dried herself did she turn to me with a cocked eyebrow. 'Well? Do you approve of the sight?'

'How could any man not approve?' I said, I think gallantly.

'Oh, really,' she said, and this time she laughed. 'You are a poor fool, aren't you?'

I confess that this is one woman I perhaps will never understand.

We left the house soon afterwards, descending to the road.

She took me up to a small alehouse not far from her home, in which there was a good fire roaring, and I gladly took a seat while she ordered a thick barley broth and small ale. I took my share with pleasure and devoured the bowl, resting my ale near the fire. I had a dagger at my belt, and I thrust this into the fire until the blade was good and hot, and then stirred the ale with it until it was warmed through.

I was racking my brains by this time. The food was good in my belly, and the beer was helping, too, but I still had the issue of money. Now that I had been forced to hire Humfrie a second time in a week, I needed more. I couldn't use the Spaniard's cash, since that had gone the way of all things in London, into the pocket of a thieving scrote with the morals of a starving rat – unless I could somehow find the man responsible, and I didn't know how I could do that. What, go and speak to a man, and say, 'There's this man who has stolen a purse I meant to have for myself'? No, I didn't think so either. No one would agree to help me, and the only ones who might would be the sort of men who would cut my ballocks off to see how long it would take me to eat them, and then go and take all the money for themselves.

And where would I find such a man, anyway, someone who would know who had stolen the purse? Falkes was the only man I could think of, and he was out of the way, by some means devised by Blount, I suspected. There was no one else who was so professional about enforcing the rule of villainy in the city. No one who was an enforcer . . .

I was sitting there some moments before Agnis leaned over and pressed her delicate forefinger to my chin, lifting my mouth closed again.

'Have you been thinking again?' she said.

'I have had a brilliant idea,' I said.

'You're going to see Blount.'

'No: a *much* better idea than that!'

It took me a little while to track down Humfrie. He was not at the usual places where I would expect him, and in the end I gave up and asked some men who knew him better than most. I was directed to the cockpit of a large inn over the other side of London Bridge.

The inn was called the Gorge, and it was a conventional enough large hostelry, two storeys high, with handrails about a walkway to each of the chambers. The building was shaped like an 'L', built around a large courtyard with rooms on the right-hand side and opposite the entrance, while the third side on the left was given over to stabling for the horses. I asked inside the bar and was directed to the rear of the building, where there was a large, barn-like building, from which emanated a series of horrible noises: men roaring with excitement, and the screeching and raucous clucking of cockerels locked in mortal combat, or waiting their turn.

Entering by the great doors, which were large enough to enclose a wagon, I found myself in a dark chamber. Gradually, my eyes accustomed themselves to the dim light, and I could see that near the entrance was a series of wicker cages, inside each of which was a cockerel. Nearby, a small circular pit had been dug, around which an eager circle of faces leered down at the pair of cocks belting five barrels of shite from each other.

This was a daunting sight. Excuse me, but the sight of an animal's blood does little more for me than that of another man's. These creatures were going at it like two fishwives arguing over a herring, hacking at each other with their talons, wings flailing to keep their balance, pecking and stabbing at each other all the while. The men were delighted, but for me it was just, well, repellent.

I was pleased to see that Humfrie did not appear to take any pleasure from the sight. He was at the rear of the crowd, eyeing the two cocks with a sort of professional interest, but not with the keen desire to see maiming or death dealt by one or the other combatants.

He saw me and barely acknowledged me. His eyes met mine and I saw them sort of narrow ever so slightly, and then he returned his gaze to the pit. I wasn't sure, but it looked to me as if he didn't want to speak to me. Well, be damned to that! God's wounds, I had come all this way – south of the river, no less – in order to have a word! I was not going to be fobbed off with a grim look. I would go to him.

As I came to this conclusion, there came a roar from the pit, and when I glanced, I saw that one of the cockerels had been dealt a ferocious blow. A long, raking slash ran from beak to the middle of his breast, and he was on the ground as if winded. His opponent was plumping his feathers, crowing at the sky in glee and preparing for the fatal assault. Now he leaped up into the air, talons ready to do great damage, but when he came down, the injured bird was no longer there. He had sprung to the side, and now he pecked viciously at the other's eye, before chasing it about the pen until he caught it from behind and attacked his neck with repeated nips and bites.

I didn't want to see any more. Feathers and blood, if anything, are worse than blood on its own. Looking over to where Humfrie had been sitting, I was about to make my way to him when I realized he was no longer there. I frowned, staring at the spot, then turning all about, trying to see where he could have got to, but there was no sign of him.

Eventually, I gave up. I moved back towards the door, and there was Humfrie, only a pace away. How he managed to get so close without me realizing, I do not know.

'Master,' he said quietly.

'Is there a place away from this horrible racket where we can speak?' I said.

'Follow me.'

He took me out to a large plot behind the barn, in which a number of horses grazed. We walked to a low wall and sat on it, contemplating the view. Houses, barns and, over all, the fog of ten thousand cook fires from London. 'Well?'

I explained about losing my purse, and the need for more money to pay him. 'So, what I wondered was, whether you could speak to Mal the Loaf about the money Jeffry gave him, but also about the purse stolen from the Spaniard? See whether he has heard anything about them.'

'This is Mal the Loaf you're talking about. If he heard of a purse full of money, he'd take it,' was Humfrie's unhelpful comment.

'Not if you could persuade him that Falkes is displeased about the purse going missing.'

'He knows Falkes isn't about. From what I've heard, Mal aspires to great things for himself and thinks he can take over Falkes's empire. He's a fool to think it, because even he must know he has no brain for organization; he's much more keen on using his muscles. Oh, he's able to go find a man and break his arms or his head, maybe use that knife of his to take off a finger or two, but to take charge of a hundred men or more? He wouldn't last a morning.'

His scathing assessment was not a disappointment to me. 'Good. Because I only need him to work for a morning or so. And if he thought that this purse was important—'

'He'll steal it for himself all the more swiftly. You need it so you can pay me, then?'

'Yes.'

'Because you know I don't work for promises, don't you? I won't go chasing after this Michol until I know you have the cash to pay me. You realize that?'

'That's why I was hoping you could find a way to persuade him.'

'Oh, I can do that, right enough. It'll take a little work, mind.'

'What do you mean?'

'Mal has always been all over my Jen like a cheap tunic. He adores her, and she can't stand him. But if she were to ask him, he'd climb down into hell to fetch her a trinket.'

'Will she do it? Will she go and ask him?'

'I'll get her to ask him to find the purse because it was stolen from her. If he thinks it was hers, he'll move heaven and earth to find it, and you can be certain he won't take a penny piece from it.'

He left me then, walking quickly across the mud and gravel to the inn's courtyard, and thence out into the roadway.

For my part, I was in two minds, but I decided to make my way back homewards, thinking that not even a dedicated Spaniard would have waited all night and half the next day to capture me. I walked out past possibly the largest mound of horse manure I have ever seen, into the High Street, and up to the bridge.

Most of the damage done the previous year during the rebellion had been made good. The shot that had thundered into walls and rattled along the roads had been cleared away, the loose stones and demolished buildings tidied or burned. Apart from the shining, clean-looking timbers that lined the bridge and buildings, you could hardly tell anything had happened here.

I crossed over and made my way up towards my house. You may be assured that I kept my eyes and ears open all the way up my road. As I approached, I studied the doorways and any obstacles with great care, moving ever more slowly and silently. There was no sign of the Spaniards. Those dark eyes were nowhere apparent, and neither was his rapier, which, damn me, if it didn't seem sharper and larger than before now that I brought it back to mind. I stood ten yards from my door and studied the road again. And then, well, I squared my shoulders and set off with the confident gait of a man who had no reason to fear any man, because I was quite right and the fools had left the place. There was no sign of Spaniards or other hazards anywhere near my house.

Marching to my door, I pounded on it to waken Raphe, who would be sure to be sleeping somewhere like the lazy good-for-nothing that he was, and when it opened, I shoved it wide and stepped in.

Which was a mistake. Because before I could take a second step, my feet were knocked from beneath me, the door was slammed shut, and when I glanced up with terror, I saw that my memories of the rapier were all too good. It *was* that large, and it *was* that sharp.

I smiled up at him. 'Ah! Ramon!'

The rapier's tip approached a little closer. Not too much, but it was like seeing a mastiff's drooling jaws near your throat. A *little* closer is enough to make you need to clench your buttocks.

'Where is he?'

'I . . . er . . .'

'You know, *Peter the Passer*! He gave me an excuse and slipped away the evening before last. Where is he?'

'How should I know? I was out for the last two nights, and—' It suddenly occurred to me that Ramon, who supposedly spoke no English, was now giving a passable performance as an almost native-born Englishman. 'You speak English?'

'No, I just pretend to,' he snapped. 'Where did you take him?'

'I didn't say I took him . . .' The tip was under my chin now, and I could feel my eyes widen as I sensed the icy coldness of the blade at my exposed throat. 'Look, I don't know where he is! He asked me to find him some pretty girls, so I told him where to go, but . . .' I could feel it pressing. My skin was being compressed against the top of my Adam's apple, and I didn't like the sensation at all. 'Um.'

'Where is he? You can continue with these inventions if you like, but this rapier has not tasted blood in some weeks now, and it would love to see how your craven English blood tastes. So tell me where he is, and you will save us the effort of seeing how much energy I need expend to stab your throat and watch you drown in your own blood.'

I began to think that keeping things back was a less good idea than telling him what he wanted to know.

'Very well! He wanted to find a whore, so I took him to a place I know, the Cardinal's Hat in . . .'

'You took him to that pox-shop? Was he robbed? Did they injure him? Are they holding him for blackmail or hostage for ransom?'

I don't know if he meant to, but it felt as though he was about to pierce my spine as he spat those words. I squeaked, and tried to push my head into the floor to keep the sword at bay. 'No, no, no! He left there fine, with me!'

'What then?'

'I took him with me to a tavern, down near London Bridge.'

'Which?'

'The White Bear. It's a good little place, and he was very happy while we were there.'

'I suppose he was,' the Spaniard said with what looked to me like a sneer of contempt. Perhaps he knew the Bear as well, then.

'I left him there and came home.'

'You left a stranger to your city in a den of thieves and whores?'

'Well . . .' Yes, he clearly did know the Bear. 'Yes, but he seemed capable of protecting himself. There was no reason to think he would be in any danger.'

'Are you really so dim that you don't see the risk of leaving a Spanish nobleman in a base tavern, when all England despises the Spanish?'

'Begging your pardon, but just now everyone in England rather likes the Spanish. Hadn't you heard about the baby boy?'

'I had not heard of it the night before last,' Ramon said, and this time there was no doubt: he was sneering. 'And I doubt I will hear of it again. So you left him in there, you say?'

I didn't like the sound of that 'I doubt' bit. I would have asked him what he meant, but just now it was still my pelt I was worried about. 'Yes, of course. He had his fun with the Winchester geese, and I think they were clean of the French marbles, and then we left the stews to return to the Bear, where I left him.'

'Eh?'

'Winchester geese – the whores.'

'Marbles?'

'The French pox.'

'Oh,' he lifted his eyebrows as he absorbed this new information. Then he frowned again. 'Why?'

'Why what?'

'Why did you leave him? Peter the Passer, I do not like your face. It tells me you are lying. I think you know where he is, and I wish to know immediately, else I will pin you to the floor with my rapier!'

Now my mind was whirring quickly. 'Why? Luys told me he was just a . . .'

'He was a man sent here for a special task. We were guarding him.'

'He was no nobleman, though. I would have thought him a professional,' I said without thinking. My words touched a nerve.

'You believe that he was a professional man, out to visit the city for a lark? I think you are brighter than you make out, Passer!'

'No! No, I'm not!'

'Let us see whether you will talk more when I cut off your fingers, one by one.'

I spoke quickly: 'No! Look, I didn't know anything about him! He was there, I saw he got the women he wanted, then we went for some more drink, and that is all! I can't tell you what I don't know!'

There comes a time when a liar has to tell the truth. When a fellow decides to remove his fingers one by one, that is a good starting point. But – and it is an important but – it is important to gauge whether the actual truth – such as 'I took him to the riverside, and he was robbed and murdered' – would not lead to more dire consequences than the removal of a finger or two. At such a moment, the best thing to do is to tell a lie, but tell it *really* convincingly. If you can, convince yourself before speaking it. That way, you may just live to regret the loss of a forefinger or two.

I hoped so.

'Yet you did not protect this foreigner in your city. You took him to places of ill repute, where he could pick up disease—'

'I said, the girls don't have the clap at the Hat!'

'And then left him in a low tavern and walked away.'

'Well, it seemed better than me staying there for no reason. I was tired. It had been an exhausting day. If you recall, I saved you and him from the mob! And this is the thanks I get!' I added bitterly.

Ramon peered at me more closely. 'You swear this?'

'Yes. I took him to the brothel and then to the Bear. I swear it. And then I left him and came home. It was late; I was tired.'

'Where were you last night?'

'I was at St Paul's Cross when the news came of the baby. I went with some men there to drink and celebrate.'

'Yet when you saw us yesterday, you fled.'

'Was that you? My eyesight . . . But why did you chase me? And where's my doublet and cloak?'

I suppose the look of baffled indignation on my face was convincing in some way. He relented, enough to allow the stabbing pain to reduce somewhat. Suddenly, he stepped away, his rapier all but forgotten in his hand. One of his men was still standing with his back to the door, so I couldn't rise and run, much though I desired it. Instead, I remained where I was, rubbing my throat where he had pinked it, and thinking poisonous thoughts about foreigners coming to London. I had come to the conclusion that all should be weighted with chains and dropped into the river, when he turned and fixed me with those terrible dark eyes once more.

'Master Passer, you took young Diego to harlots and low drinking places. You deserted him at the Bear. You have broken the rules of hospitality which exist even in this most satanic city. My friend Diego is somewhere in the city. You will find him and bring him to me.'

'But – a moment, please – *me*? What can *I* do about finding him? I am only a private fellow, servant to Master John Blount and—'

'I suggest you be silent a moment. I know all about you. I know Master Blount is a servant to Sir Thomas Parry, the comptroller to Lady Elizabeth. With your contacts, it should be easy to track down our friend.'

'I need my doublet and cloak first.'

'Then you had best hurry. We left them in the street.'

That was a knock. I would never see them again.

'When you have found him, I would hear of him, his where-abouts and his condition. You have a day. Bring news of him to me at once.'

'But—'

'Because if you do not, I will see to it that you are packed in a barrel and shipped to the boy's master by evening tomorrow. He will be most interested to meet you.'

When they had gone, I went straight to a mirror. It felt as though I could breathe without opening my mouth, and I was convinced I would find that there was a new rapier-sized hole in my throat, but fortunately there was nothing. Only a small dot of soreness which, when I rubbed it, smeared a drip of blood over my shirt.

I bellowed for Raphe, who ambled along some moments later. 'Didn't you think not to let strangers into the house? What were you thinking?'

Raphe pulled a chicken leg from his mouth. He had sucked the meat from it and was sucking the bone itself. 'They were your friends. You brung 'em in yourself.'

'But the man threatened me!'

'I didn't know. I was in the kitchen. You didn't come home last night. I got you a capon, too. All roasted.'

'Good. I am starving. I'll eat it cold.'

'Had to throw it away. Didn't think you'd want it.'

'Throw it away?' I stared at the chicken bone in his hand.

He defiantly replaced it in his mouth. 'Mmm,' he said.

'Fetch me my old jack, my pale brown one, and a clean shirt, hosen and hat,' I said. I wasn't going to bandy words with him. I was already in a bad enough mood, both for the threats and the loss of my best clothing. Raphe wandered off, and when I was sure he was gone, I went to the fireplace. There was a loose stone in the left side of the chimney's wall, and I scrabbled at it now. The stone came free, and I stuck my hand inside. This was my emergency store of funds. There were several pennies inside, and I pulled them out. I had lost my purse and would need another, but merely holding those few coins in my hand made me feel happier, as though they could ensure my safety once more.

Soon I was dressed again in clean clothing. My old doublet had been my pride and joy last year: faun coloured, with a soft, lovely feel; now it was stained and marked in various places where I had bled over it, or rolled in other people's blood. Although the best woman I could find had done her best, nothing could hide the fact that it had suffered.

I stood outside my door, my few coins held in a leather pouch which I had slipped inside my waist, the laces tied to my belt. At least a foist would find it less easy to grab my money from in there, I thought.

There was no one in the street whom I recognized. That was itself a relief.

I turned to the south and made my way towards Ludgate. I had to find Humfrie and see whether he had persuaded Jen to be reasonable.

Humfrie found *me*.

I had hunted in amongst all the taverns near St Paul's without luck, when I decided I needed refreshment and expended some few of my pennies on a coffin of minced beef and a quart of good ale. When Humfrie appeared, he walked straight to me, as though he knew all along that I would be waiting there for him.

'I've spoken to her.'

'And?'

'She said yes, if she gets half the money.'

'What?'

'She's my daughter,' Humfrie said, a little shame-faced. 'I suppose I brought her up to negotiate.'

'She can't do that!' I protested. 'I need that money to pay *you*!'

'Perhaps you can find some more?'

'Perhaps you can negotiate with Jen about your own share!'

He looked at me mournfully. 'Do you think you could negotiate with her? No? Then why do you think I can?'

'Because you're her father!'

His face grew longer. 'That's why I can't. She knows how to make me agree to her every demand.'

'This is ridiculous!'

'What can I say?'

I shrugged. 'Will she come with us?'

'We can ask.'

Jen was in a back room at the George, enthusiastically getting herself outside a large pot of wine. She always used to drink cider or ale when I had first met her, but recent months living with me had persuaded her that it was less ladylike, and now she insisted on the worst red piss she could buy.

'Hello, Jen,' I said. Humfrie stood at my side, a sycophantic smirk on his face.

She studied me for a moment, then lifted her chin and turned to her companion, a slimy little bag of rats called Simeon. I'd met him before. He was not too bad at purse-cutting, but a more devious little weasel-faced lick-spittle . . . well, I never liked him, let's leave it at that.

'Do you remember this toad, Simeon?' she said now.

He turned his attention to me. It made a change from staring down her cleavage, I suppose. Unconsciously, I found myself clenching my fists. She had been a good companion for a bedchamber gallop, and to see the little strumpet being fondled by this oily runt made my blood warm.

'Him?' Simeon said. 'He's just a second-rate purse-snatcher, isn't he? I'd heard he learned under Bill, when he was the fence-master near the river, but Bill was never much good himself.'

'Yes, I've always been unsuccessful,' I said sarcastically. 'Do you remember my silks, Jen? In my large house? All the silk lining my best clothes?'

'Yeah? What happened to them, then?' Simeon sniggered.

Before I could answer, Humfrie cleared his throat. 'We're off to see Mal, Jen. Will you come with us?'

'Mal? That bonehead?' Simeon said, and gave a little laugh.

Simeon had one of those laughs that is a cross between a horse whinnying and a stylus scraping down a slate. It made me shudder, and I gave him a look of contempt. 'I'll be sure to tell him what you think of him,' I said, and was rewarded by a look of absolute terror.

'You should be careful about threatening people with men like him,' Jen said tartly. 'I don't think he'll like to see you much.'

'All I want is—'

'To find some money, I know. Well, I don't know if I can help you there.'

'I just want you to speak to him.'

'Ha! Yes, but then you won't share the money, will you? I know you, Jack. You're unreliable. Leaving me alone while you went off with your floozy! I shouldn't have to put up with that.'

'Yeah. And she's happier with me, anyway,' Simeon sneered.

'I find that hard to believe,' I said.

'She's with me, isn't she?'

'I'm sorry,' I said to Jen. 'Second best is always hard, I imagine.'

'You callin' me second best?'

'No,' I said. 'You don't even measure, you shit-sack!'

'I'll have your guts!' Simeon shouted.

Humfrie stepped a little closer to me. 'Sorry, Simeon, but this fellow is useful to me. I won't have anybody try to harm him for now.'

'Oh, yes? What, you think you can stop me, old man?'

That was a mistake. I knew it, and from the look on Jen's face, she did, too. She flapped a hand at Simeon while fluttering her eyelashes at her father, who was standing like a man bound to a tree. His face was white, and his stance that of a man held taut by unimaginable emotion. It almost seemed to me that the whole of nature paused as if cocking an ear for the inevitable explosion. Birds, I imagined, stopped their singing and twittering to listen; dogs searching trash piles for the odd delicacy halted; even hogs snuffling in the alleys stopped their foraging. For an instant I thought Humfrie might draw a knife and explain to Simeon in stabs of one syllable that his words could be construed as rude, and although I do hate the sight of blood, this was an opportunity I would not have missed for the world. But then the world stopped teetering, birds returned to their songs, dogs snapped up things unmentionable, and the hogs sauntered on. Humfrie's tension relaxed and a small smile appeared on his face.

'Yes,' he said. Suddenly, his hand snapped out. He caught hold of Simeon's collar and pulled. There was a mild squeak, which might have been the bench on which Simeon was sitting, but might have been the man himself, and then he was sprawled face down on the floor, his right arm up in the air, the wrist gripped firmly in Humfrie's hands. I saw Humfrie's foot lift, and then it slammed down into Simeon's back as Humfrie twisted. There was a crackling sound, and I suddenly had an urge to throw up.

Simeon gave a sharp yelp and was still.

Humfrie dropped his arm. 'Child, I need your help.'

'What have you done to him?'

'You're not so old I can't put you across my knee, you know, Jen!'

'You've killed him!'

I chose to be quiet at this point. It was obvious to me that Simeon was breathing, but I could see that this was a case where paternal persuasion would weigh more effectively with the strumpet. And I had no wish to see Humfrie irritated with me in the same way as he was with Simeon.

Humfrie's face had coloured now. 'Don't talk wet, maid! I dislocated his shoulder. He'll be fine. But you will need to come with us.'

'Why, just to help Jack? I'd rather be sent to the Tower!'

'Just this once, can't you pretend you're a helpful child to your father?'

'After what you did to Simeon?'

'He was being rude.'

'*Rude*? You'd kill a man for being rude?'

'He's not dead!'

'And all for some money!'

'I paid a fortune to see you raised properly, Maid!'

'Oh, yes? What, like that old sow Maggie, who you paid to tup her every evening? She was a very expensive nursemaid for your daughter, I'm sure!'

'She was . . . a good woman,' Humfrie said, but he had reddened, and I saw his head drop a little as though ashamed.

'She was good for one thing, I know that now!' Jen said.

'Ow! My arm, I—'

Without looking down, Humfrie brought his foot down and Simeon yelped and was silenced again. 'She was a good, kind woman, and she looked after you well, while I was out at work.'

'Work! You were doing things for others before my Thomas came.'

'I helped him.'

'Yes. And now he's disappeared.'

'We still need your help,' Humfrie said.

'Then I want half the money.'

'Come, Jen,' I said. 'If you can help us, you will be saving my life.'

'Your life? So what?'

'I have been threatened with death if I don't find these purses. There are men here who want to take advantage of your father and me, now that Thomas is no longer here. They say, "Falkes is dead" or "Thomas Falkes? He can't stop us now!" and they plan to take over all his operations.'

'All?'

'Aye, all. From the strumpets to the thieves to the gambling. And you know what happens at times like this? The first people who'll end up taking a dive in the Thames wearing chains bound to a stone will be the men who were most helpful to Thomas. All those who helped him and supported him – they'll be the first to disappear. Especially once Mal the Loaf tries his takeover. He won't do well, but he'll want to get rid of those he sees as his competition. People like your father. And me.'

She lifted an eyebrow at that and glanced at her father.

Humfrie nodded with a hangdog look.

'Oh, very well. Just this once. But I still want half.'

Mal was not a prepossessing sight.

He was definitely one of those men who tends to run to muscle, with the largest and least used being the one inside his skull. It was fresh, his brain, by which I mean he used it as often as a chicken. And if you have ever looked after chickens, you will know that I mean him no compliment when I say that.

He was no taller than me, but he didn't have to be, because he was so wide he had to turn sideways at doorways. His chest was like a barrel, and his arms could barely touch the sides of his ribs, because of the overdeveloped muscles on his arms. Hands that were as short and stubby as a collection of sausages, but were thick with strength, hung at his side when his mind was at ease, which was often, but as he walked, they clenched and released with his steps, making his advance towards a man alarming. It looked as though he was thinking about pummelling you to death.

His face was different. Whereas his body gave the impression of malevolence and aggression, his face was often clear of all emotion. He looked like a man who was waiting mildly for the next thought to occur to him, rather than a man planning the downfall of his previous superior. He had deep brown eyes, a round face, and thick eyebrows that almost met over his nose. The nose, though, was more descriptive of him. It had been broken so many times that now it resembled a vegetable that had been pounded with a hammer: squashed, pulverized, and left as a grim reminder of what any man could expect were he to stand in the path of a fist large enough to knock Mal down.

''Allo, 'Umfrie,' he said.

He was standing in the gambling den that Falkes had created all of five years ago. There were many people in London who disapproved of such places. Bowling alleys were not the places of relaxation and mild entertainment that they could be in a country tavern. Here in the city they were the dives where men would go to enjoy gambling and whoring in all their forms. Those foolish enough to be gulled into putting down money for a game were those who could most easily be fleeced. Thomas Falkes knew that only too well when he set up his little bowling alleys, and he made sure that those who wanted to visit had every amenity at their disposal, from ales and women to the gull gropers who would offer to help the poor victims by loaning them money at exorbitant rates of interest. Any man who refused to pay their debts would have to meet with Mal to explain why, and he was hard of hearing when people asked for sympathy.

'Mal,' Humfrie said.

Mal ignored me. He nodded once to Jen and then returned his attention to the meat pie in his hand. Gravy oozed and dribbled down to his stomach, but I suppose he didn't notice. He was only wearing a poor, rather threadbare jerkin over his shirt – not that he would have cared if it was a silk jacket worth a king's ransom. Some people have no idea how to look and behave in company.

'What is this, 'Umfrie?' he rumbled.

'Have you heard that Thomas is on his way back?' Humfrie said.

'No!' Mal's eyes widened. 'When?'

'I don't know. But there are some things that he'll be worried about. Jen, his wife here, is keen to make sure that all is well, but Thomas was asking about two purses that you are looking after for him. The ones that Jeffry of Shoreditch gave you to take care of.'

'They're nothing to do with Thomas.'

'Oh, good. You can explain them, then. I was worried Thomas had been lied to about them. So you have them both?'

Mal scowled. 'Yes.'

'Where are they, Mal?' Jen asked.

Mal did not answer. He was staring at Humfrie, his expression darkening.

'Mal?' Humfrie said.

It was rather like watching a filthy rainstorm on its way. You know how it is. Sometimes, when I was a lad, I would run away from home and sit up on a local hill and watch the weather. From up there, I could look out to sea, and from miles away I could see the storms coming. Sometimes as fast as a flight of geese, others as slow and stately as a swan on a river.

The thunderstorms were always best. The thick, black clouds darkening the sea beneath, the waves turning grey and evil, as though a blanket was being drawn over the world, while flashes erupted deep within them. They were always exciting, their raw ferocity thrilling rather than terrifying – until I saw a tree struck only a few tens of yards from me. That was enough to curtail my interest in observing storms.

Watching Mal's face was a bit like that, as though he was about to start spitting lightning and rumbling like thunder that was not far enough off.

'You come in 'ere and try to threaten me about those purses? You try to tell me I should be passing 'em over to you? Do you have any idea what they were for, eh?'

'No, but I'm sure Thomas will want to know,' Humfrie said, as if unconcerned.

''E'll want to know about the purses, will 'e?'

'What do you mean?' Humfrie said.

'You don't know everything, do you? You come 'ere, spinning some cock-and-bull story about Thomas coming back, when you all know 'e's dead! Even 'e knows it, since 'e saw to it that Thomas was captured!' he added triumphantly, pointing at me.

I confess, this was a new thought that I had not considered. I knew that Thomas had been captured back at Woodstock, but as to what happened to him after that, I had no more idea than, well, Humfrie.

Humfrie clearly wasn't so convinced of my innocence. The look he gave me was one of his milder glares, but I still had the feeling that I had been pinned to the wall behind me. 'Tell me, Mal, what is said to have happened to him?'

''E met Master Blackjack there at an inn. 'E was going to catch Jack, but although 'e had two men with him, Jack managed to call the local officers, and Thomas and 'is men was caught and executed on the spot!'

'No, they weren't,' I said. 'They were captured, yes, but only for a minor affray in a tavern. No one would have hanged them for that.'

'They wasn't: they was executed as threats to the realm,' Mal said sneeringly. 'They were caught just down the road from Woodstock Palace, and everyone thought they was planning on breaking in and rescuing 'er.'

'How do you know that?'

'Because one of 'is men came back and told me!' Mal said gleefully. 'Didn't expect that, did you?'

Humfrie bent his head. I didn't. Not because I didn't like the backsliding, devious felon or his companions, you understand. Of course I didn't, but it wasn't that, just as it wasn't because I was no hypocrite. I could pretend sorrow for another man's passing whether I knew him or not, if there was a possible gain in it for me – such as a weeping widow to console, or handy purse dangling within reach – but no, this was for the sudden reflection that if Humfrie thought I had lied to him, or not told him all the truth about Falkes, he might take it into his head to forget his earlier words about disliking inflicting pain and seek to persuade me not to lie again.

It would not matter that I had no idea about Falkes's death. I couldn't prove that, of course. So it was quite likely that at any moment Humfrie might decide to turn on me. And if *he* didn't, what about Jen? She could well decide to launch herself on me. She was never all that logical, after all. I was just considering that Mal had no great liking for me either, and eyeing the distance between me and the door, when Mal suddenly beamed with happiness. It was as if the thunderstorm had miraculously abated, and instead the sun came shining through the clouds.

'So you see, friend 'Umfrie, that all this is unimportant? It don't matter, since Thomas is not coming back. And, I'm sorry, Mistress Falkes, for your loss. It must be a sore surprise to you to learn this. Still, it's a bastard wind that doesn't blow anyone any good, ain't it?'

'What do you mean by that?' Humfrie asked.

Mal set his head to one side. He looked like a pensive frog who's just swallowed an over-large fly, his eyes still bulging with the effort. Mal never found thought particularly easy. 'Think about it: you can 'ave your job still; Jen doesn't have to worry about her 'usband finding out she's been entertaining every free man in the city; and I don't 'ave to worry about giving up the two purses.'

'What were they for?' Humfrie asked. 'I saw him give them to you, and he looked relieved afterwards.'

Mal gave him a sly look. 'If anyone asks, they was gambling debts.'

'So you didn't do anything with it?' Humfrie said. 'You still have it?'

'It's my money,' Mal said flatly. 'No one else is taking it.'

'What do you mean to say about me?' Jen said at last.

I had seen the slander brewing in her as soon as Mal mentioned that men had enjoyed playing hide the pudding with her. Her tone now was one I recognized. This time I took a step towards the door. I've already mentioned thunder and lightning, and if you knew Jen, you'd know that the way the air was fizzing now had nothing to do with lightning from the sky. This was coming from her. Pretty soon plates and jugs were likely to start flying.

Humfrie turned to look at me in a contemplative manner. In his eyes there was a sudden cold ruthlessness which quite unmanned me. If there had been a seat nearby, I would have collapsed into it. As it was, I smiled weakly at him, convinced that any moment now I would have my life ripped from me. I stood tottering, a smile of blank terror engraved on to my face.

You see, Humfrie must have realized that his partnership with me was rather pointless. I had no money with which to pay him now. All I had was a nebulous relationship with a master who would no doubt seek to remove me since I was little use as an asset to him. After all, I had killed the wrong man and couldn't possibly kill the man he wanted me to. And I couldn't even pay my hireling to do it for me. What, really, when it all came down to it, was the point of anyone keeping me around?

So I waited. If I could have bolted, I would have. However, when your bowels have turned to liquid, and your legs can barely support your weight, trying to run is not so appealing. I felt about as capable of running as a new-born foal.

'Look,' I said, desperate for an escape. I was too late.

'You, Jack? I don't know why you wanted to come here today, but it saved me going to find you,' Mal said. He interlaced all his fingers and stretched his arms. All the joints cracked like ice breaking underfoot. I felt the gorge rising.

'Mal?' Humfrie said.

Mal stopped and glared at him. 'You can keep your job, yes.'

'No, not that. I was wondering about this *other* purse. It was stolen the other night. I think someone's been stiffing you.'

*   *   *

'Stiffing me? What do you mean, "stiffing me"?'

Mal's eyes had narrowed into hard little chips of jet. Suddenly, the thunderstorm was back.

'Thomas always kept a close eye on larger robberies. He didn't want to lose the money when someone took a rich man's purse, did he? Have you heard about the man who was robbed and murdered the other day over at the river's side? Jack brought him there, but someone killed the man and took his money. And there was a lot in it, Jack reckoned.'

''Ow do I know Jack didn't kill 'im and steal 'is purse?'

'Me?' I squeaked. I must have been convincing, because Mal gave me a really disdainful look.

Humfrie said, 'Perhaps if you tell us who normally looks after the stretch of the river from the bridge up towards the Temple, we can ask him and maybe bring in some more money.'

Mal considered, and then the sun broke through once more. 'A good idea. First, though,' and he turned to me again. His hand lifted towards my throat, and I watched it approach without the faintest ability to do anything.

I don't know if you have ever seen a man hunting a hare? They are not the brightest of creatures. If a huntsman comes across a hare in a field, he will crouch down, remove his cotte or cloak, prop it on a stick, and then creep around, giving the hare a wide berth. Nine times out of ten, he will be able to get behind the hare and simply knock it on the head, because the daft animal will keep watching the garment, rather than the moving man.

Well, in that room, I would have said that I was the gawping, terrified hare, and Mal was the hunter. As I stood there, watching his hand approaching me, I knew that my time was done. I had gambled my all, and it was not good enough. I was about to end my days with a dim henchman's hands squeezing the life from my neck. I just hoped he wouldn't want some fun before, like maybe seeing if he could snap off each of my fingers first, or cutting my nuptial tackle away to satisfy his bestial amusement.

And then, all of a sudden, I realized that I was not the hare. He was. Because all the time he stood there staring at me, a huntress was stalking him, and just as he was about to reach out and throttle me, Jen gave a shrill cry and launched herself at him.

I saw his eyes widen with horror, and then she was on him. She scratched and gouged at him with her rather blunt nails. 'What do you mean, all the men of the city? ''Sblood! You think you can make an accusation like that of a lady and get away with it, you dull-witted shag-bag! You shit-for-brains! You think I'm just some slut you can insult?'

All the while her hands were clawing at him, and when he tried to reason with her, her dainty foot snapped out and flattened his codpiece. It must have crushed his tarse and tackle. I winced, and I saw Humfrie flinch; Mal gave a great roar of agony.

She continued all the while. 'You think I'm just some bitch-booby, you great lummox! I'll soon—'

She would have gone on a lot longer, I have no doubt, but at this point he decided to stop her assault. One hand grabbed a wrist each, and then he gripped both in one hand.

'You mad whore,' he said, and drew back his fist.

I couldn't watch. One blow from that lump would detach her head, I was sure. I turned away, and there was a sort of soggy, nasty sound, a bit like a hammer striking a cabbage: crunching and wetness were roughly equal, and deeply unpleasant. When I turned back, Mal was on his back and Humfrie was thoughtfully slapping a rock- or sand-filled leather sack against his palm.

He looked up at me. 'He was going to hurt her,' he said simply.

'Thank you, Father,' Jen said. 'Oh, I knew I could rely on you!' She threw her arms about his neck, and he gave me a look of embarrassment, as if to say, 'Children, eh?'

The two of them turned about and made their way from the room. At the doorway, Humfrie turned and saw that I was still rooted to the spot.

'Are you coming?' he called.

'Do you think he was injured, Father?' Jen asked as we walked away from the bowling alley.

I looked over her head towards Humfrie. He studiously avoided my eye. 'I'm sure he—'

'Jen! He's dead!' I shouted. I was still feeling queasy. It was not that I cared about him, you understand. Let us be sensible, the man was a torturer and murderer. He wasn't the sort of fellow I was going to weep tears over, especially since I was pretty sure that Mal had intended murdering me. His expression when he looked at me had not inspired confidence. Nor had the sight of his fingers reaching for my throat.

'We are no nearer finding any money, are we, Father?' Jen said.

Humfrie looked at me. 'No, but I think I'll do the job anyway,' he said. 'It may be useful in the future to have men in power who have made use of me. If the men that Jack here knows think I can do a good job for them, it may help me if at any time I need their support.'

'Yes,' I said. Not that I would mention his name, of course. Blount may well wonder why I had decided to sub-contract my killings, after all, and he could decide that he could cut out – or cut down – the middle man.

Besides, there were other things to concern me just now. First, who was this man who had brought news of Thomas's death; second, where was the Spaniard's purse; and, third, where would Mal have put the other two? And what did he mean about Jeffry's two purses being "gambling debts"? Mal had worn that sly expression when he had said it, and then said that the money was his own. I didn't believe him at all. Yet what other reason could there be for the two purses being handed over so willingly? And why would Jeffry look so happy at giving them up? He was the sort of man who would be desperate for any spare money, and the idea of throwing away two purses of gold would appeal to him as much as going to a barber to have all his teeth pulled out with pliers. Jeffry would prefer to sell his daughter into slavery than do that.

Thinking about teeth, I suddenly had a vision of Ramon again. I had to think about what I could say to Master Ramon about the events that led to Luys's death. He would not be happy to hear that I had learned nothing, nor that his master was, sadly, dead. I had a flash of memory, which mostly involved his eyes staring down the length of his blade. It was not reassuring.

No, I had to think of something I could do or say usefully to protect myself. Perhaps I should merely take what I could from the house and run? There were plates of pewter and silver that I could convert to cash. It may be difficult, but it is better to be alive and aware of problems than dead and have none.

With this in my mind, I prepared to take my leave of Humfrie and his deplorable daughter. The silly strumpet could have had me killed in there. I owed her nothing after the shock she had given me with Mal. 'Well, it has been good to learn nothing from Mal,' I said. 'So now, I had best try to—'

'I will seek out this Michol and see how best to remove him,' Humfrie said. 'You had best wait in your house until I speak to you, in case I need you to help me.'

'Can't Jen help you?' I said, not unreasonably. After all, she was his daughter.

He looked at me, and his look gave me to understand that he didn't think Jen would be the perfect accomplice. I don't know why. To me she seemed eminently suitable.

'Very well,' I said, with as much grace as I could manage. 'But I do have other things to do as well. I must see if I can learn what did happen to Luys.'

'Why?' Humfrie asked.

'Because his men asked me and I don't want them playing rapier practice with my body.'

'Just invent something,' Humfrie said. 'They're Spaniards. They'll never know better.'

It was tempting, but I also wanted to learn what I could about the purse Luys had been carrying. Mal had not told us who was Thomas's officer for that stretch of the riverbank, but now I had an idea I might be able to find out. If I could, I would be able to sidle out of the city before anyone noticed me. 'I will be back at my house before Vespers.'

He looked at me very straight, but then nodded. 'Very well. And then we shall see what we need to do.'

'Yes,' I said, and took my leave of them, turning and striding back towards the river. I had an idea.

* * *

There are many men who make their living from gamblers and their gulls. Being in the bowling alley with Mal had reminded me of another place, only a bowshot from where Jeffry and Luys had both died.

It was an elegant-looking place from the outside. There were no piss-stains at the walls, and the pile of garbage waiting to be collected was of only a moderate size. The building itself was a bit of an oddity, because the frontage was mostly brick, filling in the gaps between the timbers. It was the sort of place that spelled comfort and good manners, and indicated that any visitor should feel safely at home here.

I walked past the front and down the side alley to the door that led to the kitchen. Here I rapped at the timbers.

Of all the places that Falkes had opened in his time as the master of the city's felonious fellowship, this was one he could not copy. He generally tried to take over the bowling alleys and gambling dens that he favoured, but every so often one would evade him. This, because it was partly owned by the Lord Mayor and certain of his acquaintances, was safe even from Thomas. His companions, and especially those who aspired to great positions in the city, persuaded him to leave this institution alone, and largely because he had so many others to manage already, to the surprise of many, he did.

It was not the sort of place that would welcome a man like me. When I was a mere thief of other men's purses, I was frowned upon. Now that I was grown to be a great man, in my own way, I was still ignored by the men who would frequent this building, because I was known to be a member of Parry's household and, as such, a supporter of Lady Elizabeth. To be popular in this place, a man must be an enthusiastic supporter of Queen Mary, *not* her half-sister.

The door opened and I was confronted by a man with a sharp face, pale in colour, with a dimple in the middle of his chin. Grey-green eyes peered at me with a slight frown. He was slight in build, with a fringe of sandy hair that ran about his ears while leaving his pate bare, as if it had washed away in the last rains. The look he gave me displayed a sort of world-weary resignation. It was the sort of look the bottler to a duke would use when answering his door to a beggar.

'No,' he said firmly, and would have closed the door, had I not taken the precaution of shoving my boot in the way.

'Come, now, Hugh. That's no way to treat an old friend, is it?' I said with an evil grin.

'Is that you, Jack? Christ's ballocks, I thought it was some peddler . . . What's happened to your doublet?'

I glanced down at my old clothes. 'Until yesterday you would have been impressed. But I was robbed of my doublet and cloak, and had to put on old clothes.' I saw the way his eyes slid down my doublet. 'These are my second best.'

'Only second?' Hugh said.

Hugh was one of the old school. He had learned his basics at the western side of the city, where there was a better quality of gentleman, and a superior form of bodyguard to go with him everywhere. To dip your hands into the purses over in that part of town, you have to be quick and careful, and – if you're spotted – even quicker on your feet. Hugh was very quick and capable, which is why he had this job now.

'How goes it, Hugh?' I said.

'What do you want?'

'There's no need to be like that,' I said, hurt. 'Can't an old friend come to speak with you now?'

'Yes. But what do you *want*?'

You see, Hugh had been invited into this special gambling den because he was a known master of thieving from the pockets of the rich and generally foolish. That was one thing, but there was another aspect of his skills that impressed his new masters: the fact that he could do it under the noses of the bodyguards employed by the fellows who knew their own limitations. He could take the money from a purse even when the guards were watching him, knowing that he was likely to be a thief.

With such skills, he was soon in demand as the perfect man to monitor the gambling dens where the most money was being used. Now, with an irony that was surely only to be found in London, the man who was perhaps the scourge of the majority of gambling hells of the city was the man employed to ensure that no one was robbed. And since he knew of my past and my skills as a foist, he was naturally keen to know what it was that made me so interested in his own place of work.

'I'll not have you harming my business here,' he said.

'No, of course not,' I said. 'But what I was thinking was that perhaps you might have seen something.'

He gave me the sort of look that a parent reserves for their child who has just been discovered in an untruth. 'I have seen many things, Jack. Get your foot out of my door.'

'But this was only two evenings ago. A man was killed in the entrance to the alley up near the wharves.'

'I had heard there was a body. There're often dead men found out that way. It's been taken to the nearest pub to wait for the Coroner, I expect. Serves the fool right. You don't go to the wharves unless you want to risk your life. It's full of sailors up there, and you know what they're like. They'll stick a knife in your belly as soon as look at you.'

'I don't think this was a sailor, Hugh. I was on the wharf. I just put the fellow down because he was tired, and when I got back to him, someone had killed him.'

'What were you doing there?'

I could hardly say, 'Oh, just killing a man,' so I gave him a grin and indicated that I had been busy with a wench.

'Your smile would turn milk rancid,' he said. 'What were you really doing?'

'I can't say. Honestly, I truly cannot. But it was not anything to do with the man. And when I came back, I had a lump on my head the size of a goose's egg. Look, it's still here!' I said, turning my head.

He expressed an extreme reluctance to touch my scalp. 'I'll believe you this once,' he said. 'So what has it to do with me?'

'Nothing. But the man had a magnificent purse, which to me looked heavy enough to be full of gold.'

'Stolen?'

'Not at all. It was his own. But when I found his body, the money was gone.'

'So you were cultivating this fool, but another thief got to him first and knocked you down into the bargain? Ha! That's good!' he laughed.

I was unimpressed with his amusement. 'So?'

'I didn't see anyone coming into the place that evening with a large amount of pelf, no. There were few enough in that night, to be honest. Only the Chamberlain, and a few of the Aldermen. The gambling wasn't very brisk, and the girls weren't busy, so it was easy to keep an eye on things, and you know me: I always watch for possible thieves.'

'You didn't see a man with more money than he would usually hold?'

'Several. But not the sort who'd wander the streets killing strangers to steal their money.'

'Oh.' It was disappointing, but hardly unexpected.

I withdrew my boot and was about to give him a farewell when he frowned. 'There was one . . . but no, it'll be nothing.'

'What?'

'Your friend, the Lawyer. He was here with a young maid who was worth looking at. Only a little cheap tart, but such a bust – you had to see it to believe it was real. Flashing eyes, too.'

My mouth began to fall open as he described Agnis in perfect detail.

'What do you mean, what was I doing? I was out, having fun, wasn't I? Why shouldn't I have a bit of fun in my life now and again?'

She was in her noisome little chamber at the top of the ladder when I reached the place. After all, it was close by Hugh's establishment. 'What were you doing going to the gambling den with Abraham?' I demanded.

'I was having a drink with a pleasant man who doesn't shout at me all the time! What's it to you, anyway? I was just having a bit of fun. He took me there to show me how he gambled. Didn't seem very good at it to me, mind. He lost almost everything.'

'How much?'

'Quite a lot. Not a huge amount, but, well, I don't think he has a lot to lose, does he?'

'No. You're right there.' This news had sent me thinking hard about Abraham. 'What, did you follow me?'

'No! How could we know where you were? We finished
our drinks, and Willyam suggested a game, and we all went
walking up the road. I was coming back here anyway, and
they said they'd walk with me to protect me. It was a good
idea. It was late. Should I have ignored their offers? What
right do you have to make me walk about alone in danger in
the dark?'

She spoke firmly and with a growing passion. Her eyes
flashed and her bosom heaved, and I could not help but stare
and smile.

'You can keep your eyes off my assets, too,' she declared.
'You stayed here one night, and now you think you can own
me, do you? No man owns me!'

'I thought you said that Master Blount was your master?'

'He is a man I can work with, nothing more. Why should I
want a master? I had a husband, and he died. Any other man
will die, too. So I waste my love and affection and efforts on
someone who'll die? Does that make sense to you? It doesn't
to me! You men, you just think about a woman as something
to warm your bed – you don't care about us as people, do you?
You would take me now, and then what? You'd walk away
without a backward glance. You wouldn't care if you'd broken
my heart, left me with child, or given me the pox! Well, I'm
not foolish enough to fall for your languishing glances, Jack
Blackjack, so be away with you! You will not share my cot
here, so go find a floozy who'll let you into hers.'

'I don't want to do anything like that! I was just asking
because the man I was with that night died out in the alley. You
didn't tell me that the others were all here with you that night.'

'What if I had? They are your friends, aren't they?'

Ah, and there she had a point, you see. Because the three
were comrades-in-arms of a sort. There is a camaraderie
between men who participate in the military, in the law, and
in the more flexible industries such as the one in which I was
employed. However, I was about to point out that there was
a significant difference between the trust involved between,
say, two soldiers who have fought and survived a battle, and
two thieves who tried to rob the same man; and then I recon-
sidered. After all, I had experienced battle with a man at my

side who was as keen to kill me as I was to kill the enemy, and I had lived with a small group of criminals who had, some of them, been happy enough to see me lying in a ditch with a knife in my belly. Perhaps there was more of a similarity than I would have thought originally.

'Besides,' she continued, 'Master Abraham actually did fetch me home, which is more than *you* did!'

She had a point there, too.

'Well?' she added, folding her arms and staring at me with a raised eyebrow.

'Well, what?'

'What now?'

'I don't know.'

'Have you found Michol yet?'

'No, but my friend Humfrie is doing that for me.'

'Your friend . . . Do I have to explain everything to you in simple words?' she sighed.

'I don't need to stand here and be insulted,' I said.

'No. Not when there are so many others prepared to stand in line to insult you,' she said sweetly. 'But for now, since I'm the only woman present, I'd best take on the responsibility, you poor fool. Who is this man Humfrie?'

'He . . .' I hesitated. I didn't want her to get to hear that I had to use an unofficial murderer to carry out my executions. 'He's a friend who performs certain confidential tasks for me.'

'Like what?'

'Such as finding your man Michol,' I said with some asperity.

She nodded. 'Then you had best meet him as soon as possible to learn what he has discovered.'

'Yes.'

'Where?'

I felt my mouth open and shut again. 'He said to meet me at my house.'

'When?'

'Before Vespers.'

'Then we should be on our way.'

'You are coming with me?'

'I don't think I can trust you on your own, do you?' she said, not unkindly, but as she crossed the floor, she slapped my cheek like a mother patronizingly patting a foolish child, so not exactly trying to spare my feelings either.

When he saw Agnis waiting with me, Humfrie's face went as still and expressionless as a statue's.

'It's all right, Humfrie,' I said. 'She is a sensible woman and keeps her mouth clamped shut.'

'That's good, Master,' Humfrie said. 'But she will wait outside while I have a private word with you.'

'That's not necessary,' I said.

'But she will wait outside.'

With a sense of irritation, I rolled my eyes and looked over to her. She smiled, but as I looked at her, my ballocks froze to balls of ice. That's how cold her expression was as she inclined her head graciously to Humfrie and strode from the room.

'What do you mean by being so—' I began, but he cut me off, his voice little more than a hiss.

'Are you truly this confused about the world? She is a woman, so she cannot be trusted to keep her mouth from flapping with her friends, and she is an unknown person when it comes to serious business. How do you know she is not the paid informant of your enemies? How do you know she is not the person come specifically to destroy you?'

'She is just a young widow, Humfrie!'

'How do you know that?'

'I've seen her house. She would not live there if she had any choice.'

'How do you know that is her home?'

I laughed, and then caught sight of his expression. For an instant the air expelled in humour was blocked by incoming air. It was as if Mal's hands had managed to reach me at last and were choking me. I managed to clear my throat after a moment's gurgling, and said, 'Who else's home would it be?'

'You tell me you want an assassin to help you, because you work for rich, powerful men. Now you have no money, you have been told not to kill the man you pushed into the Thames, and you have to kill another man, and you cannot see that letting a woman like her into your affairs could be dangerous?'

'We need to kill this Michol. He's a danger for some reason.'

'You don't even know why, do you?'

'Yes! He has been spreading lies about the Lady Elizabeth, I expect.'

'You expect! He is very friendly with the French.'

'Well, there you are, then!'

'You told me that he was an intelligencer for the French. Who told you that?'

'I don't know!'

'Was it her?'

'Maybe – what of it?'

'You have a reputation, Master Blackjack. You should protect it carefully. You wouldn't want to have others start to play with it, would you?'

'I . . . others play with it? What do you mean?'

He rolled his eyes this time. 'Master, you are a confessed assassin! If people are told that is what you do, how safe do you think your position here, in this house, would become? If anything ever happens to the Queen or her husband, where will people come looking? If a certain wealthy man dies suddenly, who will attract the blame?'

I confess, this was an aspect of my position that had not occurred to me. Certainly, I had no desire to broadcast my new job to everyone, but it had not struck me that if it became common knowledge, then every single assault or murder could easily be placed at my own door. This had an instant effect on my bowels, and I was forced to lean against the wall, a hand pressed against my belly.

'I cannot run risks, you understand,' Humfrie continued with a brutal ruthlessness.

'I . . . of course not, no.'

'So, if news were to break out that you were an assassin, you would obviously seek to reassure people that you had nothing to do with such things.'

'Well, I suppose.' I stopped. Suddenly, the full impact of his words struck me. 'No, I mean, of course not – by 'sblood, no, I'd never peach!'

'Any man taken to the Tower will talk after a while. So before you could be arrested, I would be forced to take action,' he continued, as relentless as a fox in a chicken yard. 'I could not afford to risk that you might speak of me or Jen. So it would be a precautionary death. Performed with great reluctance.'

'Yes, right . . . of course, no . . . I see. Um.'

'So I may well have to remove the young lady. She could be a threat to us both.'

'No, look, she is innocent in every way, I assure you.'

'You give me your word?'

'Yes!'

'And if you discover reason to doubt her word, you will inform me?'

'Yes, yes. I swear it.'

'Good.' He considered me a moment, and then spat into the palm of his hand and held it out.

It was one of those old-fashioned oaths, clearly. At least he didn't demand our oaths to be sealed in blood, I suppose. I spat into my hand and we shook on it.

At last we could ask the women to rejoin us.

'Where is he?' I asked.

The evening was coming on too swiftly already. Humfrie agreed to return in the morning, and I settled to enjoy an evening with Agnis. My plans did not accord with her own, sadly. She was much more keen to speak about the man Michol than I was, especially after Humfrie's careful warning about her and her flapping mouth.

I could begin to comprehend his concern now. She talked solidly, without concern for Raphe and anyone else who might be listening. Her speech was as unrestrained as her breasts, which moved so entrancingly as she drew breath. She was fascinating. A couple of times I attempted to sidle a little nearer to her, but every time I tried, she managed to evade me. In the end, although I can always handle my drink, I discovered that it was growing more difficult to speak and try to maintain her interest. You know that time when you first drink cider? Some men get fighty and stupid, but I found that I was fine, able to count, swear, laugh – everything. But after three pints of rough cider, when I tried to stand up, I toppled to the ground. It was as if my legs had been cut away. This was rather the same, except suddenly I found that my mouth also failed. I tried to stand and fell on my face immediately. With my mouth working, but nothing intelligible escaping me, I was confused and somewhat alarmed, but then Agnis put her arms down to me, and I was aware of a lustful surge running through my body. I tried to pull her on to me, but although my arms rose, I had no command over them.

It was a curious sensation, to know that she was lifting me to a sitting position. Then lovely Raphe appeared. Giving me a look in which disgust and amusement were equally mingled, he went behind me. He tried to put his arms about my chest to lift me, but my own shot upwards and I slid through to fall on my arse again. Although Raphe attempted to pick me up in this manner three times, each was as ineffective as the last, and eventually he released me entirely, standing at my side while, I confess, I giggled a little.

'I can't get him up,' he said rather pathetically.

He pushed and I was allowed to fall forward over my own lap, and then I felt two delicious cushions on my back. Agnis slipped her arms under my armpits and whispered breathily into my ear, 'Cross your arms.' She took my right wrist in her left hand, my left in her right, and hoisted me. In a few moments I found myself on top of my bench near the fire, a bucket by my head, and my head resting on her lap.

'This is a lovely place,' I said. Her bodice ballooned over me and I strained to reach it, but her hand slapped mine away.

'More of that and you will be sleeping on the floor. Your floor will be less comfortable than mine.'

'Can't I just—'

'No.'

'You might find you—'

'You want me to push you to the floor?'

No, I did not. With the effects of the wine, the comfort of that delightful pillow beneath my head, and a mind wondrously clear of all terrors, I closed my eyes and was soon fast asleep.

The following morning, I could think, I could reason, I could recall, and I could scare myself into fabulous terror at the thought that the Spanish were coming to get me any time soon.

I also felt as sick as a dog, by the way. True fear can do that to me. When I get absolutely appalled with perfectly natural fears – such as those of having my cods cut from my body, seeing my fingers cut off, that sort of thing – I can become a gibbering wreck in moments. While I can be as courageous as the next man when I am in a moderately strong position, there is little better guaranteed to show me in a terrified funk than the thought of pain or death.

Just now, of course, I had two main concerns. Ranked in order of seriousness, these were: what would the Spaniards do when I could tell them nothing (that I dared confess to) about the end of their friend; and what would Blount do, were he to discover that I had killed the wrong man? Possibly still worse, he might learn that I honestly could not stick a knife in a man with whom I had no quarrel. He would be certain to consider that a serious character defect, one that could have a severe impact on my own enjoyment of life . . . if only for a short period.

However, it was not, of course, only the fear that was having this impact on me. In large part, it was due to the head from the wine the night before. But it did not seem to me that I had drunk so much. I recall some wine early in the evening, and perhaps a flagon or two with the meal, and perhaps another after our meal . . . but that was not so far from a man's usual daily consumption. It was not as though I had mingled ales with wines and burned wines, which were usually my disaster of choice. And Agnis had joined me in some of the drinks, too, so I was not alone in my consumption. Still, the fact was that my head was not feeling normal this morning, and neither was my stomach. I could not look at the plate of eggs and greasy bacon that Raphe set before me with his own slightly green grin.

'What's the matter with you?' I demanded, but quietly. My head was not of a mind to enjoy loud noises.

'I feel a bit unwell. I will be fine,' he added quickly, not wanting to give me a reason to expel him.

'Well, see to it that your work is unimpeded,' I said sternly.

Glancing down at the trencher before me, I quickly averted

my gaze and gave a firm smile to Agnis, who sat at the table next to me. She looked as beautiful and calm as a swan, I thought. When I had woken, I was alone on my bench, but she had kindly draped a couple of thick blankets over me, and I had not been chilled. I think she had also set a cushion beneath my head, but it was on the floor when I woke. It was a kind thought, however. And a woman who performs such kind little gestures must surely care for the man for whom she performs them, I thought. I tried to smile at her.

'Is it very bad?' she said.

'No, not at all,' I lied.

She laughed aloud.

There are times when you really have no interest in a man – when it seems as though every step you take, the fool appears to be underfoot and you spend your life tripping over the bastard. Other times, you can search high and low, and never catch a glimpse of the man you seek.

This was one of the latter.

First thing in the morning, Humfrie and his daughter appeared at the door, and we left my house soon after completing our breakfast, although we did have to stop for a while at an alley near Aldgate while I successfully deposited the greasy eggs and bacon into a corner. Humfrie looked disgusted, but it wasn't my fault. I have never felt worse. Still, with the search ahead of me, I felt better for the loss of my excess baggage, as it were. Then we bent our steps to Michol's stomping ground.

We searched for him near his home; we hunted down near the docks where we were told he had been working; we haunted the alehouses and taverns nearby; we looked in the pie shops and inns; we visited every bowling alley; we dropped in to every legal, illegal and slightly suspect gambling hall and cockfighting ring. Desperate, I even thought to see if there was a duel being fought anywhere, but I was told that the last was finished for the day.

Twice, I could have sworn – or at least, I thought – that I saw that other man again. A man with his face entirely concealed beneath a cowl, his body hidden in robes. It was unsettling. I began to wonder if this was a man sent by Blount to follow me, or a Spaniard, or . . . but there my imagination failed me. And each time I thought I saw him, when I peered more closely, there was no one there. Only the usual London mobs.

Seeing me staring back, Humfrie glanced up at me. 'Seen someone you know?'

'No . . . no, I don't think so.'

'Then stop staring back like a woman searching for her lover!'

In short, we found neither sight nor rumour of the man. It was infuriating.

Humfrie, as the afternoon progressed, was growing more and more short-tempered. 'It's bad enough being paid nothing for all this effort, without wearing out my shoes.'

'Yes,' Jen declared. 'It's not our fault we can't find him. You should promise us more money if you want our help.'

'Why don't you sell the necklace I bought you?' I said nastily.

Her hand went to her throat at that. I knew how much the capricious little noddy had liked that damned trinket. It was the reason Falkes had come to realize his wife was fondling another man's cods, when the silly tart had worn it while out walking with him. Falkes was never forgiving or unsuspicious, and the sight of that necklace was enough to send him into a paroxysm of rage that nearly resulted in my death. As it was, Jen was very lucky not to have been chastised. I wonder whether that was because Falkes, even in his more homicidal moods, still wasn't quite suicidal enough to try to attack Humfrie's daughter. He knew from first hand just how deadly Humfrie truly was.

'Now, now,' Humfrie said soothingly. 'We are all in need of refreshment, that's all.'

As luck would have it, we had reached the door of one of the meaner alehouses, a place we had already looked into that morning. Humfrie went inside, and we stood outside. The street's kennel was full and somewhat dammed by turds, and I was idly watching a rat slink across the roadway to tuck in, when Humfrie appeared in the doorway. The rat scurried back whence it had come.

Humfrie had ales in both hands and passed these to the women before returning inside. A short while later he brought two more and sat on a bench against the wall with every sign of satisfaction. 'Here's to the successful completion of our task,' he said.

'That's all very good,' I said. 'What if we can't find him? We can't do what we need to if we don't find him, can we?'

'Oh, I wouldn't worry about that,' he said.

'Wouldn't you? Let me remind you that this whole affair is rather serious to me! If we don't do what we need to, I will be in trouble with my master! This could cost me dearly: my clothes, my house, everything! I won't be able to pass business on to you if that happens!'

'Why would he do that to you?' Humfrie said, tipping his pot back and drinking deeply before fixing me with a beady eye.

'Because it matters to him! He doesn't explain such things to me, though. He wants this blasted man removed, for reasons best known to himself.'

'It is because the man is fomenting trouble,' Agnis said. She looked around at us, although she stiffened when her eye lit upon Jen. 'I overheard a part of a conversation, in which Master Blount spoke with a man who told him that this French agent seeks to weaken the Queen, and open affairs for Mary, Queen of Scots, to take the English throne.'

'What?' Humfrie said. 'This bastard wants to sell us down the river so we become vassals of the French?'

'How could that be?' I asked, confused.

Humfrie shook his head – whether at the perfidy of the French or at my obtuseness, I am not sure. 'Mary, Queen of Scotland, was raised in France. She is French to all appearances, and she is engaged to the Dauphin. That is the French King's heir.'

'I know,' I lied.

'So, if the French could have their way, they would have her installed on the English throne as well as the Scottish one. She would swiftly be married to the King of France, uniting all three kingdoms: Scotland, England and France. That would make the French invincible against the Spanish. She would form an impenetrable barrier to Spanish ambitions. The Spanish empire would be split in half, with the Netherlands north of France, and the rest of the empire to the south. As things are now, ships can sail the English Channel, but if England was united with France, and both coasts guarded, it would be possible to block any transports or other shipping from navigating it, and the northern empire would be cut off completely.'

'How do you know all this?' I asked.

'I listen to merchants,' he said.

Agnis was nodding agitatedly. 'Yes, that's what Blount was saying.'

'How did you hear about it?' I asked. I knew Blount of old, and it was highly unusual for him to speak uninhibitedly in front of others. Usually, he would supply just enough inform-ation for his servants to carry out their tasks, considering that the less they knew of his plans or aims, the better for all concerned.

'He was having a meeting at a tavern when I was in there, and he had me wait in the next room. I could hear every word.'

'You were listening at his door?'

'Yes.'

I looked at her with some respect. To listen in to Blount's conversation was an act of courage. If he had realized, he could well have put her on the top of his list of 'People I don't want to hear of again'.

'That was very brave.'

'Thank you.'

'Are you both finished?' Humfrie said.

'Well, at least we know why now,' I said.

'Yes.'

'But it doesn't help us find him.'

'No?'

'No,' I said more firmly.

'I suppose not,' Humfrie agreed. He set his drink down. 'So you continue hunting for him, if you like.'

I looked up. The sun was out, and it was sweltering already. My armpits felt sticky and my back ran with sweat. 'I suppose we could always stay here a little longer.'

Agnis exchanged a look with Jen. 'Are you serious? You have been talking about how badly we need to find Michol, and now you want to drink away your afternoon here?'

Jen agreed. 'Father, come along! We need to discover where he is!'

'I'm staying here a little longer,' he declared, and thrust his chin and legs out, crossing his arms. He was the very picture of obstinacy.

'I'll buy us a drink,' I said.

Both the women made sounds expressive of contempt and annoyance, and span on their heels, walking away down the lane. A hand reached out, I saw, towards Agnis's bottom, but before it could connect, she had whirled around, whipped out a knife, and the man withdrew his hand with a yelp.

I smiled and walked into the dingy interior.

It was a short walk to the bar, a plank set across a trio of barrels, and I called for two quarts of their best ale. While they were drawn, I turned and glanced about the room.

There was a loud party at a long table, and as I glanced about, one of the men was bellowing with delight. 'Come on, Michol! Even at St Olave-towards-the-Tower, they must have . . .'

And I saw him.

There was no mistaking him. As Blount's original note described him, Michol was a happy-looking fellow, perhaps in his early thirties, and the description of a man with a paunch who looked as though he enjoyed his life was fully justified. Apart from that, his clothing was not of a bad type. It looked to be of a stolid, workaday form, with good, bright colours, although little of the expensive silks that a man like me would require to demonstrate his status.

But there he was, sitting at a bench, smiling and laughing with other men. It was the kind of sight to make a person feel as if the grey clouds of misery and despair were suddenly burned away under the beaming glory of a full summer sun.

I did think to go to him and join in with his little party. The men were clearly discussing a game of cards, while there were some women with them to lighten the mood with alternative diversions.

One of the prettier wenches gave a raucous laugh and slapped the face of the man on whose lap she was sitting, but her hand left no mark. It was not the angry smack of an offended maiden, but a jestful tease, tempting the man to greater efforts.

I allowed my eyes to flit over the other women in the group, and all were a sight to please a man's gaze. As I moved on through the crush to the bar and ordered the drinks, I circum-ambulated the people at the table, and it was as I was talking to the pretty maid serving that I caught sight of the skinnier woman on the farther side. It was enough almost to make me spit out my beer.

She had been sitting with her back to me when I had entered, so I had no idea who this was at first, but now I could see her plainly: it was Jeffry's daughter, whom I had seen at his house on the day I had gone hoping to find news of his money.

Except now she was no ancient wench who was weary from cleaning up after an inveterate gambler, but a woman in her early twenties, if I had to guess, with sparkling eyes, and if her upper carriage was a little lighter than Agnis's, there was still enough to fill both hands.

What was she doing here, though? I had left her deep in misery, convinced that she was about to lose her house, knowing full well that no matter what her father managed to do to recover any income, he was sure to squander it on cock-fighting, bull-baiting or the time it took for a snail to crawl up a glass. Now she was the glittering beauty in this gathering. Her dress must have cost someone a pretty penny, and she wore about her dainty throat a necklace that gained more from quantity than delicacy. The weight of gold involved was enough to sink a small wherry.

It was astonishing to see her there, but my eye was drawn back to the man who must soon die.

For a man whose death warrant was signed, he had every appearance of health and happiness. I had no reason to dislike the man, except for the fact that he was the source of consid-erable embarrassment to me, since he should be dead and Jeffry alive, but I wasn't going to hold that against him. Not in the time he had left, anyway.

And then my thoughts were dislocated as someone else entered the room.

It had not occurred to me that there might be a second entrance to this tavern, but there was clearly a door at the rear which gave out to a yard where drinkers would go to piss. While I stood there, I saw a couple of men walk in from that direction. It was the second of the two that made me almost drop my ale. I must find Humfrie. I had news for him.

Gathering up my beers, I tried to duck my head to be as unobtrusive as possible as I squeezed and pushed my way out from the place, spilling only a very little of the beer on my way.

'You took your time,' Humfrie said.

'Did you know he was in there?'

'Oh, so ye saw him too? I wondered if you would,' he grinned. 'That was why I thought we might as well remain here. More fool those two women for not trusting me! They can enjoy their walk while we wait here for him to come out, and then one of us can follow him and do what is needful.'

I put a hand over my eyes. The sight of the woman and the man in there had quite unmanned me.

'What is it?'

'At his table, there was a woman. It was the daughter of the man we killed at the wharf.'

'Oh? Jeffry's daughter, eh?'

'Yes. How did she come to know Michol? She is sitting in there right at his side.'

'So? Maybe their fathers knew each other?'

'Yes? *How*, I wonder? Was it a shared interest in gambling? Perhaps both liked to watch cockroaches racing? Or seeing which window pane would attract the most raindrops in a storm?'

Humfrie was watching me with that steady, grim stillness that I was coming to recognize. 'What's the matter with you?' he said with great preciseness.

'What's the matter is that Mal the Loaf is still alive.'

'No,' Humfrie grinned. 'I think I can be fairly certain that he wasn't going to get up again after the tap I gave him.'

'Oh,' I said. 'That's a great surprise, then, especially to

Jeffry's daughter. Because his ghost just walked into the tavern there and gave her a welcoming kiss.'

You know those moments, when you are gaily going about your daily business, and suddenly something strikes you in the face like a recently caught pike? I don't mean a polearm, of course, but the fish. I mean, if you were hit by a polearm, there would be little humour in it.

There was a time when I was in a hurry to get somewhere, back when I was still living with my father, and there was a series of fields that had ditches dug all about them, to prevent flooding, and where the ditches were wider, a helpful fellow or two had installed bridges to facilitate crossing. However, most of these bridges were little more than broad planks with a handrail on one side.

One day I ran across with urgent abandon. A man in front of me, walking the same way, was striding along in a powerful style, and as I was on the bridge, he thought it would be a fine thing to call his dog, a great shaggy black thing built like a pony. Unknown to me, his brute was at the far side of the bridge behind me. So I was unaware, when the man whistled, what this could mean.

The first I knew was a thunderous sensation on the plank as the hound sprang on to it. Then I became aware of the wood bouncing before I received a sudden buffet at my knee as the mongrel slammed past and pelted onwards.

He was fine, of course, but he completely up-ended me; my feet slid on the slimy surface, while my knees collapsed, and in an instant I was upside down in the ditch, my shoulders wedged against the ditch's walls, my legs waving in the air.

For a few moments, the hound returned, head set on one side as though contemplating the foolishness of humans who decided to go diving into ditches. Then, with a valedictory shake of his head, which had the unhappy effect of depositing several strings of drool on to my upturned face, he responded to another call from his master and trotted off.

I have often had cause to think that, were the ditch full of water, I would have drowned, and anyone who knew me would speak of the foolhardiness of anyone who could slip and fall into a stream in such a ridiculous manner. Who, after all, could have guessed at the canine agency of my death?

But that was plainly one of those moments in which I felt I had been hit about the face by a cold, wet fish. And I was now granted the sight of someone else who was struck with the same sensation.

Humfrie goggled at me. For a while, he looked like a bull that had run at a man, only to find that the man was painted on a rock wall. He was dumbfounded. As though in a mild daydream, he reached into the bag at his side and withdrew his little leather sack. He weighed this in his hand as though suspecting someone else had been fiddling with it, and had perhaps replaced the sand and stones inside with pure fleece.

'No, he can't be alive after that,' he said doubtfully.

'Go in and see for yourself. You know him. You can't miss him just now. He has a turban of muslin wrapped about his head,' I said, thoroughly enjoying Humfrie's discomfort. After all, no expert in any field enjoys being shown to be wrong. I suppose it would be like an alchemist having absolute, incontrovertible proof that all his efforts for the last thirty years had been barking up the wrong tree.

Humfrie stood, tugged at the front of his jack, took a great gulp of ale, and sauntered into the tavern.

A few minutes later he returned, this time sinking half his beer. 'Yes, it's him,' he said pensively. 'I cannot have hit him hard enough.'

'Obviously.'

'But it is interesting that he is with the man Michol,' he continued, eyes narrowed. 'If what you said is correct, and Michol is acting for France, I am surprised that he would meet and socialize with a man like Mal. Men who have such an interest in politics that they seek to overthrow a queen rarely meet socially, in my experience. How did they meet?'

'Both are Catholic,' I suggested. Since King Henry's creation of the new English Church, Catholics had become an underground body, and even now, with Queen Mary's sweeping away of so much of her father's religious reforms and the return of the Catholic Church, many adherents were rumoured to meet in secret. It would be no surprise if these two did.

'So? You think Mal would let religion get in his way?'

'Perhaps politics to them is less important than gambling?' I hazarded.

He gave me a look of admiration. I confess, I threw out the comment more as a sarcastic reflection, but he was plainly taking it seriously. 'Of course!' he declared. 'They must be seeking to make money together in some manner.'

I nodded and smiled knowingly, wondering what on earth he was thinking. Then I returned to the matter at hand. 'Michol doesn't know you, does he?'

'No. He is completely unaware of me.'

'So getting close to him should be easy enough. What do you think? Get him into an alley where you can strangle him? A knife in the dark?'

Humfrie nodded. 'Something of that nature.'

'Well, I had best leave you so you can follow him.'

'Yes.'

He was still studying me with a quizzical look in his eye. It was the sort of look that made the hackles rise on the back of my neck. 'What?'

'I just had an idea,' he said. 'After all, I can do little while Mal remains in there. If he sees me, he will likely want to come and chat about my attack.'

'So you will need to remove him before you can kill Michol. I see.'

'I cannot go to him without him chasing me away. If he does, then I will not be able to follow Michol later, will I?'

'No.'

'So, we must have someone else go in there and let Mal see him, so he can be tempted to pursue the hare.'

'But there is only you and . . .'

My mouth was in need of Agnis's finger again. I gaped like a carp, mouth flapping uselessly. 'But that would . . . I can't do that . . . What if he catches me?'

'I would think that you would be entitled to the defence of preventing a murder. His of you!'

'Which is fine, except he would take more killing than an elephant! Look at the size of him! You thought you had killed him yourself, but there he is still! If *you* can't manage it, how in God's name do you think I can? God's wounds, it's mad! *You're* mad!'

'All you have to do is let him see you. If you run, he'll give chase, and with his head the way it is, he will not be able to run too fast. Just go quickly, and he won't be able to keep up with you.'

'No. I can't do it. I won't do it!'

I entered the tavern as quietly as I could. After all, if the man refused to notice me, it wouldn't be my fault. I could hardly be blamed for being unnoticed.

They were all sitting, and I walked around them, so that I could avoid meeting either Jeffry's daughter's eye or Mal's. I had thought that I could wander through, buy a drink, and saunter out in front of Mal. Now a slight difficulty became clear. If I were to do this, then I would be in plain sight of Mal from the moment I turned and faced the table. Since his attention was fixed in that direction, I would have to run the gauntlet to escape the tavern. It was moderately full, so that meant I would have to force my way past twenty feet of slow-moving, aggressively resentful manhood to make it to the door, while all Mal would have to do would be to stand and move four feet or so to cut off my escape. I may be no gambler, but those looked like odds that were not in my favour.

Standing at the bar, I tried to escape the conviction that his eyes were boring into my back. I stared disconsolately at the ground before me, but found no inspiration there.

I came to the conclusion that I had two choices. First, I could return the way I had come in, and hurry out and tell Humfrie that Mal had not seen me. That would risk Humfrie's contempt – well, I was used to that from many people. I could bear his disdain, I was sure, in exchange for my life.

The second option was to go out and then return so that Mal could see me while I was still nearer the door. That way, he would have the handicap of all the people in his way, and I would be able to escape more swiftly. At least by that means I would be more likely to get outside with a firm grip on my life. It appealed much more.

There was, of course, the third option of running out through the door to the yard as though I wanted a piss. This only occurred to me now, because as I stood there contemplating my options, I was growing ever more aware that my bladder was full. Now, I don't know about you, but for me, if I am to run away from someone in a hurry, the very last thing I want is a heavy load of ballast on board. But to go to that door would involve walking back in full view again.

Then another thing came to my mind. The door to the outside could have a second exit. If I went out there, I might be able to gain access to an alley or side lane that could take me away from here. I could run back to my house and . . .

And meet with the Spaniards and be reintroduced to Ramon and his Toledo steel. That was no option. Where else could I run? Without money, I had no choices. I had to accept the danger of Mal the Loaf's breadknife.

I turned to face my enemy.

He didn't see me. His own face was turned to Jeffry's daughter, and the two were laughing and joking like lovers.

And then I saw Agnis. She was staring at me from the doorway, half hidden behind the door itself. Her eyes were fixed on Mal, and as she looked across at me, I held up my hand.

It was a moment's thoughtlessness, that was all. She was there and looking as attractive as only she could, and I was anxious and trying to think of what to do for the best, and seeing her was like seeing an inn after a long and dangerous journey, a refuge and sanctuary against all the dangers that surrounded me.

So, yes, I lifted my hand. And she saw me. Pretty much at the same time as Mal.

You have to admire men like Mal. There he was, sitting with a pretty maiden at his side, in a room full of people, and yet even at such a time, even with a head that must have hurt as much as if a dozen bulls had tried dancing on it, even with the men about him who would surely have protected him against any obvious attack, he was still alert and watching for danger.

It just goes to show that a vicious, evil, murderous halfwit really should not be underestimated.

I stood goggling in horror as our eyes met across the crowded room, and for a moment I considered trying to make it to the door – but it was very obvious, very quickly, that to try that would be suicide. Even as I considered it, I saw that Mal was standing – Christ's Blood, he was huge! – and starting to move towards me, like a great ship of the navy getting underway.

It was really impressive, in a hideously horrific manner. He sort of swam through the crowds; he swept with his left arm, and four men found themselves inexplicably moved a yard or so to the side; his right arm duplicated the motion, and another three men were relocated. With each move of his arms, he took a step towards me. At first his progress was slow, but he began to pick up speed, while I could do nothing but remain where I was, transfixed with terror. I felt as though my feet had sent out roots. A slight murmur, or perhaps gibbering, may have left my lips, but that was all.

I have heard that snakes can so terrify their prey that the rabbit or mouse is incapable of escape, and all the while that their eyes are held by the snake, they are fixed like a bird to a limed branch. My eyes were gripped by his, and I was unable to move.

It was truly petrifying. While I stood there, I had flashes of my life pass before my eyes. It was a depressingly short display, and most of it was not inspiring. I remembered things like my father strapping my arse after he found I'd raided his beer savings; waking from a horrible knock to the head to discover I was lying next to a dead man; stumbling over a woman's corpse. Why do such things happen to me? And, now, the one man I had wanted to see dead was making his way towards me with every intention of skinning and paunching me like a rabbit, if his expression was anything to go by.

And then there was a miracle.

The latest man to have been barged aside by Mal's arm was unaware of the cause of his sudden translocation and decided to take umbrage.

He was a slight little figure, and my first thought was that he would be crushed like an egg under a hammer, but it only goes to show that a man's first impression can be significantly in error.

The initial encounter completed, Mal was about to move on past, when the smaller man turned. Like many others during Mal's onward progress, he had to blink at the size of Mal's massive torso. What he lacked in height, as I have hinted before, he more than made up for in breadth.

But while others took a short glance and quickly decided that they had not been seriously discombobulated by their sideways movement, this fellow was clearly either so drunk that he didn't realize he was staring at his personal Nemesis or so foolish that he didn't reckon Mal was dangerous, and he pushed Mal in the back.

Mal was not a man to intentionally allow an insult to go unnoticed. He turned, and it was rather like a mountain turning, I would imagine. I haven't seen one, but I can easily believe that there would be a similar sense of shock to see a mountain rotate. I'm sure I heard a grating, rumbling sound, as of rock moving against rock, but I could have imagined it.

There was a look of incomprehension on Mal's face. He and the little man stood staring at each other, and from my vantage point I could see the play of expressions that shifted over Mal's features: from surprise to shock, to bafflement, and finally absolute rage. He lifted a fist like a ham, and I prepared to see the small fellow's head spring from his body and bounce around the room. I flinched at the thought.

I heard a loud 'Oof!' and when I opened my eyes, Mal was rocked back, his hands on his belly. The small man with the death wish was light on his feet, but he packed a punch like a sledgehammer. Darting around, he punched twice for every one of Mal's, and although Mal moved as swiftly as he could, wherever his fists were aimed, the little man was no longer there.

'Keep still!' Mal bellowed, anguished.

There was another flurry of blows, and the fellow danced around Mal, slamming four rapid punches to his kidneys, then, under a flailing fist, landed a punch on Mal's throat that had him reeling.

But that was never going to stop the inevitable. A jab from Mal missed, but before the opponent could spring up and hit him again, Mal's left fist shot out. It seemed to move quite slowly, compared with the quick-fire blows from the other, but even moving slowly it carried weight. It met the other's cheek, but that had no visible impact on the speed of the fist. The fist continued on its forward movement, and from where I stood, I could see the small man's body curving in a delicate arc, both feet leaving the ground, as though his face was now glued to Mal's fist.

He disappeared from view, and I felt a momentary sadness. The man had fought well.

And then I looked up into Mal's face and the spell was broken.

I ran.

The yard outside was in a terrible state. If I had been the owner, I would have been ashamed.

Ahead of me, a wall enclosed the yard and blocked my path. To the left there was a wall which, my nostrils informed me, was where clients went to relieve themselves. There was a pit nearby, and I didn't need to look to know what that was for.

On the right was a large mess. There was an old cookpot, a couple of barrels, but mostly it comprised of timbers, lathes, lumps of plaster and shingles, where once had stood a small extension to the main building. Clearly, it was no more. Beyond that was another wall, but this was the wall to another building, without window or handhold. I could not get away in that direction. Further to the left was another house, with timbers and plaster falling apart. There were hand and footholds aplenty, but none looked as though they would hold my weight.

I took this all in with one glance. My only possible escape was over the wall before me, but it stood at least four feet over my head. I had little chance of leaping that. Not that I had any choice. I heard shouting from behind me and ran for it.

When I was much younger, I was quite agile. Yes, I had a small frame and was not known for my strength, but if I was asked to leap into the air, I had some ability. Once, I remember, I sprang into a tree to escape a ravening hound that clearly had rabies or something similar. It was a horrible experience, and I am sure I leaped four feet into the air to snatch at a branch high overhead. After that, I always believed that a man could somehow jump astonishing distances when in dire need. As I was now.

Alas, my theory was to prove that whatever the abilities of a youth, it was many years since I had been that young. Perhaps my comfortable living over the last year has taken its toll.

At full pelt, I ran to the wall, springing up and reaching for the top. I slammed into the wall, the breath knocked from my body, my hands scrabbling wildly. It seemed to me that I hung there for some while, as though I had been snagged on hooks. And then I realized that my feet were still on the ground. Absolutely on the ground, as though planted. It was hard to believe, and I stared down with some surprise. Somehow I had landed without noticing. I leaped up again and could see that the top of the wall was tantalizingly close: only a matter of a couple of inches or so from my fingertips when I jumped, but nearly two feet away as I stood there.

There was no handy foothold or loose brick by which I might pull myself up. Nothing. Only . . .

I hurried to the collapsed building. There must surely be some kind of box or barrel in there, something I could put in front of the wall to help me clamber over.

There was! It was a barrel, quite ancient, and I picked it up and set it down, and climbed up on it, wobbling precariously, expecting at any moment to feel Mal's ham-fisted grab for me, but there was nothing other than a roar from inside the tavern, as though Mal was remonstrating with another member of the fraternity in there.

I stood upright, wobbling on the circle of safety, reached up, and just as my fingers gripped the top of the wall, I had a sickening sensation.

There are many very clever fellows who assert, so I'm told, that in life it is vital to remain steadfastly positive, no matter what. They think, and I have little reason to doubt them, that the good Lord will listen to those who do their best to help themselves, and He is more likely to look on such folks favourably and lend a helping hand. In my position, He should have seen me as a perfect case. I was in danger of my life, yet here I was, struggling on manfully, clinging to the top of the wall over which, if I could only clamber up, I would find safety.

Perhaps these clever fellows have had different experiences from me, because personally I find that no matter how positive I try to be, the sad fact is that I routinely find myself gammoned. At the final hurdle, I learn that I was deceived to be so optimistic. As on this occasion.

My fingers were on the top of the wall, and I was just smiling with relief when this little premonition of disaster crept into my consciousness. The sickening sensation I mentioned was a sort of rocking, slipping feeling, as if I was on a ship crossing the Thames in the foulest of wintry weather. I don't know whether you have been caught in a gale on the Thames – I haven't – but I can imagine it would be like this. The ground was moving, as though the soil was itself turning to water. My feet trembled, then wobbled; they seemed to have turned to jelly. Suddenly, they could not support me.

Of course, my legs were fine. This was the consequence of my selecting as a support a barrel that had been thrown out on the rubbish heap. Perhaps, if I had thought this through, I would have realized that any barrel set out there was likely to be rotten.

There was a crack, and the topmost bindings that held the staves together snapped. Suddenly, released from their captive cooperage, the staves flung themselves free, like so many condemned prisoners on their way to the gallows who unexpectedly find their wrists unbound.

With no staves, the barrel top disappeared from under my feet. I was suddenly without support, dangling by my strained fingers from the brickwork of the wall. I know that my eyes widened in horror. Safety was over there, on the other side of the wall, and all I needed to do was lift myself up and drop to the other side of the wall. I heard a high keening noise and realized that it was the breath whistling in my throat as I strained my arms to lift myself over. I scrabbled with my feet, but my boots were not made for such climbing, and I could not find even the smallest lip or groove. Instead, I felt my fingers relinquishing their hold.

I had time to reflect that if this was all the good that

positive thinking could achieve, then God was a practical
trickster. I was betrayed, I thought, and He was responsible.
I fleetingly felt a sense of guilty remorse for such an irreligious
idea.

Not that it mattered. I fell.

Falling always seems to take a long time. Have you noticed?

I have had some experience of falling. There was a time I
was scrumping apples from a neighbour's orchard, when the
irate owner saw us, and I fell from that tree flat on to my
back. Seeing the farmer approaching, I left the apples behind
and fled as fast as I could. I had already experienced his
vengeful punishments before and had no desire to do so again.

That time we had escaped, too, me and my two comrades
in theft. We found our way to a thick hedge, where we knew
of a decent hollow, and we would have got clean away, if only
our friend, always known as Whelk for some reason, had not
farted in the effort of restraining his laughter just as the farmer
drew level with us. But for that, we would have evaded capture.
As it was, I got a flogging to go with my sore back.

This time was different, though. I fell, aware of the sound
of splashing from nearby as the staves, or some of them, fell
into a puddle or something. Their precise location was unimportant to me. I fell into the barrel, and although much had
disappeared, when I tried to move my feet to regain my balance,
I suddenly found myself toppling. The bottom cooperage, you
see, was intact, and my feet were entangled. I overbalanced
and fell back.

The odd thing was that I did not fall to the ground, as such.
Yes, I was lying horizontal, I was sure. My legs, snared as
they were in bits of barrel, were resting against the ground,
and yet my head and chest seemed to be suspended in mid-air.
That was the thought that came to me: that I was floating. I
whipped my hands out to either side, replicating Christ's cruci-
fixion, giving me my second blasphemous thought in as many
moments. You know how sometimes a feather can seem almost
to hang in the air over a candle? It will flip, whirl, turn, and
sometimes rise for no apparent reason. That was how I felt.
Except there was something else making itself felt. A certain

smell. Not the repellent odour of burning feather, either. This was infinitely worse.

I mentioned before that there was a wall, and nearby a pit. The pit was not the well. It was a 'necessary' for those for whom a mere wall to piss against was inadequate. In falling, I had managed to topple so that the whole of my upper body was dangling over this cesspit, and the smell that rose from it was hideous in the extreme. I do not know what sort of food the denizens of that tavern were prone to eating, but whatever it was, it must have been an unhealthy diet.

All thoughts of Mal and his breadknife left me. Just at that moment, the only thing that I could think of was that his knife was much less terrifying than the thought of falling headfirst into a well of . . . well, it didn't bear thinking of. It would not be a pleasant death, drowning upside down in a deep pit filled with ordure.

My hands reached the edges of the pit without difficulty. My left hand met with a damp slipperiness which I didn't want to think about. Whatever it was, I held on. Just now, holding on was the only thing on my mind.

Have you ever been forced to hold up weights with both arms outstretched? At first it is easy. You compliment yourself as a splendid fellow for being able to show such stamina and fortitude. And then a slight doubt comes to mind. It is the tremble in one arm, a slight sensation of weariness, like the first little flakes of snow that herald a blizzard. Only a tiny tremble. Nothing more. But it is the precursor to disaster. You become aware of the tendons on the upper side of your shoulders, and a kind of red-hot agony begins to spread from the shoulders to the upper chest, the arms, and in a short time you are ready to scream and rail against the torture.

Now imagine that you are suspended over a terrible pit, and you know that your fate is not a gentle death, but drowning with . . . *that* in your mouth.

No, Mal's knife seemed oddly unexceptional.

Which is lucky, because as I was thinking this, I heard a snigger. I looked up into the upside-down features of Mal.

'Oh! Hallo, Mal!' I said.

*   *   *

I have a very fixed memory of that sight. If someone ever tells you that the sight of a man upside down is amusing, you can tell them from me that there is a world of difference between the smiling features, say, of a paternal-looking fellow with an affable smile, and the angry, vengeful, rage-filled glower that met my eyes. It was like looking into the face of the Devil himself.

'Hello,' I said again, and smiled.

I daresay that his view of me was little more appealing. Still, suddenly his black mood seemed to dissipate, and he grinned. That was itself a scary sight. 'You're a bit stuck, ain't you?' he said.

'Yes.'

'You need help.'

I could not argue with his reasoning. His logic struck me as sound. However, while I had been hoping for a helping hand, Mal had other ideas. He carefully stepped around the cesspit until he was standing by my left hand. Very slowly, he placed his boot on it and began to lean with all his weight, grinding slowly.

There is nothing I can say that could possibly describe the pain of that. It defies accurate portrayal. If you have ever your-self hung dangling over a hideous depth like that, with a crazed madman trying to turn your hand into paste on the stones of the pit's sides, all the while staring into your face and smiling with a kind of fiendish glee, perhaps you'll have some idea of how I felt, but even so, until you have met Mad Mal the Loaf and seen how vicious, vindictive and evil he looks, you cannot have a true feeling for it.

I closed my eyes and screamed. Someone could have heard me, I thought. I didn't want to look up into his face, and I didn't want to fall, but I knew I must. What a way to die! What a last few moments, waiting to drown in drunken tavern guests' turds!

Over my screams, I heard a dull but pleasant sound. It was rather like a bell, but a cracked one. There was a kind of reverberation, but it died all too soon, and then all I heard was a kind of rattling and whirling. I was reminded of that disk of metal which had made such a hideous and prolonged noise in the alley when Humfrie knocked out poor Jeffry, but this time it was briefer, or else I lost interest in it as I became aware of other things.

First, I was quickly to appreciate that my hand had been seriously hurt. It felt as though someone was trying to flatten it with a red-hot iron. The pain was unremitting, seeming to thunder into flaming glory, and then sizzle slightly, before launching itself into even greater efforts of anguish. Then I was aware that it felt as though my hand was failing. I could not keep gripping the side of the well with my hand. It was impossible to maintain any kind of hold, partly because of the agony, but also because of the slimy substance that lay beneath it. And no, I still didn't want to know what it was. All I did know was that my left hand was incapable of holding me up.

'Give me your hand.'

I opened my eyes with astonishment to find myself staring up into Agnis's serious face. She reached down and gripped my wrist. 'Come on,' she said. 'What have you put your hand . . . ugh!'

Of course, the splendid girl had been quick to see what was happening when I darted out of the room. In a glance, she understood that my life was in danger if Mal got anywhere near me, and rushed to my assistance. When she reached the yard, pushing past certain unsavoury types who were, so she said, egging Mal on, she caught sight of the rubbish where the extension had collapsed, and took advantage of the broken cookpot, which explained the bell-like tone when she swung it at the back of his head.

She pulled me up, helping me disentangle myself from the remains of the barrel, and I walked with her, past the snoring form of Mal and to the door, me nursing my flattened hand against my breast. The smell from it was not pleasant, and it was clear what I had grabbed hold of at the edge of the cesspit, but that didn't matter just now. All I knew was that the damn thing hurt.

The men in the tavern drew away respectfully as we approached, although whether because of the odour I drew with me or because of fear of Agnis, I am not sure. I saw the table, with Jeffry's daughter, and I caught a glimpse of Michol in the farther corner, eyeing me with as much keen interest as any of the other drinkers. I suppose, to the inmates of the tavern, it was a rare thing to see one of Mal's victims still walking.

Outside, there was no sign of Humfrie. I didn't care. I was past worrying about purses of gold, assassins, murderers and thieves. Instead, I went with Agnis to a trough and washed my hands carefully. There was a strip of linen in a corner, and I washed that, too, before binding my hand in it. The cool felt good.

'I'm going home,' I said.

'What of the Spaniards?'

'Oh.' I had forgotten all about them in the madness of the last hours.

'You had better come back with me,' she said. 'Although it means you have ruined all Blount's plans.'

'What plans?'

'He wanted Michol dead, because that would injure the French plans to disrupt the Queen's succession. If the Queen were to die any time soon, that would leave everything up in the air, wouldn't it?'

I smiled. 'There's no need to worry about that now. The Queen has given birth to a big healthy boy – didn't you know?'

'Perhaps you didn't hear what they were all talking about in there. They were all saying that she hasn't. The announcement was a mistake.'

'All the bells, the bonfires . . .' I said weakly.

'Mean nothing,' she said. 'There is no child. The men in there were saying she gave birth to a monkey, or that she has been trying to find a child to take as her own, but there is no doubt that she has no son.'

'How could the news have been so widely circulated, then?' I scoffed.

'What, that she had given birth? A foolish serving maid? A groom with more mouth than sense? Idiots can spread lies easily enough. The main point is that we need to get to Michol quickly. Blount will be very disappointed if we don't.'

'Yes,' I said miserably. My hand hurt, and I was in need of

some brandy or strong wine. 'I need to speak to Humfrie, then. Make sure that he is with me when I do it.'

'Why? Do you feel lonely?' she laughed. 'You can do it yourself, can't you? He's only one man. You've done it before, haven't you?'

It was a statement, not a question. 'I didn't realize you knew what I did for Blount.'

'He had to explain things so I understood the seriousness of his instructions,' she said.

And I had thought her only a pretty face and exceptional top-carriage.

'We have the rest of today to plan,' she said.

'Eh?'

'Now that news of the baby is spread all over the city, there is an incentive for the French to try to do harm to the Queen, isn't there? If they can get to her and kill her, what will happen to the succession? They could impose Mary Queen of the Scots on us, and then they would march into London and take over everything. Do you want that?'

'Well, no!'

'Then we must go and do Blount's bidding while we still have time. It's the only way to protect the Queen, isn't it?'

Thus it was that I found myself a few hours later clad in a new suit of clothes that barely fitted me. Agnis had left me to go and fetch some food for us while I changed into her husband's old clothes, and on her return we ate cheese and bread with sour ale. Once she had taken a good look at my hand (now washed), she declared it merely bruised. I forebore to mention that she should try having Mal try to squash it into the cobbles if she thought it so little a thing. I doubt she would have cared. She would probably have laughed.

Later, she took me down the ladders and led the way to a place where, so she said, we would be likely to find Michol and his friends.

It was a wet evening. Since my excitement over the cesspit, I had felt myself caught in the mechanism of some gigantic machine from which I could not escape. No matter where I turned, whether it was to try to run from the city or to attempt to hide myself, or even perhaps go to speak to Blount and explain myself, it was plain enough that I could do nothing in safety. I was trapped. Events were moving too quickly for me. Mal was not dead, from the snoring he had emitted when we left him at the cesspit; the Spaniards were sure to want to find me and introduce me to Spanish steel since I hadn't given them news about Luys, or Diego, whoever he was; the Queen would be angry with me since I had killed Jeffry, although not intentionally; and now I was on my way with Agnis, for whom my earlier lust had significantly waned now that I had discovered she was a dangerous harpy who could happily contemplate cutting a man's throat. If she was so keen on the idea, I felt, she could go ahead with the commission herself. I wanted nothing to do with it. And now I had even mislaid Humfrie.

He had been at the tavern, but as so often happened, now that I needed him, I had no idea where to find him. He fled before I came out with Agnis. And although there were a number of low taverns and alehouses where I would probably be able to locate him, Agnis was determined to crack on with killing Michol.

'Come along!' she snapped when I suggested a small detour to look for Humfrie. 'You don't *need* him, do you? What, do you seek a wet nurse? All you have to do is kill the man. You have done so before.'

She was convinced that I was a crazed murderer, you see. She plainly thought that I was as keen on the idea of slaughtering this fellow as she was. It is curious: only a little earlier today I had thought her appealing. Now that reaction gave me pause for thought. I had been, more or less, a carefree, happy man, up until the moment I met this woman, and now my life was sliding towards an uncertain future that could be potentially short and very painful.

I slipped on a wet cobblestone and cursed without feeling. For a good, mouth-filling curse, I need anger or at least resentment. Just now all I felt was misery. The rain was a thin drizzle, but it seemed to soak into my clothing like a mole burrowing into a field. I already smelled like a wet dog, and I hunched my back as a rivulet of water ran down my spine.

My hat was sodden, and the felt was floppy, half concealing my face. Really, I must have looked pathetic, like some yokel visiting the city. Only, instead of staring about with wide-eyed awe like a peasant from the country, I was merely wretched.

'I think you must be very brave,' she said as we passed into a lane. 'It makes me very excited.'

'What?' I said.

Her breast was rising and falling like a sea in a storm, and she licked her lips. Suddenly, I understood her. The mad trollop thought that rattling my cods would be fun, once my hands were bloody!

I have known some mad bitches in my time, but it never occurred to me that Agnis could be one like this. It was entirely out of her apparent character to be so . . . well, I can understand women falling for me. It's very common, in fact. But this self-assured woman? I was surprised. Let's leave it at that.

Of course, the main problem just then was that I would have had trouble raising a smile, let alone anything else. The thought of having to go and kill a man in order to be rewarded with a night of passion was enough to turn my stomach, even if the thought of murdering the fellow wasn't.

She stepped closer. I could see her bodice heaving. It was all I could do not to turn and flee. But I stood my ground. It took all my resolve, but I remained rooted to the spot, and when she slipped her hands around my neck and pulled me down towards her, I felt I had to comply.

I could feel her breath, hot and smelling of something spicy, on my mouth, and then her lips were on mine, and I felt them pushing with a sweet insistence, and at the same time there was the delight of feeling her breasts flattening against me, and her groin rubbing against mine. Scared as I was, there was no way to stop my codpiece from making her effect on me obvious. She pulled away, arms still about my neck, and leaned back, her groin going like a dancer's in a vaulting school. Bawdy houses always had one or two wenches who could dance lewdly, and Mistress Agnis could have taught them plenty. I could feel the blood rushing, and it wasn't just to my face.

She smiled at my confusion. 'Later, Jack,' she murmured,

and leaned in to kiss me again, before drawing away and
pulling me by the hand after her up the road.

I was flustered, I confess. I had little time to think about
where we were going. Mostly, my mind was filled with other
thoughts, and while it's true that a woman's desire for a man
based on his desire to exterminate another did not leave me
filled with enthusiasm for coupling with her, still, it had to be
said that her soft lips had tasted sweet, and my mind could
not quite lose the feeling that I would like to have remained
kissing her a little longer.

There was a crossing over a broad road, and I suddenly
realized that we were down past the bridge, and heading nearer
the Thames.

'Where are—'

She cut me off rather curtly. 'Before you tried to dive into
the cesspit, I had found some men in an alehouse along the
lane. I spoke to some of them and they told me where we may
find Michol tonight. He's up here, near the river, at the sign
of the Mermaid.'

I stopped dead in the street. 'Mermaid?'

'Yes. What of it?'

I knew of the Mermaid. There are many different places to
go and get drunk or to buy a woman's companionship for a
while. The good ones are expensive, and the women young
and beautiful; some are good, and the women clean; some are
tatty, and the women acceptable. Others, like the Mermaid,
are places where the drink is cheap, the women available for
little investment, and where a man might easily lose more than
just his purse.

'Nothing,' I said, and I hoped she didn't hear the trembling
in my voice.

The biggest and best inns are mostly outside the city walls.
There are several down south of the bridge, some on the roads
out east from Aldgate, so I hear, and others dotted all about
London. It's easy to see why. Inns take up a lot of space, with
the need for stabling, chambers for guests to sleep, and a yard
for wagons and carts. There are such places in London, but
it's less costly for hosts to set up their establishments outside

the town, where they can offer speedy transport into the city, but where visitors can leave wagons and mounts stabled more cheaply than in the city itself.

The Mermaid, down near the Walbrook, was one of those rare places where anyone could drop in and stay the night for remarkably little, but the true cost would appear later, when the guest discovered that his pocket had been lightened, or possibly wouldn't wake at all. It was a grim little inn, with three storeys set behind a small cobbled yard. A stable allowed space for, at a push, six horses of poor quality. A well-bred mount would never deign to enter. The stablemen were experts at spotting good horseflesh, and I have no doubt many a quality mare ended up in another man's hands; poorer-quality mounts could always become steaks.

I once met a trader from Faversham who stayed at the inn almost a whole night. He was asleep in his bed, when three men entered. He was terrified lest they would set about him and injure him, but instead they all rolled themselves on to the same bed and began to snore. The host of the inn had decided that since only one man was making use of the bedchamber, he could squeeze in a few more. My friend left in high dudgeon, his mood not improved by the fact that he had paid in advance – always an error, as I will tell any visitor who cares to listen.

Outside the inn a large mermaid was painted on to the white walls. She looked decidedly raddled, to my mind. The artist had made much of her upper attractions, but his depiction of her lower portions seemed to have been painted from memory of a six-week-dead salmon. The scales looked dull and rancid. It was an appropriate image for the place: a creature that had suffered humiliation, degradation and brutality, from the look of her, although none of these could prepare her for her arrival here.

Agnis took my hand and led me to a doorway. I was glad, because it was out of the rain, and I had no wish to be any wetter than I already was. In the doorway she put her hand on my shoulder, and I thought she was going to kiss me again. I admit, I was nothing loath, and puckered in preparation, only to see that she was staring at the inn, not at me. She reached in under her skirts at her belly, and seemed to wriggle a bit. Soon her hand came back, and it gripped a nasty-looking thing.

'By 'is wounds, what on—'

She silenced me with a glare and passed the thing to my hand, slipping a key into my other hand as she did so. 'Hush! This is the weapon which John Blount wishes you to use against the man. Michol must die, so you have to loose this at him.'

'But what is it?' I demanded plaintively.

'It is a gun. A wheel-lock pistol. Have you not used one before?' she asked, and I could see that she was perplexed.

'Not like this,' I said defensively. It was a curious weapon. It was like a squashed triangle from the side. There was a barrel at one end, and at the other, I supposed, was the handle, made of wood, with a bulbous pommel, in case one shot was not adequate and the assassin needed to bludgeon his victim instead. In the middle was a circular lump of metal, with a dog, in whose teeth was a lump of shiny rock.

'You wind up the spring with this,' she said, passing me a small spanner. 'When you see him, push the dog on to the cog there, press the trigger, and the cog will spin, striking sparks from the rock in the dog's teeth. Then it will go off.'

I had already taken an intense dislike to this thing. 'I don't want this!'

'It will make a lot of noise, but don't worry about that. It will scare everyone away, and you can escape back the way we came,' she said.

I pulled a grimace. Utterly pointless, for she ignored me, but it made me feel better. 'Are you sure?'

She said nothing, but the glance she gave me was freezing. It was the sort of look I'd expect a shepherd to give on finding his dog with a lamb-bone in his mouth. I tried to smile, but it was obvious that she was more than a little disappointed in me.

'Get as close as you can,' she said. 'Point it, loose it, and run away. That is all.'

'Will he have men with him?'

'When you see him come out, cross the road to him,' she said. 'Put the dog down ready, point it, loose it, and run.'

It was all she would say, as though she was trying to inspire me to courage by repetition. Not that it would work with me, as I could have told her. I was already far too alarmed to be able to remember anything. Put the dog down, my arse!

She slipped away, and I saw her slight figure crossing the road like a sliver of shadow. If she was a professional assassin herself, she could hardly be better. A faint glimmer at a doorway showed where she was sidling along the wall of the Mermaid, and I saw her stop and peer in. She turned back to me, and then opened the door and was inside.

There have been several times when I have been forced to wait in the dark for something to happen. Invariably, it is an uncomfortable thing to do. Standing still is irritating at best, but in the chill of evening it can be an almost intolerable experience, and when it rains as well, it is worse. Then there is the standing.

It is all very well standing for a while, but then the body craves movement. A leg will grow uncomfortable, so one must bend it and move it. And the back begins to itch, so it is necessary to lean against a wall and rub it against the plaster, or to put a hand to it. But a slight scratch is only sufficient for a short time, and then it is necessary to try to keep still again, for any assassin will tell you that the easiest way to stand out in the dark is by merely scratching your nose. Meanwhile, your other leg is going to sleep, the first is aching, your nose is itching, it is cold, and the man who is supposed to be your target is noticeable by his prolonged absence. Standing there, I was reminded of my (short) period in the militia, protecting London during the Wyatt rebellion the previous year. There had been times like this then, too, when I spent an age standing staring into the darkness for no apparent reason, and hoping against hope that no one was going to try to attack the position while I was still on guard duty. Mind you, in those times I had the benefit of a good bonfire to keep me warm. Now I didn't even have that.

The darkness is a strange thing. As you look at it, it changes. One thing I have learned is not to think of ghouls or ghosts. Thinking of them will conjure them in any shadow or dimly lit doorway. You look at a darkened window and see only a pane of blackness. But look away, and you will see a hideous face leering out at you; look at a wall, and you see a pile of rubble somehow stuck together, but if you stare too hard, soon you discern faces – distorted, horrible faces, with slack, dead jaws and goggling eyes. The darkness allows the mind to take flight and imagine all kinds of horror.

And sometimes the horror is not so far from reality. I caught sight of a doorway farther up the street, and a flicker of a candle in a window was just enough to allow me to make out perfectly the shape of a man with long robes and a hood over his head. I blinked, and there was only an empty doorway. Like I say, the mind can conjure up the most hideous of spectacles.

What was I doing here? I had not set out to be a murderer. I was a happy-go-lucky fellow. All I wanted was a small sum to keep body and soul together, and I would be content. But no; instead, here I was, in the dark, getting cold, and expected to murder a man I didn't know. Where was Humfrie? He was the man for this, rather than me!

I had taken to stamping my feet to stop them from becoming numb. My hands were as bad, too, but I dared not clap them to get them working again. Apart from anything else, I was still clutching that damned great lump of metal. It was as cold as ice, and my hands felt almost as though they were frozen to it. Perhaps it was because it was an instrument of death, I wondered. Something designed solely to assassinate men must always feel like this. It had a hook on the left side, and I thrust this through the belt inside my doublet. The barrel stuck out beside my codpiece and would have looked comical to anyone watching. Anything less comical I couldn't imagine. I wouldn't say it was comfortable, but at least it left my hands free. I waved them and blew on them, before taking up the gun once more.

Turning the thing over in my hands, I studied it again. It was a clever piece of workmanship, I suppose, but so is a mill, and at least the engineer who builds a mill knows that he will help maintain life; not so the man that constructed this thing. I hefted it, and lifted it, pointing it at the far window, at the door, at the sign of the mermaid itself. There was a strange imbalance in it, I thought – a sort of *wrongness*. It was not comfortable in the hand. I turned it around, studying the dog, and how it moved forward. There was a sort of spring that held it down against the mechanism, I saw. When the trigger was released, the wheel would spin quickly and strike sparks from the dog, which held some golden yellow stone in its jaws. I saw a little lever in front of it; I touched it, and instantly regretted it.

The lever released a little cap, which had until then covered a pan full of powder. As the cap flicked up, I saw the powder, but the act of moving the gun meant that much of the powder was released. Quickly, I snapped the cap back, hoping I hadn't lost too much.

Hoping? What was the point? I couldn't kill Michol, no matter what. I thrust the gun into my belt with a sense of utter failure and incompetence. What good was I? I leaned against the door, shaking my head, in the middle of enumerating all my faults, when I gave a short scream.

A hand was on my shoulder, and a knife was at my throat.

If there is one thing that I have learned over many years of hardship and ill-fortune, it is that a squeal rarely helps a man, but it can make me feel better for a moment or two.

'You like good steel?' A man with a slight accent.

I recognized that voice. I would have cursed aloud, were it not for the fear that my Adam's apple might be horribly damaged. 'Ah! Master Ramon!'

'What do you do here? This is not where I expected to find you.'

'How did you find me?'

'The message. I was at your house all day today, awaiting your return. But when you did not appear, I decided to have a good look about London, in case you had decided to make the escape, yes?'

'What made you come here, though?'

'As I say, a message. I was told you would be here.'

'Who told you that?' I asked, really rather cross to have been betrayed.

Yes, I was cross rather than afraid. Oh, I suppose there was a little trepidation, but when all is said and done, when you've had a knife at your throat as often as I have, the thrill tends to diminish. And, of course, I had been standing there for an age thinking of killing someone, waiting in the cold and the rain with a damn silly weapon that was more complicated than an alchemist's astrolabe. All I could think of at that moment was that someone had betrayed me, and it made me angry.

'Shut up!' he hissed. He moved around to face me, pushing me back against the wall.

That was when I grew more scared. He was leaning forward, his eyes glittering unhealthily, and I could smell the garlic and sour wine on his breath from his lunch. In his eyes, there was a truly startling lack of compassion or fellow feeling. I really did get the impression that he would cut my throat in an instant.

'I have been asking about town, to find out where Luys might have gone. Did you know that he was seen with a man dressed in a blue doublet, dark-blue cloak and a red, broad-brimmed, high-crowned hat with a white feather in it, and . . .' he paused. 'Why are you wearing all this?'

'Someone stole my doublet,' I said sarcastically.

'Anyway, the man with him was dressed as you were when I first met you. And you and he walked to a tavern called the Boar—'

'It was the Bear. I told you.'

'Where you both drank with a club of friends of yours, and he was last seen walking with you and your friends down towards the river. What do you have to say to that?'

'You're quite right,' I said. There was little point in lying, after all. 'And we crossed the river with my friends and made our way to the Cardinal's Hat. I told you all this. Luys wanted to go to a bawdy house. He was desperate for a doxy. You kept him on too tight a leash, and he was mad for a night free.'

'You left him there?'

There was something in his tone now, and I felt sure that he had an inkling of my movements afterwards. Rather than run the risk of being caught in a lie, I decided that the truth would be safer. 'No. I told you: we returned to the Bear. Then he expressed a desire to follow when I was going to meet an acquaintance, and he kept with me to the wharves, but there I lost him. I was struck on the head, and when I came to, he was not at my side.'

It was close enough to the truth, while not being the *whole* truth.

He was staring at me with eyes bulging, like a schoolmaster who thinks he's just caught out the secret pilferer of his stores of brandy, only to hear a cast-iron alibi. His face registered his disbelief, but there was still the glimmer of misgiving that his original suspicion had been wide of the mark. He was not keen to give me the benefit of the doubt, but there was enough uncertainty for him to hold off his blow for now. The blade of his knife did not noticeably move, but I felt as though the pressure was slightly less severe. At least, I felt I could breathe a little more easily. The wall was soggy behind me, and I could feel the sodden shirt clinging to my back. All in all, I felt miserable. The look of contempt in his eyes didn't make me feel any better.

'You are worthless scum,' he said at last. It seemed to have taken him a while to work his way up to that as an insult, and he was quiet for a while afterwards.

In fact, he said nothing more, because as he was silent, there was a sudden eruption of noise. The Mermaid's door had opened, and a small party was leaving, with many a clap of the back and declaration of everlasting friendship. And in the midst of all the noise, I saw that Agnis had come out and was sidling along the wall behind the party. She made her way clear of them, stared at me fixedly and then jerked her head back towards the group of men.

Michol was in the middle of them.

I dare say not too many men have been thrown into a situation like this, in which they are expected to run across a street and slaughter a man. Even fewer have been expected to do so in a broad thoroughfare, with many men smiling and laughing all around the intended victim. I very much doubt that more than one man – me – has been expected to do so while standing in a darkened doorway with a knife at his throat.

She turned her gaze back to me, and this time appeared to notice that I was not alone. Her eyes narrowed, I saw, and as they did, the Spaniard spotted that he did not command my full attention. He threw a glance over his shoulder at the collection of men in the roadway and snarled, 'Always in this benighted country, there is someone else in the way!'

'It's not my fault!' I protested.

'I came all the way here expecting a good life, a long position in the employ of King Philip, and only had the one task to perform – to bring the physician to him – but no, you took him to drinking dens and lost him. He will be robbed, his body lying in the river, and my own good fortune is ruined. The physician to the Queen is lost, and all because of you, you gangrel, wastrel, pogy tatterdemalion!'

'Pogy? I'm not drunk!' I declared.

'You are hardly worth a knife,' he said. Suddenly, the blade was withdrawn and he stabbed towards me.

I had no choice. Raising my arms, I squealed and ducked. The knife slashed into the air above me, and he grunted as his forearm struck mine. There was a click, and as I glanced down, a sudden flash and eruption blinded me. It was a loud hissing and fizzing, and the smell of rotten eggs filled the air.

Ramon stumbled back, staring at his breast. 'You have killed me!' he spat as his knife clattered on the ground. He took a pace backwards and suddenly fell to his rump, staring at his breast. 'Murderer!' He patted wildly at his belly, which was smouldering where burning powder had lodged in the material of his clothes.

'*Murderer?*' That, I felt, was unreasonable. The man had been about to remove my head, after all. 'What do you mean, "murderer"? You were going to kill me!'

'Murder!' he shouted, and the party of friends over the road, who had seen the powder go off, I assume, and now heard cries of 'Murder!', began to make their way towards me. Beyond them, I could see Agnis, who stood shaking her head with fury, and as the men approached more closely, I saw the hulking shape of Mal. He saw me, too, and began to return to his parting-of-the-seas movements with his hands, pushing

Michol's friends aside like so much driftwood. 'Wait!' he bellowed.

Well, I wasn't going to do that, obviously. I took to my heels.

As I have said, it is essential, while running from people, to be unconcerned about exactly where you are going. If you begin to think of such unimportant matters, you are likely to be confounded from the start by thoughts of which road to take, whether there would be a wherry, and other considerations which, at that moment, do not matter quite so much as putting shoe leather on the cobbles and hurrying away as swiftly as you may. Not that there were any cobbles here. The road was mostly mud and horse droppings, with a kennel that was too shallow in its incline to do much more than store faecal matter waiting for the next storm.

I ran, thinking only of putting as much distance between me and Mal as I could, in as short a time as possible. As I went, there was a kind of churring noise in my ear, and as I turned, Ramon's damn knife nearly took my nose off. I had time to give a startled, irritable 'Hey!' before noticing Mal's rapid advance, and concentrated on my feet once more.

In my time I have run on many occasions. As a child, we would have regular races between the boys, so that our fathers could have something to gamble on. Other families would no doubt have horse races to give them their little thrills, but for us, it was the children. As I grew older, I learned to run from our neighbour with the orchard, whom I believe I may have mentioned already. Then there were the beadles and other officers of the law, and occasionally men who had been parted permanently from their purses. There were many men from whom I have fled at different times in my life, and it must be said that I am in some ways a fair judge of those chasing me.

There are some, you see, who are slower and reluctant. These are the officers of the law, generally, especially the late-night watchmen, who are older and do the job more as a way of keeping themselves in ale than from any wish to protect another man's goods. The youngsters are easily the worst, because they are fleeter of foot and far less cautious about the risks of injury. The young always think they must live for ever, and until they grow a little older and wiser, they remain convinced that they will remain immune from injury or harm. They can be misled, though. They don't have the experience of the older men, and if you slide into an alley and double back quickly, all too often they will be left confused.

But the middle-aged men, those who are a little slower, but determined and intelligent, these are the bane of any thief's life. He might be a man who has been made constable and sees his duty as clear, or he may be a man like Mal, with only one thought in his bull-like head, but who has stamina and patience.

Mal was not the sort of man I would have expected to set a strong pace. In my experience, most men of his size are slower, lumbering fellows who have no imagination or conviction. Mal, irritatingly, was an exception. Not only was he able to hold just one thought in his head – that of pulling mine from my shoulders – but he had the strength and speed to do so. Now, when I glanced over my shoulder, I saw that he was only inching closer, but he was gaining. That was not good.

I was near the wharves here east of the bridge. The roadway grew slippery, and it reeked. Here was where fish were gutted, I remembered, and almost slid on something that was probably best not looked at. Mal was getting closer, but he too slipped and for a moment I thought he would end up on his chin, cropping at cobbles, but no, the bastard recovered somehow and was after me again.

There was an alley, and I threw myself into it. The place was narrow and grew narrower the farther in I went, with a building on the left that projected out over the alley. I was looking for an escape, some kind of doorway or entrance to a yard, into which I could slip and slam the gate behind me, but there was nothing. The people of this alleyway had no thoughts for others. They only sought to protect themselves, without caring for the dangers of men like me who could be chased to death for want of a simple escape. It is uncaring behaviour of this kind that makes a city such an impersonal place.

On my left there was a door, and I hurled myself at it, almost gibbering with fear, but it was locked and barred.

Looking back down the alley, I could see that my pursuer was maintaining his steady pace. He bellowed at me, 'Stop, Blackjack! Wait there!' but I was not going to fall for that. I turned and ran.

And stopped. Something had slammed into my forehead, knocking me back like a ball bouncing from a wall. My legs were no longer my own, and I fell back to land in a puddle which I had time to hope was water, before the slow onset of slumber overwhelmed me, like a steady injection of quicksilver that entered my legs and rose gradually, inch by inch, overcoming my groin, stomach, up to my neck. I had enough time to note Mal's face above me, just as before, when I had dangled over the cesspit, before the heavy, liquid metal ran up into my head and I knew no more.

I have had cause to mention my experiences of waking after being struck on the head in other chronicles of my adventures. On occasion, such as at the wharf where Jeffry died, it was unpleasant. On other occasions like this, it was more agreeable. But always, with the sensation of comfort, there appears the nagging doubt: who brought me here, and what do they intend to do to me?

The second anxiety was still more apposite, bearing in mind the vision that was imprinted on my doubly aching head: that of Mal's snarling face.

I was lying on a good tester bed, in a chamber that was well decorated with carved panelling all about. There was a stool on the right with what looked like my clothing borrowed from Agnis neatly folded. Beside it was a cupboard, with a pouch and leather wallet on top. Next to that was a flask. There was a window, with blue, green and yellow diamond panes of glass. On the sill were a number of pots of sweet-smelling herbs, no doubt to keep the odours of the street at bay.

My head, I need hardly say, was pounding like a tree with a woodpecker trapped inside – a fast, agonizing sensation that seemed to emanate from just behind my left eye. When I lifted a hand to my brow, I discovered that I could, in fact, increase the pain. I let my hand fall with a sharp yelp.

Agnis was there.

At first I didn't believe my eyes. That must have been a bad knock to the head, I thought, and I blinked several times to try to clear the image, but no matter what I did, she remained there.

There is an etiquette to waking from a bad knock. First, I clenched my fists. Both there. Then I wriggled my toes. Nothing seemed out of place there. Perhaps Mal hadn't had his knife with him?

'You were asleep a long time,' she said.

'I don't know what happened . . .'

'It looks like you ran into a wall or something.'

I recalled the low beams supporting the jetty of the building. I must have run straight into it. Tentatively, I put a hand to my brow and touched it. It had come up with a lump that felt really quite impressive. 'Where am I?'

'In a safe house. It belongs to a friend. You are safe here.'

I noted that she hadn't told me anything. 'How did I get here?'

She gave me a serious look. 'I brought you.'

I frowned. She was strong enough, I suppose, but there was the other matter. 'Where is Mal?'

'Who?'

'Mal? Big man, head like a rock, hands like millstones. Tends to go about with a breadknife and remove bits of people. The man you hit with a broken cookpot.' I had a thought, and was about to feel for my cods, when I reflected that if he'd removed anything there, I would have known it. 'He was there. When I passed out, he was looking down at me.'

'He wasn't there when we found you,' she said.

'We? What happened? The gun went off and—'

'And you missed him. You should have been more careful, got a little closer.'

'I had a knife at my throat! I didn't wish to have my head parted from my neck!'

'The Spaniard?'

'Yes! He still believes I killed his fellow. I shot him. He was going to kill me.'

'So you loosed the gun at him?'

'Not on purpose,' I admitted, downcast.

'That was brave of you,' she said softly.

'Eh?'

'You tried to fight him off so you could continue with the assassination. That was very courageous,' she said, and stood. To my astonishment, she walked to me and kissed me softly. It was a delightful experience, although I confess that the effect was dissipated somewhat by the thundering pain at my brow. One headache is bad enough, but to suffer from two blows makes it a great deal worse.

'But Mal wasn't there?'

'No. There were many others following after you when you ran, men from the Spaniard's side, many from Michol's group, so perhaps Mal heard them coming and bolted?'

'Perhaps.' It didn't sound likely. I had seen Mal when he was in a bad mood. It didn't strike me as likely that he would willingly forgo the chance of inflicting pain on me, given the chance. If he was in the sort of murderous temper I had seen before, back at the gambling den, he would be likely to miss any approaching steps in the immediate pleasure of removing my fingers or head.

'I will report to Blount and let him know that you are well enough, but also that you were enormously brave.'

'Oh . . . good,' I said weakly. At least Blount wouldn't hear that I had failed abjectly. He would hear that I had been confounded by that Spaniard, and it wasn't my fault I had missed his target. Perhaps I could even negotiate a reward for trying, and for suffering this head as a result? Knowing Blount as I did, it did not seem likely. But there was another consideration. 'What happened to the Spaniard?'

'I don't know. I expect someone took his body away. Your bullet must have given him a mortal wound.'

So now I would be sought by the officers for the murder of this second fellow.

Agnis left me a little after that. She had her own errands, I have no doubt; for me, though, the opportunity of sitting in that room with a coverlet over me and my bruised head resting on a soft pillow was too good to miss. I had no idea where I was, although I hazarded a guess that I was not far from where I had run into the building. Agnis could not have carried me, and as for helping me – well, with the way my head hurt, I didn't think I could have made more than a yard even with her assistance, so surely someone had helped her. I wondered who.

There was a crash as a door was slammed, and I rose to walk to the little window. The glass was fogged with dirt, and I had to wipe and wipe at a pane to create a tiny view of the world. Opposite was another house, a mere spit away. Down below was a narrowish street, with a car travelling along it slowly, while pedestrians moved from its path, some few shouting bile at it for blocking their way. People always grow hot about being forced to slow their own passage. Below me, a woman darted to the opposite side of the road, and even from above, I was able to recognize that it was surely Agnis. No other woman rolled her entire body so enticingly fore- and- aft while merely strolling across a street.

It was a picture to make a man smile, and I did, for all of a second. Then, I admit, my mouth fell wide.

She was crossing the lane to talk to a man, and as I watched, I saw that she was speaking with a man in the shadows. I peered closer, trying to guess who it was, but the glass was too filthy. The man was wearing a hood that concealed his face, and even when I peered closely, nose against the window, I could not see who it might be.

Then I gave a shriek.

A hideous, grey flashing thing, like a hellish demon of the air, appeared before me. I sprang back, heart beating, swearing as my head pounded again, and then cursed myself for a fool. It was a pigeon.

At the window once more, I flapped my hands to send the bird off, but it merely stared at me with idiotic, empty eyes and cooed gently.

When I looked down again, Agnis and the man had disappeared. I don't know why, but it left me unsettled. Who would she be going to talk to, leaving me in my injured state? Of course, for all I knew, it could be a brother, or her baker . . . but no baker would wear a hat like that. It spoke of money. Perhaps it was the owner of this house? Why would he be waiting outside for her to meet him there?

No, whoever this fellow was, I wanted nothing to do with him. I was sure of that.

I dressed quickly and went to the door. It was locked.

There are some men who would have been downcast to be confronted with a locked door. Not so me. If you had lived in London with some of the rough fellows whom I had known, you would appreciate that no door is safe against a determined draw-latch.

I knelt and stared at the door's lock. It looked a complicated affair, but I had seen others make free with such locks with their sets of skeleton keys. However, I had none. I stood and stared at the door for a long time, and then searched the room for something suitable. I needed a fine, strong piece of metal, like a nail or something similar, or a strong iron bar to break the lock and prise the door from the jamb. Or something. But there was nothing suitable.

Sitting on the bed, I gazed about again. I had no idea what to do now. I was truly downhearted. I had anticipated a swift exit from this place, but now I was apparently trapped.

My eyes returned to the cupboard and the collection of items on the top. There was a pouch, which was heavy, and when I opened the drawstring, I discovered it contained a number of lead balls. Useful, perhaps, as marbles, but I didn't see why they were here. The flask beside it, I had hoped, might contain some brandy or wine, but it had only powder when I shook it.

And that was when I realized what this was. I opened the wallet beside it, to find the gun. It lay there, all workmanlike and oddly unappealing, in spite of the skill and effort that had gone into its manufacture. But for all that, it was a comforting sight. It was the only means I had to defend myself.

The thing was repellent. Heavy, cumbersome; but still, it was better than taking a dagger to a sword fight. When I studied it more closely, I saw that there was a mark on the side. Something put on by the armourer who made it, no doubt. A sort of T and F, the sign of the fool who wanted to be known for making things that would kill people. Personally, I would prefer to be known for making things that enhanced life, I thought. And then I thought that this thing could well

save mine. I decided to be less judgemental about the man
who made it.

I was sure it was easy to ready it. I took some powder in
my hand, pouring it from the flask, and tipped it into the barrel.
I stared into the barrel. Was it enough? How could I tell? I
put the flask over the barrel and let in a goodly quantity more.

When I took a ball and dropped it into the barrel, it rattled
down easily enough. I hunted for the spanner, which was under
the pouch, and quickly set it to the wheel, turning it for almost
a full turn, before there was a loud *click* and the wheel locked
in place. I took the dog and set it on the wheel. Then, as an
afterthought, I pulled the flask, pouch and wallet to me. The
first two had long thongs, and I pulled these over my head,
the pouch with bullets lying on my left hip, the flask with the
powder on my right, while I slipped the wallet with the gun
inside it, under my jack. It was a hellish weight, but I didn't
care. The hook of steel on the left side slipped through my
belt, binding it firmly in place.

Just as I was completing my preparations, I heard steps.
There was a snick as the door was unlocked, and then it
opened. A man was in the doorway, and as the door opened
wide, I gaped. It was growing on me as a habit. 'Willyam!
What are you doing here?'

Willyam's eyes took in the room with a quick, practised glance.
'Are you ready to get away from here?'

I shut my mouth, but my bafflement was not reduced. 'What
are you doing here, Will?'

'I saw that you had been taken. When the wench left
you, I thought I had best come in to rescue you.'

'But . . . what?'

He gave me a pitying look. 'Perhaps we can leave the explanations until we find a safe place to talk? Come with me.'

I was in no position to argue, really. I followed after
him as he led the way to a steep staircase. We descended
silently, apart from my hissing breath when I struck my forehead against the ceiling and muttered a curse. Willyam turned
and glared at me so fiercely that I almost thought I would
burst into flame. I swear, he could have lighted a fire with that

look. He turned and led the way downstairs to the front door. Here he opened the door a crack and then slipped through it, beckoning me to follow suit.

We hurried along, Willyam thrusting ahead, while I rattled along in his wake, until we came to a broader thoroughfare, and I recognized Eastcheap by a couple of the houses. With relief, I entered the great thoroughfare, and then we turned away from the Tower and headed back towards St Paul's. There was a tavern there that I knew well, and I hurried inside before pausing to consider that I still had no money. I looked pleadingly at Willyam, who rolled his eyes and waved to the serving wench. Soon we both had ales, and I downed half of mine in one, long, delicious draft.

'What are you doing, Jack?' Willyam said.

'Just trying to survive,' I said.

'Tell me all about it,' he said, and I did so with relief.

I had not realized just how concerned I had been, until now. The pressure of trying to prevent Jeffry's death, of being told to kill Michol, of knowing that Blount would be furious with me for failing in both, and then the death of Luys, being hunted by Ramon, almost being killed by him several times, and . . . well, even if my head hadn't been battered so wildly, I would still have had a headache just trying to keep up with events. It was a huge relief to be able to confess to my problems.

He listened as I spoke, his eyes growing rounder and rounder as I explained the full horror of what I had been going through – not the bits about being a paid assassin, you understand, but I let him believe I had tried to save Jeffry and had failed to help Luys.

'What of your attempt to kill the Spaniard?' he said. 'Did you succeed?'

'He must be dead,' I said. 'The gun went off in his belly and bowels. He fell like a poleaxed steer. It was horrible!'

He nodded. 'Where did you get the gun?'

'The girl gave it to me. She said that Blount sent it.'

He narrowed his eyes. 'The messenger girl?'

I suddenly remembered. 'I asked you how you found me in that room, but you didn't answer. How did you know I was there?'

Michael Jecks

'I saw you being dragged up there by her and a big man.' He shook his head. 'That woman: do you trust her?'

His question threw me. Oh, I know Humfrie didn't trust her, but she had saved my life, letting me stay with her away from Ramon, rescuing me from Mal too . . . I did not quite let my jaw drop, but it was a near thing. In the last days, the only constant had been Agnis, but now that Willyam asked that simple question, it put a number of things in a fresh light, and the light was not pleasing. 'Um.'

'Did Blount himself introduce you to her?'

I didn't answer that; I was thinking.

She had arrived as a simple messenger, as Willyam said, but all too soon she had taken charge. She had told me whom to kill, she helped me hunt the man down, she gave me the gun . . . And then something else came to me: at the tavern, while Humfrie waited outside for me to draw Michol out, when she came in and saw Mal, she had been worried. She had hidden herself behind the doorway, while the party continued with their roistering, with me standing out like a lemon in the press. What if she knew Mal, too, and was not with Blount and me, but was instead working for the Spanish, determined to have me kill not the Spanish ally, Jeffry, but their enemy, Michol?

There are times when I find that my bowels seem to turn to water.

'Oh, Christ's pain!'

'I think you need another drink.'

I left Willyam in the tavern. There was a loud group of rowdy apprentices who had entered and were singing some lewd songs about how the Queen had been getting sweaty with an ape, and that was why she'd given birth to a monkey, or some such nonsense. If they weren't careful, they would all end up in Newgate or the Tower.

Outside, the morning air was cooling to my pounding head. I couldn't wear a hat, of course. The sensation of pain was all too keen, and trying to enclose the swellings with a hat was not to be borne. Instead, I made my way along the road to Ludgate, and thence up to the Cross. There was a preacher there, giving probably the most boring sermon I have ever heard, all about fraternity or something. A group of young fellows with serious expressions listened intently, trying not to laugh while a pair of apprentices danced about and pulled faces behind his back. I walked on.

Could Agnis have been an agent all along? It was hard to believe, but the more I thought about it, and her, the more I began to see that she had grown in confidence with every meeting that we had. At first she had mentioned two names, and that was it. Then she was interested in helping to find the money and Luys's purse, but last night she had instructed me on using the gun, as well as telling me which man to point it at. She was no mere messenger from Blount! I had been made the dupe of a foreign spy!

'Oh, God, help me!' I murmured. The thought of Blount's reaction when he heard that I had been persuaded to kill the wrong man was enough to make my belly give a swoop. I had to clench my buttocks. Blount was a dangerous man – much more than I was. I dared not think of letting him know.

What could I do, though? I needed a friend. Someone in whom I could confide, someone who could make sense of my predicament and perhaps see a way through it all to safety.

I thought of going south of the river and visiting Piers at the Cardinal's Hat. Piers was a good man when sober, but at this time of the day it was too early for him. He would still be sleeping off last night's debauch. Porters at the doors of harlots' houses don't tend to get to bed early. They lean more towards rising later and enjoying their breakfast while others are digesting their lunch. Then I had an idea: I recalled the man, Master Mark, to whom Piers had introduced me a year earlier, but then I had to reject the notion. Although he was undoubtedly brilliant and had a mind like an elephant's, he was also a confidant of Blount. I could not trust him not to pass on information.

In the end, I sighed. I had no choice.

I set off to search for Humfrie.

He was sitting in the dark corner at the rear of a tavern not far from St Paul's. It was the sixth hostelry I had entered, and he welcomed me with a quiet smile, nodding to me in much the manner of a squire acknowledging a groom. His manner was high and suave, but I was not in a position to let it rankle.

'I have been sorely tested,' I said as I sat beside him.

'I hear someone tried to assassinate the Spanish ambassador Renard last night,' he said.

I choked on the ale I had just begun to swallow. 'What? Who told you that?'

'Apparently, he was out near the Tower last evening and visited a tavern. On leaving, someone loosed a pistol at him and fled. Obviously a French agent wanting to remove the Queen's best adviser. Of course, the fellows with him gave chase and got a clear view of him.'

I could feel myself blanching. The colour ran from my face so fast that I thought my hair would go white. 'But, but I had nothing to do . . .'

'You?' he said quietly, and looked at me.

'I was there, but I was trying, well, to defend myself against the Spaniard.'

'This Spanish man. Describe him?'

I gave a good summary of the man. 'He looks like a devil. Evil, narrow, pointy face, with dark eyes, black hair. Very Spanish,' I said. 'He's called Ramon.'

Humfrie was silent as I told him about the man's clothing and cloak, the rapier that was always at his side, and all the while he held my eyes with a fascination that rather appalled me. Then, as I finished, he nodded as if to himself. 'I think you have tried to attack the Duke of Aragon. He is as you describe, and he has a reputation for violence and cruelty.'

'I killed him.'

'That is unfortunate.'

'Why?'

'He is – or was – the right-hand man of the ambassador, Renard. If you killed him, you will be sought by all the men under the Spanish command as well as the men serving the Queen. However, fortunately, you have escaped without risk. You know that Mal was chasing you?'

I nodded, unnecessarily.

'It was not you who was seen, but Mal. Those who believed that they were being fired upon only saw him.'

Suddenly, I realized how it was that I had survived. Mal must have heard them giving chase and realized that they sought him, so he could do nothing to me. As soon as I fell, he had to keep running to evade his pursuers.

'What can I do? Mal will want to kill me, the Spanish will want me dead for killing Ramon, and Blount will want to punish me for believing this woman Agnis!'

Humfrie studied me. 'Find her, catch her and take her to Blount. If you bring her to him, he will be less inclined to be angry, and at the same time he may well decide to reward you for taking an enemy spy.'

It did make sense of a sort. It was certainly better than going to him empty-handed. 'How will I find her?'

'You know where she was living? Go and seek her there.'

Humfrie shook his head when I asked him to join me. He had other business to attend to, he said, which made me almost laugh. The idea that this scruffy fellow had business of any sort that could merit his leaving me alone, when I had so many difficult, dangerous things to deal with, was, frankly, ridiculous. After all, here I was, his young master, and all he would do was snap his fingers and murmur that my position was difficult.

Difficult!

I left him there without a farewell, and if it hurt him, it was intended to. This was not the sort of behaviour I expected from my servant, and since I was the man who employed him most of the time, I thought it only fair to call him such.

It took only a short while to make my way south to the river, and I had to glance at the spot near the alley's mouth where I had found Luys's body that fateful night. There was nothing to show that he had ever lain there, and I looked at it with a vague sense that things were wrong. I could almost have persuaded myself that he had never been there, I mean. If only he hadn't. If only he had gone to sleep and woken with a sore head the next morning. Still, I suppose that at least he got to bounce around with one of the Cardinal's Hat's best wenches before he died. And I got the sore head instead of him.

That was something that kept coming back to my attention as I walked. I had been hit on the front of the brow on the night Luys died. I still had the lump to prove it, a large one on the left of my head, which was balanced by the second I had won last night. Yet I didn't think I had walked into the pillar on the night Luys died. It seemed much more likely to me that I had been struck on the head by someone who wanted me out of the way. Perhaps the thief who had taken Luys's purse? Could that have been Agnis? She was strong, but perhaps not strong enough to wield a bar or pole with sufficient force to kill me? Perhaps she didn't want to, since she was struck with desire for me? Or, more likely, the strumpet had missed her mark in the dark.

At Agnis's home, I stood and waited. I was there for an age, and although it wasn't as cold as the previous evening, it was tedious. In the end, I spied an urchin and offered him money to keep a lookout for me. He gave me to understand that a difficult task like that would justify cash payment in advance. I suggested that he might like to wait until he had performed the commission, and he suggested I should consider an act so bestial and improbable with a donkey that I told him to swive his mother, then settled resentfully in my doorway again.

You will forgive my resentfulness, I know. I need not enumerate all of my various woes, since you have already heard them; however, this one seemed to me to sum up my miserable life. Here I was, considered by those who employed me as a dangerous killer, a man who could be instructed to commit murder, and yet a lazy urchin felt himself safe to tell me to do that. No one truly respected me, I suspected. They all laughed at me behind my back, in all probability, and made fun of my current predicament.

At least my companions in the White Bear didn't make jests at my expense.

I was by now feeling quite sorry for myself, and the sight of a cloud moving across the sky with a sort of heavy, yellowish look to it, promising at the very least a foul form of rainstorm, didn't help. I was just about to give up, when I glanced to the east and saw a familiar group approaching me. It was the Lawyer, Willyam, Leadenhall Bob – and Agnis.

They were walking straight at me, and I shrank back into the doorway where I was hiding. As luck would have it, as they passed me, the rain began – first a fine drizzle, but then a sudden cascade of water, as if Heaven had decided to empty all its chamber pots at once. The four paid no heed to the doorway where I was hiding, but instead bolted past me and onwards.

This was worth investigating, I thought. I trailed after them, regretting not wearing a hat, but also glad of the rain's coolness soothing my injuries. The downpour also concealed my steps. It was as loud as gravel hurled at the ground – a rattling, crackling, spitting noise that was all but deafening. It certainly hurt my head in its current damaged state.

It was when they reached a door and passed inside that I looked about me to see where they had come. And then I realized: it was the bowling alley where Mal was based.

'Best to get out of the rain.'

I nearly screamed as Humfrie tapped my shoulder, it was so unexpected.

'Come along,' he said. 'Let's get out of this weather.'

'What are you doing here?'

'Seeking to preserve my master,' he said imperturbably. He was, at that moment, craning his neck around me and peering in through the doorway. 'Come, let's go and see if we can make sense of this affair.'

He led the way inside, and I followed him along the corridor to the main gaming chamber. At this time of day it was more or less empty, and the three men and Agnis were prominent.

'Oh, I'd best leave,' I said. They were talking to Mal.

I had no desire to meet with him again. The last two times, my best view of him had been his nostrils, and that was not a pleasant sight. Now he looked even more alarming. He wore a fixed glower and stood facing the three as they spoke quietly. Then his eyes rose and I groaned as they locked on me.

Humfrie's hand grabbed my shoulder as I tried to escape. 'Come with me.'

I tried to slap his hand away, but he had a grip like a vice and he pulled me forward. I hung my head as we drew nearer and did not dare look at Mal's face. But then something like defiance flared, and I lifted my gaze to stare at Agnis. She had the decency to look ashamed, as though she could guess what I was thinking. Although, as soon as I saw that, I looked at Willyam. I had told him, and he had guessed much, so what was he doing here with her?

'You brought me a little snack, eh, 'Umfrie?' Mal rumbled. 'Good. I've been looking forward to this!'

'Wait a moment,' Humfrie said. He still had my arm in his grip. 'What is your interest in all this?'

'I just want to pull 'is 'ead off,' Mal said, as though surprised. It was obviously the most natural desire in the world to him. 'The snivelling little shite has been a pain.'

'No, not you, Mal, this maid here,' Humfrie said, pointing at Agnis.

She seemed to pale, and then bright spots of colour rouged her cheeks, and a flush began, fascinatingly, below her neck and began to rise. I was watching it with interest as she spoke.

'Me?'

'Who do you work for? The Spanish?' Humfrie demanded.

'No! I work for our Queen,' she said, and glanced at the other three.

Willyam stepped forward, his hands held up as though placatingly, and faced me. 'Agnis has to be taken to be questioned. I'll look after her.'

'Well, there's no need for that,' I was about to say, when Humfrie shook his head. 'She stays here.'

'I don't think—' Willyam began, but Humfrie didn't allow him to finish.

'No, boy. She stays.'

I nodded vigorously, as though that was the thought that had been in my own mind all along.

Mal rumbled slowly, 'What is all this?'

'She has been acting like a paid assassin,' Humfrie said. 'She wanted other people to do her bidding for her, but she has been steadily working towards achieving her master's aims. She tried to have a Spanish spy saved, and have an Englishman murder another man to foment trouble. She would have had the Englishman killed afterwards, no doubt.'

Mal frowned. It was like watching the ice on the Thames trying to move in midwinter. 'So what?'

'She's a foreign agent, Mal,' Humfrie said.

'So let's kill 'er,' Mal said. His hand reached for the knife in his belt.

'No!' I blurted.

Have you ever been in a tavern where there is a loud noise from men shouting and laughing, singing and swearing, and just as you are giving a pithy comment on one of the ugliest exhibits there, the room is suddenly hushed, and everyone hears your words with precise clarity? It was like that now. Suddenly, I was aware of my scalp creeping back on my skull as though trying to retreat behind my neck. My eyes widened as Mal slowly turned to face me. The ice cracked, and a smile slowly spread over his features.

'You, eh, little man? I owe you for two knocks on the 'ead already, and now you try to tell me what to do?'

He pulled his bread knife from his belt. I could see that the grey steel blade had already earned a shallow curve from where he had been forced to sharpen it regularly. Bread knives never earned that sort of curve where the blade has been worn away. It was the sort of erosion a man might see on a butcher's knife, but not on a blade designed for carving slices of bread.

I gulped. He approached, and I snatched my arm from Humfrie's grip. Then I remembered the gun and hauled it from my breast, pointing it at his face. There was a small tapping noise, but I ignored it. 'No closer!'

'You'll kill me, like you did the Spaniard last night?' he sneered.

'Yes!'

'I'm terrified.'

'Jack!' Agnis called.

'Not now!'

'But, Jack!'

'Quiet, Agnis!'

Humfrie sighed. 'She's trying to tell you that the ball fell out of the barrel when you drew it, Jack,' he said.

*   *   *

I looked down. The tapping I had heard was the sad sound of
a ball of lead plunging to the ground, bouncing twice and then
rolling away. In its wake was a small pile of powder. I looked
up at Mal's face. He grinned, and I snatched at the pouch of
balls on my hip. As luck would have it, the damned thing
snapped its restraining cord, and the pouch emptied as Mal
took a step forward.

It was some years ago that I last saw jugglers and acrobats.
It was up at Smithfield, during the fair, and I was entranced.
At the time I was only, oh, about sixteen years old, I suppose,
and the sight of a small, wiry fellow climbing up a tall ladder,
which was held at the base by his companion, to perform a
handstand on the very top, while the brawny lad at the base
set the ladder on his shoulders and carried the ladder and his
friend, held me spellbound. You cannot keep a London mob
quiet, but that day they were silent in wonder. And, judging
by the way that hands kept moving, men were offering good
odds on the two coming a cropper, with the topmost potentially
breaking his neck when he fell. There was an audible groan
of disappointment when their act came to an end, with the
boy at the top springing down with a somersault. An English
crowd expects blood.

But that wasn't my point. After these two, there was a pair
of jesters, who came on to much applause and performed various
feats that had the crowd roaring with delight. One balanced
himself hilariously on a log that would keep rolling. He fell,
and people laughed; he climbed back on and fell forward, and
the people cheered; he tried to stand on it, and after much
waving of his arms and outward thrusting of his chest and arse,
gradually came to a form of equilibrium, until the second jester
kicked the log, and the man was forced to gesticulate wildly,
before tumbling to the ground once more. The audience bellowed
their amusement. This was more to their taste. Raucous, rowdy,
rumbustious, the London mob thought these two were
hilarious.

And that was exactly what I thought when Mal took his
first step on to those little balls of lead. His foot tried to hold
its place on the floor, and his hands waved backwards to keep
his balance as first one foot and then the other slid inelegantly

forwards and backwards, his face registering utter dismay as the laws of balance, which his body was fully used to accommodating, were temporarily removed.

There was a sort of appalled consternation in that room as everyone darted from the path of Mal's whirling blade, because the fool didn't have the sense to let it fall. Instead, it slashed about, narrowly missing Leadenhall Bob in its passage.

And then the display was over. With a gasp, both of Mal's feet shot from beneath him, and he landed on the ground.

With my facility for common sense, I was ready to hurry from the door. The sight of Mal on the floor would be enough to make any man make for the exit, I reckon, but for me there was even more pressing urgency, since it was my internal organs that he was keen to investigate. But the best plans often go ballocks up, as I have learned over the years. I span, I set my foot on the ground ready to hurtle away, and as I did so, a kind of dull bemusement spread over me.

You see, my first foot was moving as intended, and then so was my second, but for some unearthly reason I was apparently still fixed to the spot. There are times when a fellow knows that something is wrong, but cannot quite put his finger on the issue at hand. That is how it was for me. I suppose I had the firm conviction that, no matter what, I wanted very badly to be somewhere else. My mind was entirely focused on that. As I have mentioned, when running *from* someone, the main aspect of the escape is to bear in mind that you want to be *away*, not where you want to go *to*. So while my legs moved, my brain was already halfway through the door, and when it came to realize that I hadn't moved, it did so with a form of surprise, or even mild offence. I could almost believe it was issuing a gentle rebuke to my legs for not fulfilling their part of the bargain.

That was when I realized that I had fallen prey to the same mishap as Mal. I was running on balls the size of marbles and making no headway.

And then, just as I realized the problem, I performed a significant forward dive, as I believe such gymnastics are called, and landed flat on my breast, winded. The gun tumbled from my hand, and I lay there, staring at it like a shackled hound gazing at a bone one foot too far for him to reach.

For a few moments, I didn't have a thought in my head. One occasion, sitting in a tavern, I struck up a conversation with a fellow who told me he had nearly died once, and how he felt his soul leave his body, staring down at it on the ground before him. I think I was in a similar position now. My mind was still way out in the passageway, hurtling away from Mal, and hadn't quite caught up with the idea that my body was lying prostrate.

Mal was snorting and blowing like a bull about to charge, and that was enough to call my mind hurriedly back to me. It slipped in with a soft regret, as though reproaching me for failing to keep up.

I tried to lift myself, but as I did, I became aware of something else: my ankle had been badly wrenched, and it was absolutely impossible to put any weight on it. I cast a look over my shoulder and saw that Mal was sitting upright, his face a furious purple colour as the anger rose in him. It was plain to me that he would not be in the best of tempers, and I didn't want him to catch me, so I tried to rise to my feet, but even as I was trying, I saw that another person had entered the room.

It was Jeffry's daughter. She gave a little squeak on seeing everyone in the room, and then darted across the floor and picked up the pistol, holding its weight with a thoroughly professional grip, I thought. The damn thing was so heavy that I had found it wobbling in my grip, but she took it up in both hands, which looked infinitely more effective, I noticed.

'Get away from him!' she cried.

I don't know what she thought I was likely to do, but whatever she feared, the gun had emptied itself, and I wasn't overly bothered when she pointed it at me. Especially since she didn't know to move the dog holding the flint over to the wheel. The gun was no risk to anyone.

'I'm all right, Maudie,' Mal said.

'I can't get up,' I said. 'My ankle . . .'

'I don't care about you,' she snapped at me in her charming manner. 'Just keep away from my Mal.'

'*Your* Mal?' I repeated, glancing over my shoulder.

I thought again of seeing Mal at the tavern. This wench had been there then, and Mal had gone to her. Now, of course, I realized that he was walking to his woman. At the time, I suppose I just thought he was negotiating the price of a quick rattle with her, but now I saw that there was more to their feelings.

'You aren't . . . with Mal?' I managed.

'What if I am! He's more of a man than most.'

'But, maid! He killed your father,' Bob said.

'Don't be daft!' she sneered.

'Jack here saw him take two purses from your father,' Willyam said.

'Yes, I know.'

I tried to make sense of this. 'You said your father was a dreadful gambler, that he often came here. Humfrie saw him pay over two purses. Your man here took it gladly, so I was told.'

'Gladly?'

'As if he'd just been given the keys to the Queen's jewels, is how I heard it.'

'Oh,' she said, and her eyes were on Mal. 'You soft-heart!'

I looked at Mal. It was not a description I would have used, but to my astonishment, Mal was reddening. I said, 'But if your father had brought that money back, you would still have your house! I don't understand!'

'Then you're a pretty fool, aren't you?' she said. 'I didn't think a man could be as dull-witted as you looked, but I must have been wrong. Those purses were my dowry. I hadn't realized my father had paid them over when I saw you, but Mal told me, and all was well. We marry as soon as the banns are read.'

'I . . . *oh* . . . I see.'

And I did. It made a lot of sense. Jeffry had come here not to pay off a debt, as I had assumed; he had come to give the money to Mal to help the happy couple set up their home. But . . .

'You were so angry with him when he didn't turn up. You said he was a—'

'Well, he did like his gambling. He disappeared, and I couldn't find him, and I thought my dowry was gone the way of so many pennies over the years, into a wager. My poor darling, did they hurt you?'

The whole group of us turned to face Mal at that point. His face was now the colour of a beetroot, and he held his head a little lower on his shoulders, like a man embarrassed. 'I 'ad a job to do.'

'I know, my darling,' she said with a smile that turned my stomach. To see these two cooing over each other was sickening. She, who could have been an attractive wench, given a little education with a new dress and the like, and he, who, when he had 'a job to do', was probably out snipping off a man's fingers, or sawing at his throat with his bread knife, were so ill-matched that I quite had my breath taken away. I could not speak for some moments, which was probably no bad thing.

It was Lawyer Abraham who brought us all back to the present.

'Where's the girl gone?'

He was quite right. At some point in the proceedings, Agnis had disappeared.

Humfrie was the first to recover. He took a quick look about the chamber. 'Is there another way out of here?'

'Yes,' Mal said, pointing to the rear. 'Out there.'

Humfrie took to his heels. Meanwhile, there were several of the slugs of lead nearby, and I picked up some few, shoving them into my pouch. The drawstring was snapped, but the pouch seemed to hold them still. I folded it over and slipped it into my jack before rolling to my backside and trying to stand. Eventually, Willyam came to my aid, helping me up and steadying me while I tottered. Jeffry's daughter Maudie, for that was the name Mal called her by, was still standing with the gun pointing at each of us in turn. I reached out and grabbed it, and as I did, she pressed the trigger. There was a click and a loud whirr as I took it back, and I winced, but I knew I was safe, really. The dog was not resting on the wheel, and the mechanism span it without raising a spark. I glared at her. 'You could have killed me!'

'You shouldn't have snatched it from me!'

'You shouldn't have pointed it at me!'

'What else could I do?'

'Go to your man, wench!' I snapped. My ankle was hurting like hell, and I was seriously disappointed that Agnis was the culprit who had got me into so much trouble.

'How is it?' Willyam said, looking down at my foot.

'Horrible!'

'You'd better rest it.'

I nodded.

He looked at Mal, who was now being cosseted by Maudie. Occasionally, I felt a slashing glance from his eyes, but tried to ignore it. Leadenhall Bob and the Lawyer were bemused. Only Willyam and I were fully aware of the implications of all this, I think. We exchanged a meaningful look. Gradually, we made our way out to the main door, and thence into the dim twilight made all the more gloomy by the night's cookfires, leaving the others behind.

'We have to find her before . . . before she can do any more harm,' Willyam said.

What could I say? It was plain enough that he was right. Agnis was a dangerous little slut, as she had demonstrated, and I didn't like to think that she could become convinced that I was a danger to her, and thus try to persuade someone else to try to assassinate *me*. So with Willyam helping me, I hopped and hobbled along the roadway, until we reached her home.

'You can't make it up all the stairs and ladders,' he said, staring up at the building.

'No,' I agreed with relief. It was enormously tall, and the topmost storey, from here, looked as high as a mountain to me with my blasted ankle.

Willyam glanced down at my boot and nodded. 'Well, wait here, then, and we'll see what we can do, eh?'

'I could do with a drink.'

'You want me to go and fetch you a costrel of cider or ale?' he asked innocently, continuing, 'Because if you do, I'll kick your other damned foot! I'm not a valet for you with nothing better to do than hunt down drinks for your comfort!'

'What will you do?'

'I'll go and capture her. If she's dangerous, I suppose I'll have to restrain her somehow,' he added, patting his flanks to indicate that all he had was a knife.

I could have offered him the gun, but just then, with my ankle preventing me from running away, and standing in a grim roadway as dark grew about me, I was unwilling to give up the best defensive weapon I had.

'Be careful.'

'Yes.'

I watched his back as he walked to the building, standing cautiously at the open doorway, then slipping inside quietly. I stood there, my ankle throbbing nastily, and I waited, and while I did, I checked the gun once more. I still had the spanner, and I set it to the square winding nut, turning it the three-quarter turn until the mechanism clicked. Then I lifted the pan and gazed into it. It looked empty, so I took some powder from the flask and shook it into the pan, closing the lid. There was no powder in the barrel after the ball had fallen out, so I tipped a load more in and placed a ball on top. I had seen some gunners during my time in the militia during the rebellion, and I knew that the ball had to be rammed in hard. There should be a ramrod of some sort. Soon I found that it was fitted neatly into a tube beneath the barrel, and I used it to batter the ball into place. But as soon as I tipped the gun, the ball rolled out again, and much of the powder with it.

I swore. Guns, I decided, are fiddly, foolish weapons, with more risk to the user than any enemy. At least with a decent polearm or sword, a man could be sure that the thing would work. Even a bow and quiver of arrows was better than this. A man could fire a great many arrows in the time it would take to reload a gun. And then the gun would lose its balls, and with them their powder. What good would that be for, say, a cavalryman, if he had to ride into battle holding his gun aloft, and could not trust it to hold its charge until the moment that he needed to fire it?

Perhaps the bullets were badly made, I thought, and idly picked up the one that had fallen from the barrel. It was almost perfectly round, with a thin line about it where the two halves of the mould had joined, and there was a single quarter-inch mark where the lead had been poured into the moulds, the little cylinder of lead being snipped off as close to the sphere as possible once the lead had cooled. It looked well enough made to my untutored eyes. I dropped the bullet into the barrel, and heard it rattle as it slid down, striking the sides of the tube. It was much too small. I tipped the barrel carefully, and the slug rolled out, leaving much of the powder behind.

Then I had a brilliant idea. If I had a little patch of leather or parchment and wrapped that about the bullet, it would sit more tightly. If I rammed it home, that might hold the ball in place. My shirt was made of linen, and I considered it, but it wouldn't do to tear a hole in my second best shirt. I looked about me, and there was a little piece of a reddish material trodden into the dirt. I picked it up between finger and thumb, and pushed it into the barrel's end, setting the ball on top and thrusting it home. This time the ball stayed in the barrel. For now.

Feeling quite smug, I settled myself to wait.

I didn't have to wait for long. Willyam was soon back. 'She's not there.'

'Where else could she have gone?' I wondered.

'In God's name, I had thought we would have her there.'

He was obviously very angry. I said, 'She will be back soon. This is her home. All her possessions are up there.'

'It was tempting to set the place afire,' he said. 'That would make her regret her spying, eh?'

'I dare say. I still find it hard to believe that she is a spy, though.'

'Really?'

'I just remember that first time I saw her, when she came into the Bear when we were drinking, and told me that there was a task for me. She seemed so innocent and sweet.'

'It is how women ensnare a man,' Willyam said. He looked down at my ankle again. 'Look, you need to get back to your house. Now that the woman has been discovered, we need to get you home to rest that leg.'

I was nothing loath. There was a group of men approaching down the lane, singing and making merry, and with Willyam's support I began to make my way back up the lane towards civilization. We were lucky enough to encounter a car coming from a narrow alley, and the driver agreed to allow me to lie on the back and have a lift. Willyam said he would wait for Agnis at the door to her home, in the hope of catching her when she returned, and on that happy note we parted.

Once back at my house, the car halted and I could dismount without too much hardship. At my door I bellowed for Raphe, and with relief soon heard him rattling the bolts and lock.

The door opened, and I grumbled and cursed him until the door opened.

And then I gave a sickly smile as I recognized the doorman. It wasn't Raphe. It was Ramon.

'But you're dead!' I protested.

Soon I was in my parlour, and rather than sitting where Luys had, with his twisted ankle up on a stool, I was forced to stand against the wall near the fire.

Ramon was looking very well for a dead man. I said so.

'So are you,' he said, which was not particularly comforting.

'I don't understand.'

He held up his jack. There was a black mark on it, and I suddenly realized that the ball must have fallen out of the barrel last night too. The loud noise was just powder in the empty barrel.

'Do you usually attempt murders with an empty weapon?' he said with a smirk.

I had no answer to that.

'I have heard from others that you are supposed to be a competent murderer. I find this difficult to believe.'

I gave a self-deprecating shrug. He had two of his men with him, and I wondered where Raphe was. I didn't like to think he was injured. Servants were expensive and difficult to find in London. Not that I would have to worry too much, I thought, if the look on Ramon's face was anything to go by. My days of hiring servants could well be behind me.

'Um,' I said.

'You are a thief as well, I consider,' he continued. For now he had his sword sheathed, and he was pacing up and down like a hound seeking a scent. 'You took my companion and his money. One or the other, I could possibly forgive, but not both.'

'Who was he?'

He threw me a glare, but relented. 'When your Queen became with child, everyone was happy. It sealed the wedding perfectly. However, King Philip was unsure whether she was truly pregnant or not. He wanted to ensure that the child was safely delivered, but he had some doubts. Others have mentioned these doubts, too. So he had a private physician sent from Spain, a man who helped the imperial family.'

'Luys was that physician?'

'His name is Diego. I paid him handsomely to come and look at the Queen. He arrived and demanded a night on the town, as you say. I refused. Then we met you, and, seemingly, he spoke to you and arranged to meet you and go whoring.'

'I see.' And I did. That explained much about his money, his manners and his youthful excitement at being taken to the Hat.

'Now the Queen has not delivered a child, the pregnancy continues, but the physician has disappeared along with my money. *Where is my money?*'

That last was in a bellow that made me cringe. 'I wish I knew.'

'You have already confessed to much of what happened that evening, but I still do not know when you killed him. You see, I always believe in the *why*, the *how* and the *when*. I can guess the *why*. He had much money on him, and you desired it. The *when* is also easy. It was at some time that evening, after you had been drinking. But the *how* – this is still a mystery.'

'I didn't hurt him. I liked him.'

'You were planning on taking his money from the moment you first saw him. Do not try to persuade me otherwise. I know men like you.'

'That is unfair!'

'Really? When I look at you, I feel I am looking at a younger version of myself. It is sad, for I have to kill you anyway, but I would have liked to have enjoyed your company. So, where did you leave him?'

'I had to see a man at the wharf, and I left Luys at the entrance to the alley,' I said. 'When I came back, someone had killed him. I didn't touch him.'

'So you say!'

'His body is in a tavern waiting for the Coroner!'

Ramon viewed me with disgust. 'Another dead man, no doubt! I heard there was one taken from the river . . .'

His voice continued, while I found myself seeing again in my mind's eye the sad face of Jeffry as he fell backwards into the water. All because the fool thought I was going to kill him when I was trying to save him. Admittedly, I had commissioned Humfrie to kill him, but he wasn't to know that was me, and I was trying to stop the murder. 'I've told you all I know.'

'Well, I have been hunting for my money and cannot find it here in your house, so I suppose now I shall have to kill you,' he said, and drew his rapier slowly. 'Of course, if you tell me where my money is, I may consider permitting you to live a little longer, but if not,' he shrugged, 'then all is settled.'

Now, you may be thinking: What was Jack doing, leaving his pistol in his breast? The simple answer is that I was waiting and hoping something could happen. After all, a single bullet is of little help when there are three armed men facing you. All I had was a threat. So now I drew the gun, setting the dog in place and putting my finger on the trigger. 'Don't come closer!'

Ramon put on an expression of condescension and smiled sadly. 'Tell me, do you know now that powder and balls fall out unless you wrap the bullet in a patch of cloth to hold it in place?'

'Yes!' I said, but he appeared not to believe me. His sword rose.

What could I do? I could kill him, of course, but then his companions would be sure to dice me like meat for a pie. I had one bullet, not three, and there was nothing else left for me.

That was when I had my idea. I thumbed open the powder flask, pulled its strap over my head, smiled enigmatically, as I thought, and threw it on the fire.

*   *   *

If you have never played with the black powder that people use to propel bullets and balls from guns, then perhaps you have not experienced what happened next.

When you see a gun go off, it is obvious that the powder explodes with great violence. I hurled that leather flask straight into the hottest part of the fire, certain that it would mean a fearful detonation that would so petrify Ramon and his men that I could extricate myself. As to where I would go, I had no idea. All I wanted was to escape, as you can imagine. At least this time I wouldn't be chased by a maddened Mal.

So, when I threw the flask into the fire, I expected a lot of excitement. Instead, there was a little quiet hissing and fizzing. Some of the powder had fallen from the mouth of the flask, and that was all it did: it hissed and fizzed.

Ramon laughed aloud and gabbled something in his incomprehensible language, and one of his men leaned down to the fire and took hold of pincers to remove the flask. He was laughing, too, as was the last of the three. As for my brilliant diversion? It was just one more disappointing event in a sadly disappointing life. I looked over mournfully at the man with my flask. He had it in his hand now, and he grinned as he shook it.

There is a useful principle in life which I learned that day, and that is, to treat black powder with respect.

The man shaking the flask obviously thought that this was enormous fun, right up until the moment that something made him pause. Perhaps he felt a slight tremor affect his hand, or heard something. Whatever it was, he glanced at the flask with an expression suddenly devoid of humour, and then several things happened all at once.

First, Ramon stopped smiling and snapped an order. Second, the man turned to face Ramon with an expression of shock on his face. Then the third man screamed something (I think, because my memory of the precise sequence of events grows a little hazy here) and there was an almighty bang.

I know this happened because I heard it. I didn't see much, because I had no desire to see a man detonate, and, besides, I was in the process of jumping to the floor at that moment, but piecing together the fragments of my memory and the sight of the after-effects, I think that what happened next was that the flask exploded. The man holding it suddenly found his hand had disappeared, and bits of him were flying about the room. One piece struck his friend in the cheek, which made him scream so loudly that he almost drowned out my own cries, and at the same time Ramon flinched, unsurprisingly, and gave a squeal like a pig being stuck. He was thrown to the floor, as a filthy blue-black smoke filled the room with the reek of very rotten eggs.

When I opened my eyes, I found myself lying on the floor facing a white-faced Ramon. He was confused, from the look of him. Perhaps seeing me holding the gun and pointing it at his head from a distance of about a foot was enough to give him pause for thought. He looked quickly this way and that, and I could see why: he wanted his sword. Oddly enough, I was considerably closer to him than his rapier, which he had let fall from his hand as he lifted both arms to protect his face.

Then he regained his composure. 'Kill him!' he snarled. At least, I assume that's what he said; it was in Spanish.

I wasn't going to take the risk that Ramon had told his fellow to fetch a cup of wine and a bread roll. The remaining henchman, who was still whole, was about to reach for me when I set my jaw. 'How keen are you to die? I learned how to load and fire this today, and while I missed yesterday, I won't now. I am practised. Tell your man to stand back or I'll make a hole in your head that will permanently stop any headaches!'

He stared at me, then at the gun, and finally looked up at his man and shook his head.

The explosion had shaken all of us, obviously. I was quivering like a man with the ague, and Ramon was little better. Oh, the man who had picked up the flask was whimpering, too, but after the roar of the powder, none of us could hear that well.

I held my gun at Ramon. 'There are cloths which your fellow can fetch for him to bind his hand. Raphe can show him where.'

Ramon looked up and rattled off something. The man left

the chamber and its reek of rotten eggs without regret. 'What now?'

'Get up, but don't go near your sword. I will kill you if I have to.'

He nodded, apparently believing me now. Any impression of my utter incompetence with powder and gun had left him. Perhaps he was just still deafened and bewildered by the event, but he willingly clambered to his feet and walked to my chair. I cleared my throat meaningfully, and he changed direction, taking his ease on my stool instead. His servant was white-faced and had thrust his ruined hand under his left armpit. Now he sat with wide eyes like a child. I felt quite sorry for him for a moment, until I recalled his insulting manner as he picked up the flask.

I described this event later to John Blount, and he said that probably some particles of powder had been caught in the mouth of the flask. When I threw it into the fire, some was thrown from the flask's neck, and began to fizz and hiss, and some in the throat of the flask caught light, and were still glowing when the fool shook it. It would take one glowing cinder to set off the entire flask in such an effective manner. For the moment, I was less concerned with the how and the why of the black powder's explosion, and was more interested in how I should escape my predicament.

Ramon's man returned with a pale-faced Raphe.

I said, 'Raphe, go to Master Blount and tell him what has happened here. We need an apothecary or a barber surgeon.'

'My man will wait until we return to the household. He will have a Spanish surgeon, not an English butcher,' Ramon said.

'If you want. You'll be carrying him, though, because he's bleeding all over my floor,' I said with feeling.

I wasn't joking. The man was growing more and more pale by the minute. I sent Raphe on his way, and remained staring over the barrel of the gun at Ramon. 'I don't know what happened to your man. I do know that he was killed and robbed, and later I was robbed, too. I had nothing to do with his death or robbery, though. I don't even know what was in his purse.'

'He had a fortune in gold. I did warn him against going out
with it about his person,' Ramon said. 'But he never trusted
the servants in our house. He insisted on carrying it with him
at all times.'

'I think I may know who took it,' I thought. Agnis had been
there, after all. It was close to the bowling alley where she
went that night. It was clear to me that she would have had
time. She would have seen the man slumbering. It would have
taken but a moment to stab him, cut his purse free, and be
away, back in her chamber. Perhaps she knew I was there, too,
and knocked me down. Although if she had taken the money
up to her chamber, it was singularly well hidden. I hadn't found
it, and I am usually good at guessing where someone might
have hidden their valuables.

'Who?'

'I will find the money. You will leave. The money isn't
yours, after all. And I do not want to see you again.'

He sneered a bit at that, but then his companion gave a loud
shriek, and the sound seemed to go through his soul. 'Very
well. Curse this country! Curse you!'

Raphe turned up a little later, with a fretful-looking young
physician in tow. While I stood and hopped to the chair, he
had the handless man sit on the stool. With much tutting and
hissing, the doctor stared at the man's hand. For a moment I
thought the doctor would keel over, because he went as white
as a newly limewashed wall and swayed at the sight, before
sending Raphe hunting for a bowl of warm water and cloths.

I had no desire to stay while the man's injuries were investigated and patched. He had the look of a fellow who knew
that his life had just undergone a rapid and irreparable change.
I was content to know that he would not be likely to threaten
a man like me again in the near future. His life as a henchman
was over.

Ramon clearly thought the same, because as Raphe stood
back, staring with fascination at the mangled remains of the
man's hand, Ramon snapped out an order, and he and the
remaining man strode from the room. Ramon glared at me on
his way out, but, to be absolutely honest, I was past caring

what he might think. The explosion had been so devastating that I just felt drained. I pulled the dog from the wheel on my pistol and placed the thing in my jack again. It still had its charge, and I wondered how I could empty the thing. I looked about me, wondering if there was something that I could use to pull the ball out, but as I gazed around, my eye lit on the doctor with his patient. The fellow looked yellow and miserable.

My room had looked better, too. There were black, sooty powder burns on every surface, and the mists had not completely dissipated either. There were still swirls and eddies of fumes, as if my fire had a blocked chimney, but the smell was not as pleasant as the applewood that we had been burning the last few days. And then there were the red smudges where bits of the henchman had been spat against the walls, floor and furniture. When I looked about me, I could see that one of my pewter plates had a fresh dent just off-centre, and there was something near it which I truly did not want to look at too closely.

Ugh. If only that were all. I became aware, while sitting in my seat, that there was an uncomfortable lump under my buttock, and when I lifted my backside to investigate, I found I was sitting on a blackened thumb.

That was enough. With my stomach attempting to bring up my last meal, I hurried from the room and out to the road, calling over my shoulder to Raphe to clean up the damn mess as I went.

Outside, I stopped, bent over, hands on thighs, and took several deep breaths. I still felt very queasy, and the fumes in the room had made me light-headed as well, which meant that I was suffering from the double effects of inhaling that smoke and the sight of blood. It was enough to make a man want to spew.

'Master Jack?'

I groaned. 'Humfrie, not now. I've just had Ramon in there trying to spit me on his rapier, and one of his men is spread evenly over my walls and ceiling. I really don't need . . .'

'You need to hear this, Master,' he said with certainty.

*   *   *

Humfrie took me to his house. I hadn't been there before. It was a good, new house built in the gap between two older buildings on a plot which had become vacant when the house between the two had collapsed. His house had been built to fill the gap, and it looked to me as though it had been squeezed tight, with the beams at steeper angles than the houses on either side, and a roof that was considerably higher than the others, since it had an additional storey over theirs.

'Come in,' Humfrie said, and held the door for me.

He led the way inside. The door gave way into a corridor, which was a fairly long passageway. I think the place had originally been built to be used as a shop, for there was a large chamber to the right which fronted the roadway. Other house owners would have rented this space out, but Humfrie was a very private man, I suppose because someone involved in so many illegal activities would be reluctant to share his front door with another tradesman. Still, we continued along the passageway until we came to the parlour behind the shopfront. Humfrie pushed the door wide and stood back, and I walked in.

'Hello, Jen,' I said, and then recoiled, scrabbling at my breast for the gun. 'God's Wounds! It's her, Humfrie!'

Inside, as I entered, Jen was pouring ale from a costrel into a mixture of cups and a tankard. It was not her, but Agnis, who sat wide-eyed and clearly terrified at the side of the table facing me who had made me yelp with alarm.

Humfrie closed the door and looked at me reproachfully, pushing the gun's barrel away and down with the palm of his hand. 'You need to be careful with that thing. Have you seen what gunpowder can do? Put it away, Master Jack. Agnis has a story to tell you, and I think you should listen.'

I reluctantly took my seat on the bench that was offered to me, and put the gun on the seat beside me. I wasn't going to put it away – not yet. And then Humfrie frowned at me and pointedly glared at the gun. Without enthusiasm, I picked it up and shoved it under my doublet again. 'Well?'

Agnis looked up at Humfrie and Jen before starting, but then she fixed her eyes on me. 'I didn't know, Jack. I'm really sorry, but I didn't guess. When he came to me and told me his name was Blount, and would I bring a note to you saying it was from him, I thought little of it. At first I thought it was a practical jest at your expense, and he let me believe that. But then, later, he told me he was actually an agent for Sir Thomas Parry, and I saw no reason not to believe him. He swore that if you or I were to get into trouble, he would save us.'

'Hah!' I exclaimed. 'You're telling me that was Blount? He wouldn't put himself out like that. If there was no advantage to him, he wouldn't lift a finger.' Saying that, I had a sudden recollection of removing a digit from my seat, and the thought brought back my earlier attack of nausea.

'He gave me the note and told me to give it to you. Then he told me I had done well. He seemed very content with things, and kept saying I had done very well and we made a good team. Later he told me that although I had done well, I had to help you to perform your task. He told me to help you to find Michol, and that evening, when we got to the tavern and saw him there, he told me to give you the gun, and get inside the tavern to warn you when the men were coming out.'

'You are just pulling the wool over our eyes,' I burst out. 'I know who you really are, Mistress Agnis! You are a spy for the French, and a thief!'

'But, Jack, how could you think that?' she demanded with her hands outspread. 'What have I done but save you when you have been in danger?'

She did have a point. After all, I'm no expert, but I had always believed that a spy would act as a seductress, tempting poor fools into her bed with the offer of delights rarely imagined. Agnis had instead pushed me away at every opportunity. Most of the time she'd let me understand she viewed me as little more than something found on the sole of her shoe.

Jen nodded to her. 'She's not the sort Blount would have taken on. Look at her, Jack. She isn't cut out for this sort of work. She fell for his patter, that's all. He played her like a gittern. You can't blame her, just because he was persuasive.'

'Blount? He's not *that* persuasive,' I said, but then I had to admit that Blount had always known how to convince me to do his bidding. It was less that he was pleasant and charming, and more that he was perfectly happy to be a bully and threaten people into doing his bidding. I had experience of that myself.

'Well,' I said uncertainly, 'what about her manner? She grew more and more confident, especially when she was handing me the gun and showing me how to use it!'

'Blount made me more confident. He told me I was doing so well, and after we found Michol, he was delighted and told me to bring you the gun. But he had me leave it without a ball.'

'Eh?'

'It had some powder, but no slug. It was to make noise, but not kill someone.'

I gaped. The thought that I had been sent to kill someone – with an unloaded weapon! 'Ramon could have *killed* me! Hold! If Blount didn't want me to kill anyone, why did he send me there?'

She had the grace to look embarrassed. 'He said you were expendable, but it was important that the French thought they were in danger, without running the risk you could hurt the wrong man.'

'What about me? I was *expendable*, you say?' I was for a short while struck dumb by the perfidy of my master, and was about to speak again when there was a sudden draft of cold air. Smoke from the fire was blown into the room, making Agnis and me cough, although from the way that Jen and Humfrie were unaffected, it seemed to be not an uncommon event.

Jen looked disgusted. 'You left the bleeding door open again!' she said to Humfrie, who pulled an apologetic grimace and hunched his shoulders.

With a loud 'Pah!' Jen pushed past me and Humfrie, and strode out along the passage.

Agnis was still looking at me with despairing eyes. 'You do believe me, don't you?'

'Why did you agree to put me in danger? I trusted you,' I said sadly.

As I spoke, there was a loud slam of the front door, which almost made me leap from my skin.

'It's what he told me to do,' Agnis said. 'Blount told me to.'

'Well. This is nice. Can I join the party?'

* * *

I span to hear those words. Willyam had appeared in the doorway, and he held a very fine-bladed knife to Jen's throat, the tip under her chin. With a quick push and little effort, he could send it up into her brain from there. Jen, to her credit, looked absolutely incandescent. Her face was much the same as it had been once when I refused to buy her a trinket she desired: a cold fury that, if her expression was aimed at me, would have had me fleeing the place in an instant.

You'll be surprised to hear this, I dare say, but I was shocked. Yes, seriously. For once, I wasn't scared or alarmed, but simply stunned, to think that Willyam could be involved in these affairs. I had seriously believed that this was something cooked up by Agnis, and she was trying to put the blame on to Blount because it was what spies did, and in recent months I felt I had come to understand how spies behaved pretty well. But the sudden appearance of Willyam was a serious blow to my confidence on that score.

'Will?' I said dumbly.

'Yes, Jack, and ask your friend Humfrie to move into the room more, where I can see him,' Willyam said easily. 'That's nice, Humfrie. Now, go and sit next to pretty Agnis, will you?'

'But . . . Willyam, what are you doing?' I managed.

'Oh, haven't you worked it out yet?' he sighed. 'It's all about the money, Jack. It always was.'

'Eh?'

He gave me a pitying look.

I was thinking hard. 'You knew about Blount and Parry? That I worked for them? How could you know that?'

'Jack, you're talkative when you're drunk,' he said.

'*Why*, Willyam? What did you think you'd gain?' I asked, while Agnis fulminated.

'Only money. I am going to take over Thomas Falkes's gambling halls. He's not here. He has no need for them now.'

My aching head was starting to spin. 'Gambling?'

'I've been planning this for six months. Why do you think I made the effort to get to know you? A fool who in his cups cannot remember who he is, and thinks that the height of elegance is a pair of tight-fitting hosen?'

That was hurtful. 'So you are the man who knocked me down in the alleyway?'

'The night your Spaniard died? That was irritating. I guessed you had entered the alley, but I didn't know why. I knew why you were friendly with the Spaniard, or at least with his purse, so I followed you, thinking to learn what attracted you, and heard voices. When I heard you talking to Humfrie, I guessed you were employing him. And then it all became clear: you had paid him to kill for you. When you left him, I slipped into a doorway, but you came back slowly, as though you were suspicious, and kicked something that made an unholy row. It was all I could bear. There was a bar of metal nearby, so I struck you down with it. Then I took the Spaniard's purse, and his life.'

He paused, nodded to me. 'I'm sorry for the lump on your head, but I did not want you to see me. The money was to come in useful. Anyway, I wanted Falkes's businesses. They're worth a fortune to the right man. Falkes is dead, and won't return, so his ventures are all up for grabs. It would take little to stop me. I can take over Falkes's empire.'

'You think you could take it all? You think you're bright enough to run all his businesses?' I scoffed.

He wasn't upset at my tone. He grinned. 'I already have Mal on my side. He sees it as being perfect for him. A little increase in his payment, to help him with his new status as a husband. With him at my side it'll be easy enough to get the rest of the men to fall into line. If you would deign to consider a proposal, Humfrie, I would be happy to employ you, too.'

'Really? On what terms?'

Willyam grinned expansively. 'Well, my friend, we can talk about the same terms you had with Thomas, if you want? If you would like to discuss them, we can easily come to an arrangement.'

'Humfrie!' I cried. 'You can't trust him! You know that! Listen to him! He's devious, lying, cheating . . .'

Looking at him, Humfrie nodded slowly, considering, before throwing me a speculative look. 'And him?' he said, with a jerk of his head in my direction.

'Humfrie!' I pleaded.

Willyam shook his head. 'Jack is not going to be able to participate in our new venture. He's a bit too stuck in his ways. What do you think, Humfrie? Could you work with me?'

'I can work with anyone,' Humfrie said.

Will gave a broad grin and took the knife away from Jen's throat. 'Then I have no need of your daughter,' he said, propelling her with a gentle shove in Humfrie's direction.

'Hold!' I said. 'What will you do with me and Agnis?'

'I can't very well have you running about London telling others about me and what I've been getting up to, can I?' Willyam said. 'But I won't do anything to you if you promise to hold your tongues.'

'You'll let us go?'

'Certainly I will. But Humfrie won't.'

'Me?' Humfrie said. He turned to look at me again.

'Yes,' Willyam said, and motioned towards me. 'Kill him and the wench. When you have done, you'll have a job with me. Be quick.'

Humfrie nodded and cast a look at me, then he shook his head. 'I'll need your help. Leave my daughter here. You don't need her.'

'How do I know I can trust her?'

'What's she going to do, Willyam? Run to Falkes? Run to the Beadle?'

Willyam nodded, but reluctantly, so I thought, before he and Humfrie ushered us out.

I cast a beseeching look at Jen, but she shrugged with a kind of twisted grin. And that was all.

Humfrie held the door, and I stared at him with horror. I knew this man, I had hired him and trusted him, and yet now he was content to see me taken out to an unspecified place of execution. I didn't like that idea. It was not in the spirit of feudal loyalty that I felt I had a right to expect.

'Humfrie,' I began tentatively.

The only response was a rather forceful shove in the back, and a cruel snigger from Willyam which, bearing in mind how much wine I had tipped down his throat in recent years, was as unkind as Humfrie's push. I hobbled on.

After me came poor Agnis, and then Humfrie and Willyam.

'I am sorry it's come to this,' I said.

'I just don't understand!' Agnis said.

'You see, Willyam of Whitechapel has always had big plans.' I was just getting to think, and I didn't like what I was starting to see plainly for the first time.

'Oh, aye,' Willyam said. 'I've plans, all right. I'll soon be more important than Falkes ever was. He thought himself so high and mighty with his important friends, but I will be taking over all his ventures in the city. I'll be richer and more powerful than he ever was.'

'You think so?' I said.

'Yes. Shame you won't be there to see it,' he said.

I was frowning. 'That house. You found me, after Agnis took me to that room. You knew I was at the Mermaid, didn't you?'

'I was following Mal. I didn't know you were going to try to shoot someone.'

'But you had Persian pyrites that night in the tavern,' I recalled. 'Did you have that to work the gun? Did *you* give the gun to Agnis?'

'No,' Agnis said. 'I told you, that was Blount.'

Willyam shrugged. 'The pyrites? No, I picked that from a fool's pocket in the street.'

'Why would he have had a purse of pyrites?' I wondered.

'Stop talking,' Humfrie said, and I did.

Humfrie had a good idea of the place he wanted to take us, and led us down past the printing houses with their pamphlets and folio editions on shelves, and down past the inns and taverns, to the wharves. With a shock, I realized that Humfrie had brought us to the very same wharf where I had inadvertently killed Jeffry. That, I thought, was proof of very poor taste. Bringing me to be murdered at the very place where a soul was already waiting for revenge seemed to me to be exceedingly unkind.

I would have said something, but as I realized where we were going, Humfrie gave me a shove in my back, and I almost fell. I turned to give him a piece of my mind just as he pushed again, and this time my heel caught a stone, and I went over, yelping and holding my bad ankle. It was a toss-up whether my ankle or head hurt the most just then.

'Come on, get him up!' Willyam said.

There was an edge to his voice, and I realized with some surprise that he was every bit as anxious as I had been on that day when I accidentally pushed Jeffry into the water. Or when I fired the gun at Ramon. Or . . .

'Get up!' Willyam said, and I rolled over to try to get some purchase. As I did so, I realized I still had the gun in my doublet. It was such a glorious thought that I froze for an instant, mentally thanking Humfrie for his foolishness in commanding me to put it away in his house. He might be forced to regret that decision! It was still there, a massy weight at my belt. Well, at the first opportunity I would bring it out and use it to good effect. And then I wondered whether he had expected all this to happen and wanted me to have the gun on me? I threw him a glance and saw only the same, imperturbable fellow. But was there a flicker in his eye?

I rose. 'Don't worry, Willyam, I'm sure you'll be able to cope with the sight of all the blood. Not that you'll be producing it, of course. You know, the only thing harder than seeing your own blood is seeing the blood of a man you have killed. Of course, it's probably harder to see a woman you've murdered, unless you're a coward!'

As I spoke, I rose and began to increase my pace slightly. I wanted to get out of Willyam's reach, although I still could not be certain of Humfrie. I just had to hope that he was on my side. He had his knife, and from experience I was well aware that the man knew how to use it. Willyam, on the other hand, would be easier to deal with. Even if I missed my shot, I could run faster than him. Well, usually, anyway. When I didn't have a twisted ankle.

We came to the wharf and Agnis turned to me with tears in her eyes. Her bottom lip was trembling, and I tried to give her a manly, stoic smile, but if I am honest, I think that the location, the presence of Humfrie and the awareness of the knife in his hand were all sufficient to make my heart thunder rather alarmingly in my breast.

'Humfrie,' I began.

'You molested my little girl, didn't you? And then threatened her.'

'Well, I wouldn't say I . . .'

But Humfrie wasn't looking at me. He was staring coldly at Willyam.

Willyam stared at him. 'How did you know that?'

'Jen has no secrets from her pa,' Humfrie said.

'She told you?'

I broke in, 'Hold on! You say Willyam played the two-backed fiddle with her?'

They ignored me.

'Who else could she have told?'

Willyam stood with his eyes flitting from Humfrie to me and back. 'But . . . but we have a deal!'

'Remind me.'

'You kill these two, and in return you retain your post. I'm taking over Falkes's businesses, so it'll be worth your while.'

'Will it?' Humfrie said.

'I will be a better master than the fool Falkes. He was always a gross, overbearing bully, with little brain. With me running things, you'll be much better off.'

'You think so?' Humfrie said, and suddenly a smile broke out over his face.

'I think Humfrie knows who's the better man to deal with.'

Now, believe me or not, this was a surprise to me. You see, these words were not spoken by me, but by an ugly, brutish fellow who stepped from the shadows. He wore long robes and had a cowl over his face. At first, I thought it was the ghost of Jeffry, and I tried to sidle away so that Agnis was nearer, but then I realized that the fellow was nothing like Jeffry. He was heavier set and had a familiar stride.

Willyam took a step away, but he was going nowhere. He had a choice of trying to break past Humfrie or leaping into the water.

I could not help a gurgle from escaping my lips at this point. You see, the man who was speaking had pulled his cowl back. It was none other than Thomas Falkes.

I gasped, 'But I thought you were dead!'

'It's no thanks to you I'm not,' Falkes snapped. 'I was held in a cell at Woodstock until the Justices came to hear the case, and they decided that since there were no witnesses, there was no case to answer, and released me. But imagine how I felt on returning home when I learned some evil scrote had decided to try and hurt my business?'

'But, Master Blount— . . .' Agnis began.

Falkes gave an unpleasant smile. 'Sorry, Maid. I may have played you false there.'

'It was you tried to have me shoot at Michol?' I blurted.

'I learned Michol was close to the Spanish. If a known assassin was discovered trying to kill a comrade of the new King, I thought he would be tortured, and it wouldn't be long before he squealed and told them all they wanted to hear. Then you would be gone, Blount would be gone, and the Queen would have Lady Elizabeth's head from her shoulders faster'n an adder's strike. And all the time, I'd be getting back to my business.'

He turned to Willyam and his smile broadened, but it was one of those smiles that never approached his eyes, if you know what I mean.

'Willyam, Willyam, I hear that you have aspirations to greatness. You want to take over my businesses.'

'No, no. That was because we all thought you were dead, nothing more!'

Falkes was standing in front of Willyam now. 'You know, you always were a snivelling runt with no ballocks. You don't even have the courage to face me, do you? But you thought you could take over my businesses?'

Willyam struck out wildly, but he was a trained pickpocket, not an assassin. He fought like a man who was unconvinced, as though he was flailing to inspire fear in his opponent. Falkes was formed from a different mould. He had no desire to fight for the sake of the look of it. He wanted Willyam dead. He was not prey to any doubts. He clubbed Willyam's hand to one side, and thrust hard with his own.

For a few moments, Willyam didn't seem to realize that he had been stabbed. He struggled, trying to punch Falkes, trying to bring his own knife to bear, and seemed not to realize that his strength was ebbing. He pushed and slapped, but as Falkes grinned into his face, saying, 'And you won't touch my Jen again, you snivelling little prickle!' he suddenly seemed to realize that something was wrong. His legs gave way, and then he simply wasn't there any more. There was just a sad little splash from the water below.

I stared at the place where he had been. Falkes stared down, sniggering nastily, and Agnis gave a series of heaving little sobs.

'He was a nasty little turd,' Falkes said. He turned to Humfrie. 'You know what to do. Get rid of them both.'

That was one thing about Falkes, you see, He knew how to give orders. A man who has been in charge of so many others for so many years comes to understand how to issue orders. He had been doing so for such a long time that he knew his commands would be obeyed without argument. But there was a problem with Falkes's assumption. In the months since his arrest and subsequent disappearance from London, Humfrie had undergone a change of attitude. Now he knew that he had the benefit of my contracts, he could work for less time, but as profitably, while serving his country. That was how he saw it, I guessed, because he suddenly darted forward, took hold of Falkes's throat and jerked his chin upwards. His blade flashed down, and suddenly Falkes became limp.

It was all over in a moment. One second, Falkes was a bull of a man, issuing instructions like a general on his battlefield, and the next he was little more than a sack of useless flesh.

Humfrie grunted, pulling his dagger free and then casting a glance at me. 'Don't just stand there staring, Master Jack! He's heavy!'

At my own house, I opened the door with a sense of trepidation. The smell of gun smoke still pervaded, but when I walked into my little hall, I was glad to see that the worst of the mayhem had been cleaned up. There was singing coming from the buttery, and when I investigated, Raphe and the physician were both uproariously drunk. I was tempted to kick the drunken pair out, but in the end I gathered up cups and flagons of ale, and took them back to my room.

Humfrie stood with his back to the fire, looking about him appraisingly. As I walked in, he nodded to my belt. The gun had slipped, and the barrel was protruding again. 'You should be careful of that thing. I don't think you are used to such toys.'

'Who gave it to you?' I asked Agnis.

She was still in a bit of a lather, the poor wench. We had taken a while to take all the best items from Falkes before consigning his body to the Thames, and I was glad to discover that he was carrying some coin. Humfrie and I shared this bounty, before we rolled him over the wharf and into the waters. Falkes floated down the way a little, his arms moving as though he was rowing himself, face down, and then slowly sank, disappearing before he had travelled twenty yards from the wharf.

'Well,' Humfrie said. 'That's that.'

'Aye,' I said.

Agnis made no sound, apart from the chattering of her teeth.

'Don't worry, maid,' Humfrie said. 'You are safe.'

'But . . . but they're both dead!'

'Yes. They weren't good men, maid. And both wanted you dead, so you're better off without them both,' Humfrie said philosophically. 'And now I think we should be away. Jen will meet us at your house,' he added, glancing at me.

She did, too. We had only been there a short while when she knocked on the door and entered, demanding a flagon of my best wine. All I had was the stuff I had bought in for the Spanish guests, and I fetched what was left. The depleted store told me what Raphe and the physician had been drinking.

'I don't know how I shall explain all this to Blount,' I said.

'Explain what?' Humfrie asked.

'Michol, Willyam, Luys, Falkes . . .'

'He doesn't need to know anything about them,' Humfrie said firmly.

'But they are all dead.'

'Michol isn't.'

'Well, no, but the others are.'

'All the better. They can't argue.'

'We killed them!'

'No, *I* did. And I would prefer to know that my part in their removal was kept secret between us.'

'What should I tell Blount, then?' I demanded irritably.

'What did he ask you to do?'

'Kill Jeffry.'

'And you did. You can tell him that. If he asks about other men, remind him he didn't ask you to kill them.'

It was, I reflected, perhaps the best thing to do. There were some aspects that I didn't understand, still. 'How did Willyam get the idea to take over Falkes's operations?'

Here Jen had the good manners to blush. 'I didn't mean any harm by it!' she protested. 'We were just talking about this and that, and he asked about Thomas, and I may have said that he wasn't about any more. So he started thinking he could take it all over.'

'And Mal?' I said.

Humfrie nodded. 'Mal isn't bright enough to think these things through. Willyam spoke to him and told him that Falkes wasn't coming back, and Mal thought he'd take over the bits of business that he understood. Not that he did. But now his wife is trying to persuade him to leave London with her. The dowry will allow them to buy a little alehouse, where they can look after her brothers or sisters or whoever she wants. Mal is quite happy to leave the city.'

What I still did not understand was the position of the Spanish physician, whom I knew as Luys. 'I suppose the Spaniard was killed by Willyam,' I said. 'He left Agnis at the gambling hall, went back, and tried to knock me down as though he wanted to put the blame on me for the Spaniard's death.'

'And meanwhile he killed the Spaniard and took his purse,' Agnis said. 'He was using that money to gamble all night.'

'But why did the Spanish bring a physician here in the first place?' I explained what Ramon had said to me earlier in this room.

Humfrie nodded. 'Perhaps he told the truth when he said that Philip is concerned. Sometimes childbirth can be a terrible time for a mother.'

*   *   *

And, of course, now we know that is the truth of it. The two midwives who were looking after the Queen during her confinement had raised concerns about the supposed pregnancy, and others had already spoken to her husband, but received short shrift for their words. The physicians knew best, they were told. The Duke of Aragon, my friend Ramon, decided to take matters into his own hands and brought his own physician, my friend Diego, or Luys, to inspect the Queen, but before he could, Luys was killed by Willyam.

The physicians were baffled as the pregnancy continued. After the false alarm, there were no more joyous peals of bells for the Queen's happy result. Silence reigned from her palace where she lay or sat waiting, and gradually the matter of her child and pregnancy was forgotten. There was nothing official, but the lack of announcements was deafening, and the population began to worry once more about the royal line, and whether she would ever be able to give birth to a child to ensure the accession.

It wasn't likely. Her husband left the country soon after, to go and join his armies trampling over France. Without a sire, the dam will not whelp.

And all the while, in the darker corners of palaces, in undercrofts, in chilly woods, in filthy taverns, men began to plot and discuss and agitate, and Princess Elizabeth, I have no doubt, began to hope and pray.

And me? I was happy.

I said nothing to Blount, but one day a messenger arrived from him, with a small purse of gold. It was not as large as Luys's purse, nor so heavily filled, but I didn't care. It was enough that my efforts had been appreciated.

Not, of course, that Blount ever mentioned Jeffry again. Blount was content to learn that Jeffry had disappeared. Once more he was convinced that he had made a good choice in hiring me to do his dirty work, just as I was delighted with my selection of Jen's father.

Jen did not return to me. She chose to take her own path to purgatory, and somehow managed to buy a large and imposing house near the river, where she held fantastic parties with a select group of influential friends, who were guaranteed to join her because of her bevy of very high-class courtesans. Jen never told me from where she found the money for this investment, but from some subtle hints that Humfrie gave me, she had access to a certain amount of Falkes's profits from the last ten years. She knew where the money was hidden, and Falkes had no use for it any more.

Agnis? I didn't see Agnis again. The idea that she could have been persuaded by Falkes to give me a gun, knowing it was without a ball, so that I could be captured and tortured, caused even her many attractions to pale in my eye. She disappeared soon after the affair. Not in a nasty manner: she decided that she had seen enough of city life. I once heard Humfrie say that she had family in Norfolk, and I believe that she returned there. The air of the city, after witnessing two murders, and perhaps the guilt of knowing she almost caused my death too, was not to her taste. Outside the Mermaid, she had thought herself bold and brave, but when it came down to it, and she was herself threatened with death at the hands of Humfrie, whether ordered by Falkes or Willyam, she learned that her courage had precise limits.

So life continued. Humfrie spent much of his time in the taverns near St Paul's, waiting for the days when I would go to him and suggest a fresh target. I spent my own time happily whoring and drinking, and occasionally beating Raphe. Life was good.

But I continued to carry my pistol when I walked abroad. Just in case.